MARQUESS OF FORTUNE

A LORDS OF FATE NOVEL, VOLUME 3

K.J. JACKSON

First Edition: February 2016
ISBN: 978-1-940149-14-1
http://www.kjjackson.com

K.J. Jackson Books
Historical Romance:
Stone Devil Duke, *A Hold Your Breath Novel*
Unmasking the Marquess, *A Hold Your Breath Novel*
My Captain, My Earl, *A Hold Your Breath Novel*
Worth of a Duke, *A Lords of Fate Novel*
Earl of Destiny, *A Lords of Fate Novel*
Marquess of Fortune, *A Lords of Fate Novel*

Paranormal Romance:
Flame Moon
Triple Infinity, *Flame Moon #2*
Flux Flame, *Flame Moon #3*

Be sure to sign up for news of my next releases at
www.KJJackson.com

DEDICATION

— AS ALWAYS,
FOR MY FAVORITE KS

{ CHAPTER 1 }

NORFOLK, ENGLAND
JANUARY, 1821

His head jerked up.

The crack startled him, echoing through the woods, petering out. Silence.

Crack.

Loud. Low. A smash. Something solid hitting something immovable.

Garek Harrison cocked his head. He had almost been asleep, his horse plodding along the trail. Looking to the sky, he found the edge of the moon through the tree cover just before a grey cloud slipped in front of it.

Crack.

A wail. A harpy from the bowels of hell wail. The anguished sound bounced off the trees, suffocating the air about him.

Crack.

Wail.

Crack.

Garek shook a shiver from his spine. Lost. He was utterly lost in this blasted forest, it was still four hours until daybreak, and now he had haunting wails echoing through the woods to contend with.

Nicking his horse forward, Garek searched ahead on the little-used path, hoping against hope that the forest would open up in front of him, producing a village. A cottage. A farm. Anything that would tell him where he was.

Wail.

Crack.

Wail.

The last wail choked off in mid-screech, a sob swallowing the sound.

Hell.

Garek shook his head. A woman. Definitely a woman—not a harpy ghost haunting the woods.

Against his better judgement, he tilted his head as he pulled his great coat tighter against the chill, trying to pinpoint where the sound originated.

Crack.

The wails had disappeared, but the cracking didn't cease.

Crack.

He tugged the reins to the right. Six more cracks to lead him, and Garek knew he was going in the right direction, the sound much louder, no longer just remnant echoes.

The cracking continued, methodical now. Evenly spaced with no wails, no other noise. It took a half hour before Garek broke through the low brush at the edge of a clearing. A structure stood in the middle of a flat, round area carved into the woods, the ancient white stone glowing in the moonlight.

An abbey of old. Vines attacked the building, leafless thick roots blanketing the walls—fingers from the earth reaching up, slowly returning the stone back to the ground.

Garek pulled up on the reins, halting his horse as he spied the origin of the sound.

He hadn't known what to expect—he had just been following the instinct that set him forth after realizing it was a woman in trouble.

This, though. This he never could have imagined.

In the light of the cloud-dotted half-moon, a woman stood, legs wide and braced, swinging with both hands a large blacksmith hammer at the corner stones of the abbey. The flat-topped hammer she held was heavy, and he could see her arms dip with the weight every time she pulled it back over her shoulder to swing.

She seemed to pay no heed to the cold, her black dress thin with the sleeves pushed up to her elbows. A cloak sat bunched on the ground a few paces away from where she beat upon the building. The handle of an even larger sledgehammer was propped onto the stone next to her cloak.

Her hair—not quite blond, but not a dark brown—was pulled away from her face into a half-knot at the crown of her head, a ribbon holding it tight. It fell halfway down her back, long waves that tangled with the hammer every time she set it over her shoulder.

Garek could only see her profile, but even that slight bit told him this woman was beautiful—and trouble.

He stared at her from the edge of the forest for some time—too long for his own liking—debating.

A woman slamming a hammer at an abbey in the middle of the night constituted a firm walk away. Any sane man would agree. Leave her to her hammering. Move on.

But something held him in place. Held him in place and would not let him tug on the reins. Would not let him turn his head—even as he winced every time she swung and hit immovable stone, sending shocks reverberating down her body.

And then he saw it. Saw the very reason that he had stayed in place, attempting to figure this scene out. The clouds had slid off to the side of the moon, casting more light down onto the clearing and reflecting off the thin layer of white frost on the ground.

Blood. Blood dripping from her hands.

How long had she been out here hammering, bleeding?

Garek slid off his horse. He set the reins to a nearby branch and walked into the clearing, keeping a respectable distance from her.

"Excuse me, miss, do you need help?"

She jumped, spinning, the hammer dropping to her side and hitting her calf. She looked down at the hammer, annoyed, and then up to Garek. The annoyance didn't leave her face. It also did nothing to mar her obvious beauty. Beautiful, but then, he was accustomed to spending his days looking at gaping flesh and broken bones. Still, he could not deny that she possessed an ethereal quality—a glow that rudely awakened his loins.

Wiping one of her bloody hands on her skirt, she turned back to the building, heaving the hammer up over her shoulder. "No, no. No, thank you. I am doing quite well. No assistance needed."

Garek noted a hint of sharpness in her words, yet her voice was soft and light—almost lyrical—as though she sat in one of the finest London drawing rooms.

She swung.

Crack.

Tiny shards of stone went flying, sparking—progress that Garek had not been able to see from the forest. He took a step closer to her.

"Can I ask why you are attempting to destroy this abbey in the middle of the night?"

She heaved the hammer to her shoulder. "I am tearing it down."

Crack.

"May I ask why?"

"No."

Crack.

Garek took another step toward her. He was now within her swing. If she so chose, she could bash him, but he was somewhat assured she wasn't completely crazy and wouldn't try to hurt him.

No—her anger seemed to be directed solely at the building in front of her.

"Your hands, miss. They are bloody."

"They are."

Crack.

"Perhaps you could stop for a moment so I may look at them?"

"No."

Crack.

"If I cannot convince you to stop—"

"You cannot."

Crack.

"May I help you with your destruction?"

She stopped, her arms falling as the hammer slid from her shoulder. She turned to him, and for the first time, truly gave him her full attention. "You would like to help me?"

He shrugged, suddenly questioning his own offer. It was quite clear this woman was a little addled. And fascinating. And set upon injuring herself.

"Yes. If it will lighten your burden. I noticed you also have a sledgehammer with you." He pointed down the wall of stone to the large black iron hammer. "I see you have already made progress—half of this stone is gone. Perhaps I can work on this corner while you take a moment of rest?"

"I do not want to rest."

"Then I could work on the corner opposite you?"

Her eyes narrowed at him, searching his face. "Why? Why would you help me? You do not know me."

"I am Garek. Garek Harrison. And your name?"

"Lillian Silverton." Her head cocked to the side, suspicion still deep in her furrowed brow.

"And now I know you, Miss Silverton." Garek walked to the sledgehammer, removed his great coat and then picked up the long wooden handle. He moved back to her, lifting the hammer to balance it on his shoulder. "Shall I start here?"

Her bottom lip jutted out, staring at him. "Over there." She pointed to the other corner at the front of the abbey. "You can start there. This one is mine."

With one nod, Garek moved to the other corner.

And he started swinging.

~ ~ ~

Garek's eyes went once more to the dark sky. The moon had long since disappeared, and he had never waited so anxiously for daybreak, as he did in those predawn hours.

He had sorely underestimated how much energy swinging a sledgehammer took.

Thoroughly soaked with sweat, his clothes hung heavy, sticking to his skin. With every swing, he would steal a glance at Miss Silverton. She was drenched as well, her hair matted to her neck, but it didn't slow her any more than the blood dripping from her hands did. If anything, her swipes at the stone only became more ferocious throughout the wee hours of the night.

And then finally, a ray of light broke above the trees.

She dropped her hammer.

His muscles on fire, Garek gave one last stone-shattering swing, and paused, turning to her as he let the black iron head of the sledgehammer rest on the ground. "We are done?"

She didn't look his way, her eyes travelling up her corner of the abbey and then making their way to Garek's corner of the building. A quarter of the lower stones from the corners now sat in rubble.

Her eyes flickered to him, then down to the stone on the ground. "For now."

He nodded, using the moment of her averted eyes to stare at her, truly take her in.

He hadn't been wrong earlier. She was beautiful—even with sweat rolling down her brow. He could see in the morning rays that her eyes were a peculiar light blue—set against dark lashes, which made them appear even lighter. The softest waters of the ocean.

Her brown hair was light, giving way to blond in many places. The hammering, combined with the cold, had flushed her cheeks, even turning the tip of her nose rosy.

Garek's eyes travelled down her functional black dress and stopped on her hands. The blood he had seen her wipe off on her skirts over and over again throughout the night was now smeared up onto her arms, past her wrists. She had ignored him every time he had mentioned stopping to look at her hands. And he had mentioned it often.

Her chin lifted as she looked over to him, her blue eyes questioning. Caught in his obvious assessment, Garek coughed, dropping the handle of the sledgehammer.

"Would you like payment for your services, Mr. Harrison?"

He walked to her corner of the abbey, stopping in front of her. "Only one thing."

Hands clamping into fists, her arms crossed over her belly. "And that is?"

"Come with me to some water. Let me look at your hands."

Startled, she looked down as she pulled her fists free and opened them. "My hands?" Her fingers ran over her palms, quickly trying to clear the blood.

He grabbed her wrists, stopping the motion. "Yes. And you need to stop rubbing them. I would like to look at them. Make sure there are no stone shards embedded deep into your skin. They will fester if not taken care of, and you are digging what I presume are shards deeper into your skin every time you touch them."

"Oh." She gently pulled her wrists from his grasp, letting her hands fall to her sides. He could see her fingers twitching, aching to rub at the itch of the wounds.

Her head tilted to the side as her bottom lip jutted out once more. "That is all? You want to look at my hands? No coin?"

He shook his head. "No coin."

She stared at him for a long moment, judging, and then reluctantly, she nodded.

"Is there a stream nearby? Running water would be helpful."

"A short distance through the woods this way." She pointed, her feet already moving toward the water.

Garek stopped by his horse for his satchel and then followed her through the trees. Finding a large boulder near the water's edge, he guided her elbow, moving her to sit. She fought the motion for a mere second, and then exhaustion won out and she sank, setting her hands into her lap, bloody palms upward.

Stepping down to the edge of the stream, Garek used his heel to crack through the thin sheet of ice that had formed along the bank. Several more stomps of his boot, and the ice floated away, leaving a small eddy of water swirling in front of them.

He turned back to Miss Silverton. "I would normally dab away the blood, but after the hours of your hands being unattended and gripping the handle of the hammer—not to mention the scabbing that has already happened—it will be most efficient to immerse them into the water to clean the blood away."

"Are you scolding me?"

"Possibly. This should have been done four hours ago."

She sighed, shaking her head as she stood, and moved to balance on her heels at the edge of the water.

Down on his knees, Garek grabbed her left wrist. "This will be cold—freezing."

"It is fine."

He didn't repeat the warning, just pushed her hand into the stream, letting the running water wash away the blood with only a few gentle dabs of encouragement from his handkerchief. It took longer, but he didn't want to drive any stone shards deeper into her skin.

She suffered the shock of the freezing water—admirably so— until she yanked her hand from his grasp, clutching it to her belly. "Bloody hellfire. I cannot feel my blasted fingers. You did not say it was that cold."

Garek had to hide a smile. The swearing and the sweet voice belonged nowhere near each other.

"We can wait to do the other hand until I take care of this one." He motioned to the rock, and Miss Silverton moved backward to sit.

Settling onto his knees in front of her, Garek pulled free a white linen shirt from his satchel. His last nice shirt, but also his only clean one. He shook it and then bit the edge, tearing it into thin strips.

Linen ready, he rummaged through his satchel until he found the thick leather wallet deep in the bottom. Flicking open the silver catch on the wallet, he unfurled the four leather flaps and pulled free sharp, pointed tweezers and a small scalpel from the silk lining. He set both of them on top of his bag, the silver gleaming in the morning light.

Garek paused, staring at them. Months. It had been months since he had looked at them.

"What? What are those for?" Miss Silverton's left hand flew up, tucking under her upper right arm to hide.

"Just a scalpel and tweezers. I am not about to dig into your skin with my fingernails." His fingers wagged in a curl, motioning her to him. "Your hand."

"But that is a blade." She glared at him, her hand solidly buried and not moving.

"This will not hurt."

"No?"

Garek shrugged. "Possibly a little. But it is better than leaving a shard in your hand and having it fester, then move up your arm and eventually kill you. That happens, and who will tear down the abbey?"

Her frown deepened, but her hand slowly appeared. Garek grabbed it, tilting it to the bright ray of sunlight that was fighting through the tops of the trees.

Just as he suspected, a multitude of grey shards were embedded into her palm. Some were stuck half out, some he could only see below the surface of her skin. Cradling her hand, he picked up the tweezers and made quick work of the shards that could easily be pulled free.

Garek set the tweezers on the rock next to her and picked up the scalpel. Her arm twitched away, but his fingers clamped onto her wrist, holding her hand in place, resting on the inside of his forearm. "I will not cut deep. Just surface skin to get to the stone. This should not hurt too much."

With a deep sigh, she nodded, swallowing hard enough for Garek to hear. Her face scrunched, turning from him the second the small blade went onto her skin. Garek gently peeled away layers of skin above one shard until there was enough stone to grip.

He continued on—five, six, seven shards freed without a whimper from Miss Silverton. She stayed as still as the boulder she sat upon until her face turned back in his direction.

"Your hands are delicate, Mr. Harrison. I would not have thought it for how you swung that sledgehammer."

Garek didn't answer, his concentration solely on capturing the tip of the last stubborn shard. If he didn't get it, he would have to slice deeper, and that, he wanted to avoid. He clamped the tweezers and yanked.

"Uuh. I rescind my comment. That was not at all delicate."

He looked up at her. "But the pain was short?"

"Yes."

"Then my hands were delicate." He stood. "Come down to the water. I need to clean this to make sure I got all of them, and then on to your right hand."

Miss Silverton's left hand checked and the other hand washed, Garek was halfway through pulling the stone shards from her right palm when she squirmed. He paused for a moment but kept his eyes on her hand, giving her a chance to resettle.

"How do you know to do this, Mr. Harrison?" she asked, taking a deep breath. "Are you a surgeon? You have the tools."

"I trained to be a physician, but after I took the Royal College exams and began to see patients, I realized that curing the occasional cough was not what I had hoped for. So I trained to be a surgeon."

"That is an odd choice, to descend from a gentleman to a laborer."

"Not for one that has witnessed what I have." Garek shrugged, his focus diverting to pluck at another stone. "I apprenticed for years with a man who was both a physician and a surgeon before I had to leave to…to make my way north."

"Are you visiting someone in the area?"

He glanced up to her face, then bowed his head, attacking the next shard. "No. I am in the area for work. I was told Farlington would have opportunity, but then I became lost in these woods."

"Farlington? Yes, you are lost. Farlington is a day's ride west and another day's ride north of here."

Garek pulled a stone splinter free, shaking his head. "I have never been good with directions. I had hoped these woods would be the end of the journey."

"Instead, I have only slowed you." Her left fingers scratched at the linen he had wrapped around her left palm. "Although the selfish part of me is pleased you made such good progress on those cornerstones of the abbey. Your pile of rubble was far larger than mine. You work much faster than I could ever hope."

"I am also half again your size, Miss Silverton." Garek blew free a fleck of dried blood, searching for any last shards. "You made plenty of progress. More so than I ever imagined a gentle woman could."

"Gentle?"

"Yes, your clothes, your speech—I do not imagine you are a laborer?" Garek looked up to see her face had gone pale, losing all the pink from the cold.

She shook her head, pushing him aside and jolting to her feet. "Excuse me, please. This…I have not been in my right mind. I never should have allowed you to stay…to touch me. Please, forgive me. You must think me wanton…a harlot. I did not mean to pull you into a compromising situation."

Her feet shuffled in a wide circle around him, but Garek caught her wrist before she could escape. He stood. "Please,

Miss Silverton. I do not think you a harlot. Sit. Let me wrap this hand."

"No. It would not be appropriate."

"Appropriate? We have just spent half the night swinging hammers together—and you cannot afford another minute so I can wrap your hand properly?"

She stared up at him, her eyes wavering. "One minute."

"One minute. For purely medicinal purposes."

She sat, offering her hand up with a tight, acquiescing smile.

One last check for missed slivers of stone and Garek started wrapping her hand. "Tell me, Miss Silverton, why have you not been in your right mind?"

Her head shaking, her eyes swung to the half-frozen stream. "Anger. It consumes my brain. I forget about everything, including manners, when it is in my mind. I only see the red and I cannot control it." She looked to him, her blue eyes softening. "I apologize again. It was very kind of you to stop to assist me last night, and even kinder to tend to my hands. I do wish to pay you for your kindness."

"Again, it will be refused." Garek tied off the linen along the back of her hand.

A visible shiver ran through her body.

"You are cold?"

"Yes. Suddenly very much so."

Garek wrapped his tools into the leather wallet and stood, picking up his satchel. "Let us go back. I saw you had a cloak by the abbey."

Her arms clasped to her body for warmth, Miss Silverton stood and moved past him, and Garek fell in step beside her.

A few paces and Garek looked down at her. Her cheeks were flush again, but this time it appeared to be embarrassment tinting them pink. Even though he had asked numerous times throughout the night without an answer, he was going to try the obvious question one more time. "Why do you want to tear the abbey down?"

Her eyes stayed downward on the frosted trail. "Bad things happened there."

His imagination sped, scenario after scenario constituting "bad things" rushing through his mind. Bad things happening to an innocent. Instant rage. Rage he had to quell—for she looked innocent, Miss Silverton, but what did he truly know of her other than she liked to swing a hammer at a stone building in the middle of the night?

He stopped, shaking free the horrors in his mind. Miss Silverton halted, looking up at him.

He cleared his throat. "Bad things? To you?"

Her head bowed and she started walking again. "To my father. To my sister. He was killed in there. She was alive… holding on. I found them. Found them in the blood."

"You found your father dead?"

She nodded.

"I am sorry for your loss." Garek reached up, setting his fingers on her shoulder.

Her head snapped up at the touch, eyes wide at him. She didn't fully jerk away, but she did dip awkwardly, angling her shoulder away from his hand. She either didn't want comfort, or was suddenly afraid of him. He hoped it was the former.

His hand dropped to his side. "And your sister—she is alive?"

"Barely."

"She is ill?"

"She has not recovered." Miss Silverton glanced up at him, her arms tightening around her body. "It has been a month. When I found her there were gashes—deep—in her leg, and they became infected. Green pus. Fever that will not yield. I have feared she was dead too many times since then to count."

"What is being done for her?"

"Our family physician tends to her. There are times when I think she is mending, going to be well. But at other times…" She shook her head, her look drifting to the abbey coming into view through the woods. "Our physician bleeds her, but it does not appear to help. I have told him to cease, but he insists it is the only way."

"He bleeds her?"

"Yes." Her face blanched, her eyes closing as another shiver quaked through her body. "The disgusting leeches. To see them wiggle on her body. It makes me queasy just thinking about the repulsive little suckers."

"And you have asked him to stop?" Garek could not hide the edge in his voice.

"I have."

"You are right to do so. Insist again. And again. And again. Insist until he stops, Miss Silverton."

Her blue eyes left the path to center on him. "What do you know of it? Did the doctor you apprenticed with not bleed patients?"

"No. And I have seen far too many people nearly bled to death by the practice. The man I learned from did not believe in the method, and I agree. In most cases, it appears to do far more harm than good. You need to see that he stops the bloodletting and he must drain the infection from the leg properly. If he is above the labor of it, then find a surgeon to do so."

They walked to the side of the abbey and Garek picked up Miss Silverton's dark cloak, snapping it free of frost before setting it about her shoulders.

"Thank you." Fastening the front clasp, she blinked hard and then wiped the corner of her eye with the back of her wrist.

"Is something in your eye?"

She wiped her eye again. "Maybe. One of the sparks, something flew at my eye hours ago. It is an annoyance that comes and goes."

"May I?"

Miss Silverton nodded, and Garek set his satchel down and grabbed her shoulders, spinning her so the brightest rays of sunlight aimed at her eye. His thumb under her chin, he tilted her head upward, searching her left eye. The light lit up her eye, making her blue iris sparkle, and Garek lost himself for a moment, transfixed by the shimmer and forgetting all about looking for a rogue shard.

He caught himself. Focus. He had to focus.

"Blink."

She blinked several times, and then he saw it, the smallest sliver just below her upper eyelashes dragging down across her eye.

"Would you like my tweezers or my fingernails coming at your eye?"

"Can you get it with just your fingernails?"

"Yes."

"Then no tweezers. As gentle as you were, I am not looking to repeat that scene by the stream anytime soon."

"It hurt more than you indicated?"

"You did not see? I squirmed the whole time. And I could not watch what you were doing."

"Do not blink." Garek pinched the sliver, extracting it from her eyelid. He flicked it from his fingers. "You should have said something. I could have been gentler with your hands. Better?"

Blinking rapidly, she nodded as she smiled at him. "Thank you. And know that you could not have been any gentler than you were, and I am grateful. I merely do not take pain that well."

"So the next time you are out here tearing this place down, you will wear proper gloves?"

She chuckled. "I will." Looking around, her eyes settled on his horse. "I do feel as though I need to insist on paying you."

"Point me in the proper direction of Farlington and that will be payment enough."

Miss Silverton stepped past him, going to the back corner of the abbey. She pointed into the woods. "This trail will take you north to the main road—maybe an hour's ride—but it does not veer, so it will deliver you to the road. Go left, follow the road to the west, and you should hit the crossroad north to Farlington by the end of the day. It is well marked."

Though he had only known her for a handful of hours, it panged his gut to have to leave her presence. But he inclined his head at Miss Silverton. "Then I thank you, kindly. I do hope your sister recovers well, Miss Silverton."

Garek gathered his great coat and satchel and went to collect his horse. Miss Silverton stood rooted to her spot by the back of the abbey, watching him without a word.

His foot in the stirrup, Garek was halfway up his horse when her voice, sweet, cut through the silence.

"Wait, Mr. Harrison."

Garek looked over his shoulder at her, dropping back to the ground.

She moved across the clearing to him. "Mr. Harrison, what kind of work are you looking for in Farlington? Are you to set up practice as a physician there?"

He hesitantly shook his head. "No. No practice. I am not particular of the work, just that there is some."

She took another step closer, her neck craning up to him, her light blue eyes on fire. "I am, quite honestly, a little—no, a lot—desperate for my sister, Mr. Harrison. I need her to live. And our physician does not seem capable of bringing her back to me. You are the only one who has offered me any other suggestions as to her health. As to what I can do to help her."

"And?"

Taking a deep breath, her eyes implored. "Stay. Please stay, Mr. Harrison. I will pay you. Whatever you need. I do not think I can get our physician to stop what he is doing by myself. He dismisses me—anything I say. I need help. And you have training. You can help her."

Garek's mouth set into a grim line. What Miss Silverton asked—tricky waters to wade into, he knew. The matters of life and death—what people believed a doctor could truly do for them—were constant battles between reality and hope. Thorny indeed. And it was a battle he had seen lost far too many times.

He didn't want to ask. Didn't even want to consider what she suggested. Do not get involved—advice, pounded into his head for years.

But his mouth opened, words falling before he could stop them. "Why do you believe I can help her, Miss Silverton? You know nothing of my surgical knowledge. I merely pulled a few splinters from your skin."

She stared at him, searching—searching his soul if he was to guess at what she sought.

"It is your eyes, Mr. Harrison." Her tranquil voice went low, reaching up to wrap him in its softness. "I have seen it in your eyes. I have seen more humanity, more compassion in your eyes in these past minutes than I have ever seen in our physician."

"Compassion does not heal people, Miss Silverton. If it did, she would already be well—you would have made it so."

"I need her to live, Mr. Harrison." She reached out to grip his arm, the linen wrap across her palm pressing into him. "And I am willing to do anything to make that happen. Anything. I am even willing to chance the fate of a random meeting with a stranger in the middle of the night. And I am willing to trust the compassion I have seen in you. The light in your eyes. Once you commit, you will make it happen. I can see that. You will bring her back to me."

"I cannot perform miracles, Miss Silverton."

"I am not demanding miracles, Mr. Harrison. Only a possibility—give me that—the possibility that you can find a way to heal her." Her hand tightened on his arm. Garek could feel the desperation in her fingers. "Please, Mr. Harrison, help me. I need her to live."

He stared at her, jaw clenching. If he could not help her sister...he could already see the destruction he would be forced to witness. Destruction he did not want to be a part of.

But she only asked for possibility. For hope.

Do not get involved.

He swallowed hard. As much as it unsettled him, he could not deny her that—deny her hope.

Garek nodded. "I will stay. I will come with you."

Miss Silverton's eyes closed, and she nearly crumpled with relief right before him. Only her hand, her grip on him, held her upright.

"But I warn you, Miss Silverton, if your sister is not long for this earth, I can only ease her suffering. I cannot make her live."

"I understand." Her fingers slipped from his arm as her blue eyes opened to him. "You, Mr. Harrison, are the very best thing that has ever come across me in the middle of the night."

He chuckled. "Shall I grab your hammers?"

She nodded. Garek went to the side of the abbey and picked up both hammers, heaving them up to balance them on his shoulder.

"Ready?" she asked.

"I will follow you."

Miss Silverton started off into the woods, and Garek grabbed the reins of his horse, following. He watched the back of her light brown hair swing with her gait, reminding him again of her natural radiance. But that was not the thing that gave him pause, made him question every step he took in her footprints.

No, it was her voice. Her voice alone.

The most alarming, beautiful sound to have ever floated into his ears.

A voice that could take him to hell and back, if he let it.

{ CHAPTER 2 }

Her hand on the front door knob, Lily paused, trying to ignore the rotting ache in her belly. She did not want to go inside. Did not want to face the unyielding dread.

Every moment spent destroying the abbey had helped dissipate the constant gnaw at her stomach. But just as before, every step she took back toward the viscount's main residence reversed the respite. There was one desperate second at the stables, as they situated Mr. Harrison's horse, that she thought of running, disappearing into the world. Moving on from this place. Moving on from the horror her life had become.

She gave herself a slight shake, exhaling her held breath. She could not do that to Brianna. Could not leave her in the hands of the physician and Mr. Sneedly. Her sister would be dead within a week if she did.

Lily glanced over her shoulder at Mr. Harrison, pasting a forced smile onto her face.

His dark hazel eyes narrowed at her, and she knew her smile covered nothing of what she was feeling.

"This is where you live?" His eyes travelled up the outside of the grand, three-story stone entrance. "It is impressive."

Lily turned from him, staring at the carvings in the heavy oak door to avoid answering. "I know this is not proper, Mr. Harrison, but may I refer to you as Garek? You may call me Lily." She angled her head to look at him. "I plan on introducing you as an old friend from childhood that moved away, but has now returned as a trained physician. I believe all inside will unfold more favorably if I can claim you are a trusted person from the past. So if I may call you Garek, it would lend credibility to the story."

"You would like to lie about our association?"

"I would. Anything to ease the situation. Please."

He gave her a curt nod.

Not exactly resounding agreement. While Lily could see he was not comfortable with lying, she also was not about to chance Mr. Harrison being tossed out of Weadly Hall before he could help Brianna. His reluctant nod would have to be enough.

Lily opened the door before Mr. Harrison could rethink the situation, and the heels of her boots clicked onto the marble floor of the wide entryway.

She went directly to the curved staircase, quickly moving up the steps, to the left, and down a long hallway. At the last door of the corridor, she turned the knob and stepped into the room.

Her heart sank.

He was still here. Still here with his leeches sucking the life out of Brianna. Up and down her sister's arm. Just as she had left him last night.

She cleared the instant lump in her throat, not allowing her eyes to rest on her sister's sallow face. "Dr. Rugbert, you are still here. Have you truly bled my sister all night?" Lily announced her presence with the words and watched as the rotund doctor jerked awake, slipping from the chair he had sprawled in.

He scrambled to his feet, his chubby hands running down along the lapels of his jacket. "Now, Miss Silverton, we do not need the scene from last night to be repeated. I have had quite enough pestering from you on the matter of your sister."

"Get those suckers off of her, Dr. Rugbert," Lily said, ignoring his condescending tone.

"Rubbish, Miss Silverton. Do you truly think to order me about this early in the morn? I will do no such thing. Do I need to get Mr. Sneedly?"

"You do not." Lily stepped further into the room, stopping within distance to the spit that flew from his mouth with every other word. Her arms crossed over her chest. "But I want those bloody suckers off of Brianna this instant."

He blustered, his face turning red, spittle gathering at the corners of his mouth. "I am only here at the insistence of Mr. Sneedly, Miss Silverton. Not for you and not for your sister. You do not appreciate that I am the only one that can save her. You most certainly cannot, and you had very well better start giving me the respect that I deserve."

"There you are wrong, Dr. Rugbert."

Lily could feel Garek step behind her, and Dr. Rugbert's look went up over her head. His eyes squinted in the dim light of the room. "Who is this?"

"Your services will no longer be needed for my sister, Dr. Rugbert." She stepped to the side, lifting her hand to tilt to Mr. Harrison. "This is a dear friend of mine—and Brianna's—from childhood, Garek Harrison. Garek has just arrived back in the area, and as he is a trained physician, he will be taking over the care of Brianna."

"But—you cannot—who?" Dr. Rugbert sputtered, his eyes flying to Garek. "Whom did you train with, boy?"

"I studied at Oxford and was licensed by the Royal College of Physicians years ago," Garek said, his hazel eyes hardening at the physician. "In recent years I have been fortunate enough to train with Dr. Halowell at his practice adjacent to The London Hospital. Perhaps you have heard of him? He has made invaluable advances in surgery and treatments."

Dr. Rugbert's look swung to Lily. "You cannot just dispose of me, girl. You are nothing—do you hear me? Nothing. I do not answer to you."

"I am giving you the courtesy of a few moments to remove your pets before I tear them off of Brianna and crush them under my heel, Dr. Rugbert," Lily said. "Your time at Weadly Hall is very limited."

"You insolent little twit." Spittle sprayed as Dr. Rugbert's arm flew up, the back of his hand coming down at Lily's face.

Instinct turned Lily's head, her eyes cringing as she tried to minimize the impact.

But then nothing.

She opened her eyes to see Garek had snatched Dr. Rugbert's wrist in the air, right before it made contact with her cheek.

Stunned at his speed, Lily could see Garek's knuckles straining, crushing Dr. Rugbert's arm right in front of her eyes. She jumped to the side, well out of swinging distance from Dr. Rugbert, her hands landing on the side of the bed behind her.

Garek took a step forward, leaning over the physician with his height, threat clear in every muscle. "That does not seem necessary, sir."

Garek did not tighten his grip, nor did he drop the physician's wrist.

Shock registered on Dr. Rugbert's face, his enraged bluster turning his bald scalp bright pink. He harrumphed, wrestling his wrist free from Garek.

Garek made a point to hold the physician's wrist tight against his squirming. A few long moments passed, and Garek dropped it, both men fully aware of who was in control.

Dr. Rugbert whipped around to Lily. "I will not have this insolence from you, Miss Silverton, or this...this brute of a man. I am rousing Mr. Sneedly." He charged out of the room.

Her breath held, Lily stared at Garek's profile, dumbstruck. Slowly, he turned to her, his look still seething.

Lily's eyes closed, her head dropping.

Please don't leave. Please don't leave. Please don't leave. She willed him in her mind.

But why? Why would he possibly stay now? She had not told him what he was walking into, and it was now obvious that she had just dragged him into an impossibly troublesome situation.

The sudden warm presence next to her side startled her and she opened her eyes. Garek was silent, already removing the leeches from Brianna's arm. His large hands, just as gentle with Brianna as they were with her, lifted each wiggling black sucker and dropped them into the glass container on the side table next to the bed.

Lily's stomach rolled as her eyes closed. She still could not stand the sight of them.

"He has slapped you before?" Garek's voice, low and soft, drifted to her.

Her head still bowed, she refused to open her eyes. If she opened them, she would look at Brianna. Look at the leeches. And if she looked, she would retch. "It does not matter. All that matters is that he is gone from Brianna's room."

The sound of footsteps, ominous, echoed down the hall—two sets of them. A quick glance at Brianna told her Garek was not done—he still had a slew of leeches to go.

She sprang away from the bedside, moving to the door to intercept.

Her hands flew up as the pair appeared in the doorway, immediately trying to calm. "Mr. Sneedly, whatever Dr. Rugbert has told you, I am sure he has exaggerated."

"Why am I being dragged in here, Lily?" Mr. Sneedly tightened the knot around his purple velvet dressing gown, sighing as he stopped in front of her. His eyes flickered over her shoulder to Garek and then back to her.

Close. He was too close, as he always was. His chest almost touched the linen wrapped around her palms. She would normally back away, try to escape him. But not this time. This time she was so very close to removing Dr. Rugbert from Brianna's care. She held her hands in place, hovering in midair, with her feet solid.

"I am not sure why Dr. Rugbert has brought you in here, Mr. Sneedly. I have just informed him that his services are no longer needed with Brianna. I believe it is a closed matter."

Dr. Rugbert pushed past the two of them, jabbing his porky finger toward Garek. "I have been manhandled by this barbarian—this impertinent ruffian—that Miss Silverton has dared to bring here."

"He is not a ruffian, Mr. Sneedly." Lily dropped her hands, turning sideways as she forced her voice to the utmost calmness.

She motioned to the bed where Garek still calmly pulled leeches. "Garek—Dr. Harrison—is a childhood friend from long ago. We grew up together and he has recently moved back into the area. I heard he was back from his training as a physician, so I inquired as to his availability to take over Brianna's care."

Mr. Sneedly's face went pinched, his cold glare chilling Lily's spine. "How did you hear of his arrival back in the area? Who told you? Did you leave the house—you are not to leave the estate, Lily."

She clasped her hands in front of her. "I was merely down at the stables. It was happenstance that Lawrence, our old stable master, had stopped by to check on one of the horses—he had seen it in the village when it had come up lame."

"He has no right to come onto these lands." Mr. Sneedly's voice went cold, each word drawn out long and slow.

"You already dismissed him, Mr. Sneedly. There need be no dire consequence. He was merely concerned for the horse and stopped by to check on the mare and to offer help. I do not see how you can fault him for honest intentions—caring about what had been his life's work."

One wheezing inhale, and a forced smile crossed Mr. Sneedly's face. "No. One cannot fault him for that." His glare went to Dr. Rugbert, who was staring at Garek, watching him remove the last leech from Brianna's skin. "And this man—Mr. Harrison—"

"It is Dr. Harrison, and he has also studied as a surgeon."

Mr. Sneedly's pinched eyes returned to Lily at her interruption. "Dr. Harrison has agreed to take over your sister's care?"

"He has." Lily jumped on the question. "You have, Garek, correct?"

Garek set the glass topper on the jar of leeches. He picked up the jar, moving from the bed to hand them to Dr. Rugbert, and then turned to Lily and Mr. Sneedly. "I have agreed. I am honored that Lily would request me in such a difficult time."

"An abomination. You will kill this girl if you allow this, Mr. Sneedly." Clutching his jar of leeches to his chest like a newborn babe, Dr. Rugbert stepped in front of Garek, pleading to Mr. Sneedly. "I do not need to remind you I was the only one helping her. Keeping her alive."

"True." Mr. Sneedly's head tilted, looking to Lily. "You do recall that Dr. Rugbert was specifically recommended by the viscount?"

"I do. And I, of course, appreciate the kindness." Lily offered her sweetest smile. "But both Brianna and I will be far more comfortable with a trusted friend from childhood, especially since he has the proper training. I am sure, Mr. Sneedly, that you can understand my need for a comfort from the past in this difficult time."

Mr. Sneedly sneered and then nodded. "Acceptable. But I presume Dr. Rugbert will be compensated for his time?"

Lily gritted her teeth, but forced her words light. "Yes, Dr. Rugbert will be paid well for his services. He need not worry on that."

"Dr. Rugbert, you may wait in the front drawing room." Mr. Sneedly dismissed the physician and then waited in silence, staring at the open doorway until Dr. Rugbert's footsteps receded down the hallway. He turned to Lily, swiping back the long strands of greasy hair hanging down his forehead. "This will be from your funds, Lily. Not the viscount's."

"Of course, Mr. Sneedly. I will retrieve his payment at once and bring it to you, so he has no need to return." She glanced to Brianna. Even with the commotion, her sister had not moved in the slightest. "Garek, you will stay with Brianna?"

Garek nodded and went back to Brianna's bedside.

Silently grateful, Lily left the room. A few steps into the hallway, she spun, collapsing against the wall. The top of the wainscoting cut into her lower back as she gasped, trying to catch her breath.

All of it—all of it had been such raw, false bravado on her part, her heart still had not slowed.

But it had been worth it. Dr. Rugbert was gone. Finally.

The whine of Mr. Sneedly's voice spilled into the hallway from the open doorway, cutting through the blood pounding in Lily's ears. "I apologize for the untoward scene, Dr. Harrison. A firm hand is what that chit needs—my firm hand. She has gone unchecked for far too long—her whole life I imagine. Spoiled, as far as I have seen. Of course, you knew her as a pup, so you must be well aware. But she will be much more disciplined once she accepts the inevitable."

A cough filled the room. Garek's cough, Lily could tell by the depth, and then his voice. "You have intentions toward Lily?"

"It is foregone. She is already practically mine. And the girl needs to be broken—scenes like this are not acceptable. Not that I will make it easy for her—a long breaking, so I may enjoy it, if you get my meaning, old boy."

Bile rushed into her throat.

"I do get your meaning, Mr. Sneedly." There was a definite bite to Garek's words. "And I beg you to remember that Lily is a dear friend from long ago, and I would be quite displeased were she to be taken advantage of."

Lily's breath stopped.

Silence. A long moment of silence from the room.

Then a high-pitched, forced chuckle from Mr. Sneedly. "Of course, old boy, I meant no disrespect to your association with her."

Without waiting to hear another word, Lily turned, exhaling as she escaped down the hall as quietly as possible.

She could not afford to get caught eavesdropping.

All would be lost if she set Mr. Sneedly off again—especially if he made the viscount came back to Weadly Hall.

{ CHAPTER 3 }

A sack of coins in-hand, Lily stepped back into Brianna's room and handed them off to Mr. Sneedly. He wanted Dr. Rugbert paid, so he could very well do it himself. She would have no part of ever speaking to that physician again.

Mr. Sneedly left the room, and Lily stood, staring at Garek on the opposite side of the bed. He was bent over, writing on a piece of a paper on the side table next to Brianna's pillows.

Fear suddenly gripped Lily. What if she had just traded one ill-advised physician for an even less equipped one? She had been so focused on getting rid of Dr. Rugbert, and Garek had seemed like such an easy solution this morning—the only solution, for she certainly hadn't been able to manage it on her own these past weeks.

But what did she really know of this man? He was looking for work and he had medicinal skills.

That was it.

And he could swing a hammer.

She mustn't forget that. Or that he was kind. Or that—for some god-forsaken reason—he had stumbled upon a crazy lady wielding a hammer in the middle of the night, and he had decided to help her. Silently. Without a barrage of questions.

Her eyes travelled up from Garek's large hands, along his profile, to his dark hair. He was far too large to be a healer. Too intimidating. Tall, but nowhere near fat—his frame held a healthy amount of muscle if the way he swung the sledgehammer last night was any indication.

And handsome. A man that looked as if he should be enjoying sport or a grueling ride, rather than doting on the sick. If she hadn't experienced herself the gentleness of his hands, she would never have believed he had the capacity.

But he did have the capacity. She had seen that this morning. She had to trust that instinct.

He set the quill down next to the ink jar and straightened, looking across the room at her. The concentration in his eyes disappeared, only to be replaced with obvious ire.

Lily's heart started to thud hard in her chest.

"You brought me here to fight battles for you, Miss Silverton."

"I—I what?" Her feet shuffled backward until she could lean out of the room and glance down the hall. Empty, thankfully. She pulled the door closed. She couldn't afford Mr. Sneedly overhearing any of this conversation.

"Dr. Rugbert. Mr. Sneedly." Garek's deep voice cut across the room the second the door clicked shut. "You brought me here to fight your battles, Miss Silverton. Battles I am not suited to wage."

Lily moved forward, stopping at the opposite side of Brianna's bed, her fingers wrapping themselves into the coverlet. "I…I brought you here for my sister. My sister."

"Yes. That I can see." His eyes flickered down to Brianna, then up to Lily, pinning her. "And also for me to trounce the physician who has obviously been overly generous with the back of his hand on your face. And also to buffer you from the other man who has every intention to claim you. Claim you and break you."

Lily's head bowed, her eyes landing on Brianna's face. Her sister's cheeks were sunken and grey. How long had it taken the last time Brianna was bled for the pink to come back to her face? Lily searched her mind. She couldn't remember.

Her chest tightened. If only Brianna would wake up. Wake up and tell her what to do. Her sister always knew what to do.

Words crept from Lily's mouth, almost a whisper. "I need you to stay."

"You need far more than that, Miss Silverton." The harsh edge still lined his voice.

"Yes." Her chin lifted, defiant. "Yes—I need you for Brianna—and I need you for all those reasons."

"I do not take kindly to deception, Miss Silverton. Nor to being cast in the role of champion."

Lily uncurled her fingers from the coverlet, her hand waving over her sister's prone body. "All of this—this is much more complicated than I first disclosed. I know that. I did not tell you this morning because I did not want you to say no."

"So instead you try to trap me here with guilt? I see your sister and become beholden to stay?" He shook his head, drawing back from the side of the bed. "You overestimated me, Miss Silverton. I do believe I need to leave this home. I will do you the courtesy and wait until Dr. Rugbert leaves this place. I am sure you can procure another physician to look after your sister."

Stunned into silence, Lily watched as he turned from her, gathering his leather wallet of instruments from on top of the bureau and placing them into his dark satchel.

"I am alone." The three words slipped from her mouth, soft, beaten, carrying all of the pain she had suffered the last month.

His hands stilled, hovering over his bag. Slowly, he pulled himself to his full height, his arms at his sides. But he did not turn around to her.

She took a deep breath, trying to break the vise on her chest as her hands curled into fists over the coverlet. "I am alone, Garek. I have no one." She exhaled a shaking breath. "I am scared for Brianna—scared for me. And I know full well what Mr. Sneedly wants of me. I do not know what I can say to you. I cannot change what is, I can only apologize for not telling you everything before we arrived here."

She waited in silence. Silence that grew thicker with each second.

His head turned, his hazel eyes finding her, boring into her. "Tell me now."

She stared at him, stunned once more. A flicker of compassion had returned to his eyes. A light—a light to hold onto. She needed something so desperately to hold onto.

He motioned to one of the wing chairs by the fireplace. "Sit. Tell me. I do not promise to stay, but I will listen."

It took a long moment for Lily's fingers to uncurl from fists. Her eyes fell to Brianna. If she couldn't convince him to stay, if she had no one to care for Brianna...

She swallowed hard, realizing she had just gambled every last hope by bringing him here. He had to stay. He had to.

Lily couldn't pull her gaze from Brianna's closed eyelids. "Have you examined her leg yet?"

"No. Just a quick glance. I need more time to examine it properly."

"So you saw the wounds? Saw the five slices across her calf?"

"Yes."

"It was how I found her in the abbey. Blood all over her. Smeared on her face. Her arms. Her lips. I did not think she was alive. Dead. I thought her dead, just like Papa. He was clean, just the blood from his neck. But he was the one dead. She was the one alive—tied to a chair, covered in the blood from the wounds on her leg."

"What happened to them? Who did it?"

"I do not know. I only know what I walked in upon at the abbey."

Garek moved to the foot of the bed. Close, but not too close. "You need to sit before you collapse, Miss Silverton. You are swaying. Exhausted."

She shook her head, not able to look up at him. Not able to clear her mind of the images of blood and death before her. Brianna was clean now, but Lily could still see exactly where the streaks of blood had marred her cheeks, her forehead. Still imagine. "I am fine. I can stand."

He sighed, moving to her side of the bed within arm's reach. "Who owns this estate? A viscount? Why are you here?"

Her look snapped up to him. "Oh, I suppose you do not know. This is—was Viscount Friellway's estate. I speak of the eighth viscount, not the current one. I have lived here at Weadly Hall my whole life. My father was the viscount's most trusted advisor. The viscount was like an uncle to me—more—he was our family. But he died five weeks ago. He was killed. And then my father. And now Brianna is so close to…" Her words slipped into silence as her eyes dropped to her sister.

"So who is in charge of the estate now?"

"The viscount's brother—he is the new viscount, the title, the estate are now his—he has let us remain here. But he left for London soon after his brother's death." She looked up to Garek. "I have not seen him in weeks and he left Mr. Sneedly in charge. Mr. Sneedly is his cousin."

"He calls you Lily."

"Without my permission." Her head shook, her eyes closing. "I have only known him a month. It is a privilege that was taken, not offered. He has taken everything from me."

"What else has he taken?"

"He dismissed everyone. Every last servant. There is no one I know here now. People move in and out of this room and I recognize not a face. They bring food, tend to the fire, but they avert their eyes. Do not speak. I have nothing, no one from my life, except for Brianna."

She looked up to Garek. He had moved closer, his hand was under her elbow, holding her steady. She hadn't even noticed him doing so, but now prayed he wouldn't remove his hand and let her drop.

"This was my home, Garek. My home. It was happy. And I have lost everything. Everything except for Bree. She is all I have left. And she is not even here. I am alone. Alone and I am sorry I did not tell you the truth of the position I was in, but you were the first person that…"

"That what?"

"That has looked at me with…compassion. I have been alone, drowning in looks of pity, looks of lechery. But you—last night you looked at me and genuinely wanted to help me—or so I thought—or so I wished—or maybe I just put that upon your face because I needed it so badly, someone to care."

Stopping her words, she realized the complete spectacle she was making. She pulled her elbow from his hand, only to find he was right about her exhaustion and she swayed.

Her palms went down to the bed, propping herself upright as she bent over, her chin on her chest. "I am sorry. I do not wish to put all of this upon you—it is not right—these are my problems and I had no right to bring you here. To involve you. I will still pay—"

"I will stay." His low voice cut her off.

It took a long moment for his words to forge into her brain, and when they did, she sank, landing on her heels, her forehead burying onto the bed. Relief ran through her body so raw it turned her muscles to jelly.

His hand came down, landing on her shoulder. "I will stay, Lily. But only if you will sit and eat something. Sleep."

She craned her head upward to him, her temple resting along the bed. "You will? And Brianna?"

His cheek cocked upward, almost into a cringe. "I will do everything in my power to make her well. But I need to first truly assess your sister's leg. I cannot promise anything—cannot promise miracles."

Lily nodded.

Miracle or not, what was standing in front of her was hope.

Hope she had not had in a very long time.

~ ~ ~

His fingers crinkling the edges of the vellum, Garek stared at the half-legible scrawl of his oldest friend, Joseph Tangert. The ink on the last two lines of the letter was thicker than the rest, as if the quill had split, and they were the ones Garek read over and over.

After numerous denials, I was finally allowed to see him for five minutes. Your uncle is holding well, considering the situation. Though I must suggest you conduct your business with post haste.

A deep breath, and Garek carefully folded the note, slipping it in along the back edge of his leather satchel. His uncle was fine. For now.

Garek looked about the room Mr. Sneedly had shown him to in the opposite wing of the house.

Barren but functional. A small bed, now rumpled, a wooden chair, a flickering fire in the fireplace. He had slept in much worse. Yet after only two hours of sleep, he had awoken, sprawled there, staring at the shadows chasing across the white plaster of the ceiling. Maddening, but usual, as he rarely slept for more than a few hours at a time.

Restless and giving up on the bed, he had lit a candle to look at the letter—reassurance that this detour from Farlington would not do harm.

The letter hidden away, Garek threw on his linen shirt and black trousers, and stepped out of the room, candle in-hand. He moved through the grand home as quietly as possible.

He wanted to check on Brianna again, for when he had left her hours ago, her breathing had been steady but shallow. Draining her wounds had improved her leg, but Garek still could not tell if she languished because of the bloodletting, or because of the infection from the cuts on her calf. Cuts that should have started to heal weeks ago but still looked nearly as raw as the day they happened.

Garek stepped into Brianna's room. The fire had died down to low embers so he held the candlestick high. Two lumps in the bed.

Toes light on the floorboards, he walked to the bedside. Brianna was still flat on her back, unmoved from how he had left her with her left calf now above the covers, the wounds freshly drained, cleaned, salved, and wrapped in linen. The coverlet draped over the rest of her body, up past her chest, with her arms lying limply on top.

To the right of Brianna on the bed, Lily was in a blue robe, curled on her side, her face toward her sister. She had one hand on Brianna's upper arm, her breathing even and light. Her bare feet stuck out from the bottom of the robe, and Garek wondered if they were frozen. A definite chill had seeped into the room without the blaze of a full fire.

Garek moved to the side of the bed where he could reach Brianna without disturbing Lily. He set the candlestick down on the side table and his fingers went to the side of Brianna's neck, noting her pulse. Still weak. The back of his hand to her forehead told him she was warmer than she had been hours ago after the leeches were removed. A small encouragement.

He pulled back, moving down to Brianna's injured leg, but his weight creaked a floorboard.

Lily instantly flew upright, her eyes wild around her until she saw his face. Her hand went to her chest, her shoulders collapsing in relief.

"Lily, I apologize," Garek whispered. "I did not mean to wake you. I was just checking on your sister and I did not expect you to be in here."

Lily's feet curled under her backside as she waved her hand in the air. "No. It is not a bother. I do not sleep well and am easily roused." Her fingers went behind her to rub her toes.

"Do you always sleep with Brianna?" Garek bent over Brianna's leg, pulling back the linen wrapping to check the cuts. For as much pus as he had removed earlier, large swathes of her skin had already re-swelled. He could feel Lily's eyes intent on him.

"I do. I am afraid…afraid if I leave her…"

He glanced up to her. "She will pass?"

Lily nodded. "I do not want to miss it if..." Her words choked off. "I am afraid it will be like it was with my father. He was alive one moment. And then the next time I saw him, he was dead. Just gone. I did not get to say goodbye. Did not get to hug him, bury my cheek on his chest, just one last time."

Garek reset the linen and looked to her as he stood straight.

Her head bowed as she wiped away a tear sliding down her cheek. "I am sorry. I do not mean to cry. They demand I do not cry. Please do not tell Mr. Sneedly. I try. But when I am tired I...I cannot stop my mind."

He stared at the top of her head, her brown hair loose around her face, shielding her from him. She looked tiny. Fragile. A mere wisp of the woman that had banished Dr. Rugbert from this room hours ago.

Garek had to fight the stark urge to go to her, to collect her in his arms and cocoon her from everything this place had brought down upon her.

He had only known her for one day, he reminded himself. One day, and he was already too invested in her.

"I will not demand you stop anything you need to do, Lily." His voice came out rough, surprising himself as his chest tightened, her obvious pain cutting to his heart.

Far too invested.

To avoid watching her, witnessing her anguish, Garek walked around the bed, going to the fireplace and placing two split logs onto the glowing embers. He grabbed the fireplace poker, absently jabbing at the bark of the logs until they lit.

The fire climbed, sending warmth into the room, and Garek turned back to Lily. "Come, sit, Lily. Warm your toes while I finish with your sister. They must be freezing."

Wiping the corners of her eyes, she looked over her shoulder at him. "You have more to do?"

"I would like to remove the pus building upon her calf again."

Lily nodded, scooting off of the bed and stepping past him to sit on one of the matching damask-covered wingback chairs angled to the fire. She promptly held her feet straight out, toasting her soles close to the fire.

A half hour later Garek had tended to Brianna and resettled her leg. He blew out the five candles he had lit for light, looking over the bed to the fire.

Nuzzled into a corner of the chair, Lily sat curled up, her toes now gathered under her robe. She had been silent since she sat down. Garek couldn't tell from his angle if her eyes were closed, but he presumed she was sleeping.

He debated for a moment on whether to wake her so she could crawl back into the bed, or to just let her sleep in peace.

Choosing the latter, he picked up the one candle still lit next to the bed and stepped lightly to the door.

"How is she?"

Garek turned back, walking deep into the room and stopping opposite the chair Lily sat in. His hand went to the top of the empty wingback chair next to him, rubbing the cloth as he looked down at her. "It is a good thing her body is still fighting—still fighting the infection."

"Can I help her at all? Help you? I have wanted to do something—anything for her since it happened, but I do not know the slightest thing about wounds such as these. And Dr. Rugbert was insistent I not go near her leg."

Garek's jaw tightened. "Insistent with the back of his hand?"

She waved her fingers, unwilling to answer. "He is gone, that is what matters. And I want to help—I want to do something worthwhile, not just stare at her as I have been. I have been helpless, and I hate that about myself. I want to know how I can help her pain. Can you show me?"

"It is...messy."

"I do not care. Please. She is my sister."

He relented with a nod. "I can show you. Next time I drain her leg, I will teach you. And I will show you how to mix the salve and the herbs for pain."

"Thank you." Lily's arms clasped over her belly, holding herself as her head shook. "You have done more for her in one day than that blasted idiot Dr. Rugbert did in thirty."

"You are still angry with him?"

"Yes. But even more angry at me. I could not rid him from this place by myself. I should have been able to, but I had to depend on a stranger to do so."

She looked to her sister on the bed. "Bree could have done it. She would have just made it so. But I...I did not know what to do, and it took far, far too long to stop him." Her eyes whipped to Garek. "And I never even did do it—you did. If not for you, he would still be here, his suckers all over her body."

"Do not minimize yourself, Lily. You were the one that brought me here."

She sighed, her gaze going to the fire. "I just never imagined I was that weak. My life—my life was so easy before this. Carefree. I had never thought of myself as weak—we were the Silverton sisters—bold and bright and vivacious. But it was easy to be that way when there was money...love...comfort surrounding me. There was never a need for me to show my spine. My father, Brianna, they took care of anything and everything uncomfortable."

Her head tilted as her look travelled back to him. "It is just one more loss to add to the list—who I imagined myself to be. The reality of my weakness is not nearly as becoming."

"I believe the stone abbey would dispute you on that statement. You are aware you swing a mighty hammer?"

She chuckled, the firelight sending a sparkle into her blue eyes. "Thank you. Truly. You did not need to stop last night. You did not need to come back here with me. You did not need to stay. You did not need to do any of it, but you did. You are the one with an admirable spine."

With an uncomfortable half-smile, Garek grabbed the poker, flipping the logs, and then moved backward to sit on the chair opposite Lily.

"Why did you stop last night?" she asked.

"At the abbey?"

"Yes. I do not know any sane man that would have come upon me and stopped."

Garek shrugged. "I have never encountered a woman swinging a hammer, attempting to destroy an entire building in the middle of the night. And I imagine I never will again. A smart man does not stumble upon a scene such as that and dare to question why it was put in front of him. That is fate. The smart man just gets off his horse and does what is demanded of him."

"So I could have just demanded you work on the abbey while I watched?" The corners of her eyes crinkled in mischief. "Demanded you kick Dr. Rugbert out? Demanded you heal my sister? And do I get to make demands from here on? I have a list. It is long."

He laughed. "Let us not go crazy, Lily. I do appreciate that I was asked on all of those accounts, rather than told. And now I am properly frightened of the list you are sitting upon."

"As you should be." She smiled wide, her body relaxing into the chair. "I like pretending you are a friend from childhood, Garek."

"You do? Why?"

"It gives me comfort—even if it is imaginary." Her hands dropped to her lap, her fingers playing with the frayed edges of the linen bandage wrapped around her palm. "I like that you call me Lily…it has been so long…so long since someone has said my name. Bree, my father, the viscount—even to hear the servants say Miss Lily. But not now. Now all I hear is Miss Silverton, and I do not even turn my head to that. Mr. Sneedly may call me Lily, but it is so far from right that I strike it from my ears."

She waved her hand, dismissing the sadness that had crept into her voice. "I just wish it were actually true—that you were a childhood friend. Silly, I know."

"Not silly. And if it is any solace, as long as I am here at the Weadly Hall, it is true."

"It is." She smiled at him, warm, genuine, and Garek could feel himself getting lost in the sparkle in her eyes.

"But heaven forbid Mr. Sneedly discovers differently—that I lied." She sighed, rubbing her forehead. "I am entirely anxious to leave this place. Anxious for Brianna to heal so we can move from here."

"Can you leave your home that easily?"

"Yes." Her answer was immediate, no emotion. "This place bears no resemblance to the home I once knew. Mr. Sneedly took care of that quite handily."

"Where will you go?"

"I do not know. I believe Papa's estate was quite healthy, but I do not know the specifics. I know we have adequate dowries. I have been waiting for Brianna to wake, to tell me, to decide. Papa included her with everything about the Silverton estate and holdings, but I know nothing. Bree will have a place for us to go, a plan. I have just been waiting."

"That has been hard?"

"Yes." Her eyes left him to stare at the fire. Moments passed before she looked to him, her sweet voice raw. "She will wake, Garek? You will make it so? She will heal?"

Sheer, desperate hope burned in her eyes.

Garek knew he should kill it, or at least temper it, as the dark veins spreading up Brianna's leg told him she was far from surviving. But he couldn't do it. Couldn't be the cause of Lily's face falling—of hope deserting her and leaving her alone with the desperation.

He nodded, meeting her clear blue eyes. "I think she will, Lily. I think she will."

~ ~ ~

"Is this right?"

Garek looked up from the mortar bowl where he crushed herbs for more salve. Lily had just set salve on the top two of Brianna's cuts and was starting to unfurl the strip of linen wrap around her sister's leg.

"It is," Garek said, watching Lily's eyes concentrating on Brianna's leg. Her hair pinned back in an upsweep, tendrils fell from the backside, brushing Lily's neck as she moved.

A full week he had been sneaking glances at that profile, and he was still startled every single time at her beauty. A natural beauty she did nothing to flaunt. Nothing to bolster. She was far too concerned for her sister to give attention to such trivial matters.

"Please, would you mind?" She looked to him, apologetic smile on her face as she held up the linen in her hand. "Just your hands to oversee, not do."

With a nod, Garek set the pestle into the mortar and moved across the room to stop directly behind Lily. "You know what you are doing, Lily. You need to trust yourself." Nevertheless, he bent, his arms settling around her as he laid his hands along the back of hers and aligned each of his digits to her fingers.

She nodded, her hair tickling his cheek. "I know. You trust me. But I do not trust me. Ever since I wrapped it too tight that once and her toes went blue, I have been nervous. Your hands feeling what I am doing are a comfort."

Lily started wrapping Brianna's leg with the strip of linen.

"A touch looser."

Lily let out a sigh, her hands relaxing under his. "Yes, I can feel it, now." She circled Brianna's leg with the cloth several times.

"Good," Garek said, his eyes closing for a long breath as he tried not to inhale the scent of her hair. Citrus. Lemons. She always smelled bright, even in this sickly room.

She turned her face to him, her nose almost touching his cheek as she smiled. "I want to strangle the infection away. That is my problem, I have determined."

He looked down at Brianna's leg. Lily had finished wrapping the two cuts. How long had she been waiting for him to move from her? Garek's hands left the back of hers, his fingers trailing even as he abruptly took a step away from her body.

He exhaled, instantly regretting having to move from her, and hoping she never got good enough at the wrapping that she wouldn't ask for his help.

Garek walked back to the table, picking up the pestle. "That could very well be—you have been nothing but angry at that leg of Brianna's, so I do not think your problem is confidence." He smirked at her. "So to temper your annoyance with her leg, how about moving onto draining the next two cuts?"

Lily wrinkled her nose, turning to pick up the syringe. She hated draining the pus and infection, he knew. But each time he asked her to do it, she did so without complaint. Tortured faces, yes, but no complaints.

She pulled the side table close to her and set to work on clearing the next two cuts. It only took a few minutes for her voice to interrupt the clacking of his pestle against the mortar.

"Take my mind away from pus, Garek. If I have to do this, at least I can be thinking on something else."

"What would you like to think about?"

She paused with the syringe, pulling herself straight and looking out the window at the grey sky. "How about this?" Her hand swept over his set of surgical tools splayed along the side table. "Tell me what you meant last week when you said it was easy to become a surgeon after you witnessed what you have."

Garek's look slipped downward from Lily's face to the gleaming silver tools as she turned back to work on Brianna's leg.

"My uncle had paid for my education at Oxford, and I had earned my physician's license only six months before I disappeared into the war on the continent. I quickly learned the only useful doctor on those battlefields was a surgeon. Tapping upon one's chest and taking a pulse did little good for a man with his leg blasted to pieces. So as fast as I could, I learned everything and anything I could about how to properly put a body back together after trauma."

Garek's mouth went to a grim smile. "So many deaths. But I was actually useful. Saving men in a very real way. When I returned to England, I wanted to learn everything I could in the field of surgery. So I apprenticed for years with a doctor who was both a physician and a surgeon—the best in the country, a genius."

"Dr. Halowell?"

"Yes. But it was expensive, his tutelage. And then I had to leave."

Lily glanced up at him, her eyebrows arched. He recognized he had abruptly cut his story short. But he wasn't about to speak to why he had left London.

For all the questions in her eyes, she let the topic slide. "You have only mentioned your uncle. What of your mother, your father?"

Garek's hand on the pestle sped. One testy topic to the next.

"My father died when I was three, I then had a stepfather until I was seven when my mother died." His voice was curt—too curt and he knew it.

Lily's eyes whipped to him, but then she hid her face, setting down the syringe to grab a wet sponge. She concentrated on cleaning one of the cuts on Brianna's leg. "Your voice softens when you mention your uncle, Garek. I assume he was kind to you?"

"He was a good man, my uncle—my father's brother. He raised me after my mother died. He taught me what it was to be a man. To take responsibility for my life."

Lily nodded, not looking his way. "And your stepfather?"

"Not a good man. But he did teach me how to fight in his own way."

"His own way?" She set the sponge down and expelled dark pus from the syringe into a bowl on the table.

"He enjoyed beating me several times a week. But those were the good days."

Lily turned fully to him on the chair, her blue eyes focusing on him. "And on the bad?"

Garek's hands stilled, and he dropped the pestle and mortar to the table. "He would beat my mother."

Lily inhaled, her lips sucking inward as her hand went to her belly.

"She died at his hands, thrown into a brick wall—it was why I became interested in medicine. She died with her head in my lap. Her bloody head. Bruised cheek. Temple split open." His eyes shifted to the fire, his head shaking as memories of a little boy filled his mind without warning. "I could do nothing. My hand over the wound on her head. The warm blood squeezing through my fingers. Begging her to wake up. Begging."

He heaved a breath, his eyes shutting hard as he pushed long dead images from haunting his mind. "But she didn't. And I could not help her. I did not know what to do."

Lily's voice, soft and sweet, eased into the air. "So your uncle took you in?"

Garek realized she had moved from the bedside to stand in front of him. He opened his eyes to see her gaze liquid with tears, one slipping down her face as she looked up at him. Not only sympathy in her eyes, but true, guttural pain at what a little boy had suffered. What he had suffered.

He swallowed hard, nodding. "Yes, my uncle did. The first time I met him was at my mother's burial. He came up to me, a big, burly man with lots of furs around his neck. 'You can come with me boy. Get in the carriage,' he said. He sat me down across from him as we rolled away, and all I could do was look back to the mound of dirt, the dark grey headstone disappearing from the corner of the window."

Garek's fingers went to the back of his neck, rubbing. "He stared at me for at least ten minutes, and then he banged his cane on the floor of the carriage, his booming voice filling the air. 'You are of age soon, boy, so what is it that you want most in life?' he asked."

"What was your answer?"

Garek shrugged. "That I never wanted to have to watch someone I love die again."

"Garek—"

The pain echoing in the one word made him cut her off. "My uncle smiled at the answer—big and rollicking, and then he settled back on his seat. 'Well then, boy, let us make that happen,' he said. And that was it. I have been on no other path since."

"Garek—"

He opened his mouth to cut her words short again, but her hand went onto his chest, stopping him.

"No. Let me speak. I can see you do not want me to expound on how horrible her death was for you—we can both clearly recognize it was. I just wanted to say that your mother must have been a remarkable woman, to raise a boy that would take what could have been a lifetime of anger and instead, turn it into a lifetime of compassion." Her fingers curled on his chest. "You do her honor, Garek."

His throat clamping, Garek nodded, having to force words. "She was remarkable, Lily."

"Then you were lucky." Lily's hand dropped from his chest and she spun, slowly walking over to Brianna. Her voice was thick as she stopped by her sister's leg. "You said no salve on these two cuts, correct? They are ready to wrap if you would observe again?"

Garek followed Lily, assuming the same position behind her as earlier. His hands slid along the back of her hands—smooth still, even if her skin was slightly rougher from the many washings in the past week.

Lily started to wrap the linen around the middle two cuts in Brianna's leg.

Perfect.

Garek contemplated for a moment on correcting her on some minor thing, just so she wouldn't abandon his help.

Instead, he cleared his throat, his voice low over her shoulder. "What happened to your mother, Lily? You never speak of her."

"She died in childbirth."

"How old were you? Do you remember her?"

"She died having me." Lily looked over to Brianna's face, rushing on. "But Papa and Bree made sure there was never a moment where I felt I missed having a mother. Bree has always taken care of me, and Papa—he was the best father, always had time for me. And the viscount was the best uncle, even if we were not related."

"Did you always live here at Weadly Hall?"

"Yes, always. We have always been this happy family. Well, at least until…"

Her hands sped, tightening the linen strip. Garek squeezed her knuckles, stilling her.

Her chin dropped. "Too tight?"

"Only for the last go around."

She loosened the cloth, going around Brianna's leg again, this time, agonizingly slow, but in control.

"You miss him, your father?"

"Every day." At the end of the cloth, Garek's hands dropped away and she leaned forward, pinning the wrap so it didn't unwind. She stood straight, her eyes on Brianna's face as her back brushed across the front of Garek. Her fingers fiddled on the sheet of the bed. "I miss him until my heart pains me."

She spun, looking up at Garek. Tears had flooded her eyes again, even as her mouth stretched wide in a flat smile.

"But missing Papa is not going to bring him back. Not going to heal Brianna. So I am trying to move, and keep moving, whether I want to or not. I have to—Bree needs me to." She glanced over her shoulder to her sister. "Even if everything within me is dark—heavy, I can move. I can put on a smile. Fake life."

He needed to resist.

He knew it.

Yet Garek lifted his hand, slipping his fingers along her cheek, his palm cradling her jaw.

She didn't resist, her head tilting, her blue eyes closing as she leaned into the touch.

"You do not need to fake anything in front of me, Lils."

Her eyes flew open. "That—Lils. It is what Bree calls me."

"I should stop."

Her fingers came up, wrapping along the back of his hand cupping her face. Holding him in place. "No. Please do not. It is a comfort. Just as you have been every minute since you appeared by the abbey."

A tear escaped out past her eyelids, sliding down her cheek. Garek's thumb moved up, swiping it away.

She offered an apologetic smile. "You must be tired of wiping my tears. Again and again when I break."

"I am tired of nothing, Lils." Garek stared at her lower lip, thick and plump. Waiting to be kissed, whether she knew it or not. Waiting to be sucked, bitten, loved. He inhaled, calming the sudden throb between his legs, the urges he had no right to even broach.

She nodded, her blue eyes wide, watching him.

He needed to leave this place.

Leave before he couldn't. Leave and finish what his responsibilities demanded of him. Leave before he failed this woman.

Garek cleared his throat, the only thought in his head spilling from his mouth before he could stop it. "What if your sister does not come back, Lily—what if I cannot save her?"

Her smile at him widened. A true smile, crinkling the corners of her eyes. "You will save her, Garek. There is not a shadow in my mind that doubts it."

He tried to hold the frown from forming on his face before he dropped his hand and turned from her.

Staring at the small jars from the traveling apothecary on the table, Garek let the frown settle.

If Brianna died.

Hell.

What Lily would go through.

The look she would give him.

He gave himself a shake.

He could not watch Lily suffer like that. Could not watch her be destroyed.

{ CHAPTER 4 }

"You lied to me."

Left hand landing on her hip, Lily skidded to a stop, her stance wide in front of the main entrance to Weadly Hall.

Her right hand flattened onto her chest as she gasped for air, craning her neck to stare up at Garek atop his horse. She had seen him approach from the window in Brianna's room, and running through the house to meet him on the gravel drive had left her little breath for words.

His face darkened, grave concern etching his brow. "I did?"

"You told me two weeks ago you thought Brianna would wake." Lily kept her voice even as she squinted, the cloud-covered sun a wispy orange spot behind his head.

He offered one slow, careful nod. "I did say that." He swung his leg over the horse and jumped down from the saddle.

"But you did not just think it—you knew it." A smile spread wide across her face. "You must have known it."

"What?"

"Bree—she woke up, Garek. She talked to me. Not fevered mutterings. True talking. Her eyes are clear—lucid." Lily could hold it in no longer. She ran at him, her body crashing into his as she tackled him around the neck. "She is awake. Awake, awake, awake."

Lily could feel the relief sweep through his shoulders as he laughed, wrapping her in his arms and swinging her in a circle.

He set her to her feet, his hands going to her shoulders to pull back and look at her face. "She woke while I was in town?"

Lily nodded, giggling at the disbelief still in his eyes. "She did, Garek. She woke and we talked—she is sore all over—weak—but she smiled at me. Said I looked horrible. Asked me why my hair was in such disarray. She is confused, but awake—truly awake."

Garek's eyes closed, his head shaking. A smile crept onto his lips.

Lily clamped her arms around his neck again, smothering him in another hug with a laugh. His arms hesitated and then went around her back, clasping her to his chest.

"You did this, Garek. You." Lily turned her mouth to his ear. "You brought her back to me. Thank you—I owe you so much—everything."

He peeled away from her again, his hands moving up to cup her face. "No, you did this, Lily. You are the one that saved her from Dr. Rugbert. The one that has not left her side. The one that has refused to give up on her. The one that brought me here and convinced me to stay—against my own better judgement, I must say."

Lily stared into his dark hazel eyes, the blue flecks vibrant in the warm glow of the sky. "And your judgement now?"

His lips were on hers in one swift motion, kissing her.

Shock fired through Lily, but she didn't pull away, didn't resist the sudden tingle down her spine. Didn't resist because it felt so natural—so exactly what she should be doing in that very moment.

Even though she had been consumed with Brianna the past weeks, she knew full well she had grown overly attached to Garek.

It had been impossible not to.

Minute after minute, hour after hour they had spent together in Brianna's room. What had felt like a lifetime with this man.

And though Lily hadn't allowed her mind to fully drift into these waters—into thinking of Garek as more than her sister's physician—there had been far too many nights, deep in the dark, where she had watched him, imagining this very thing.

Imagining his arms around her. His lips on hers. His voice low and heated, uttering her name. In the darkness of night, in weakness, she had not been able to stop her wandering thoughts.

In a rush, every denied thought of Garek flooded her mind and she let her lips mold under his, the sensation sending her dizzy and leaning into him for support.

He drew away. Soon. Too soon. But then he looked down at her with heat so clear in his eyes she wondered how he managed to break the kiss.

"There. That is my judgement, Lily." His fingers pressing into her back, his voice dropped to roughness. "I was very wrong to have doubted staying here, to helping your sister. And I have found myself at the maddening point where I have been denying myself this very act—kissing you—for days. Do I need to apologize?"

Her eyes dove downward, staring at the lapel of his great coat as her fingers moved to her own lips, gently touching the warmth of where his skin had been. "No. No apology. Not in the slightest."

Her look crept up to meet his. "I was curious how that would feel, how you would feel. I imagined this—late at night, watching you in Bree's room. I was curious, but I never imagined it would be so…breathtaking." Her fingers slipped off her lips. "And I had never dared to think you would want the same of me."

He smiled, one of his hands releasing her body and coming up to brush a loose lock of hair from her temple. "Do you always say exactly what you are thinking, Lily?"

"You have not yet learned that about me?"

"I have, but with this—I am surprised by such candor—the lack of coyness."

"Well, I can attempt to be more coy, if you would like. It would make Bree happy—she hates my inability to filter my words."

"I do not mind. Especially in this instance."

Her fingers went to the lapel of his great coat, fingering the edge. Head tilting down, she looked up at him through her lashes. "You have been waiting how long to do that?"

"Quite coy." Garek chuckled, squeezing her to him as his free hand slipped along her jaw. "But if you must know, I have been staring at you for days over Brianna's bed, Lily. Watching every movement you made. Looking forward to the smirk you get on your face when you want to ignore death and tease me to lighten my mood. Make me smile."

Without warning, his hands dropped away from both her jaw and her waist to cross behind his back. He moved a step backward, leaving her suddenly very cold in the chilly air.

"But you do not owe me a thing, Lily. I did what I did for Brianna because I could help, not because I wanted something from you. If you tell me that this, that what I see in your eyes, how you look at me, is not there—is not true—then I will never touch you again. I swear it."

Her heart pounding at his words, at the mere thought of him never touching her again, she took a step forward, leaving no space between them. She looked up to his eyes. "You already have your answer, Garek. You see the truth far too clearly in me."

"And you are far too honest, Lily." His arms withdrew from behind him, and his hand went to her temple, his fingers following the line of her hair into the simple braid she had weaved. "Then you should know I have wanted to do this for weeks—hell, since the moment I saw you swinging that hammer in the moonlight. And then these last two weeks—every second has only magnified my want of you."

Lily inhaled, her breath caught. "Truly?"

He nodded. "Are you scared?"

"You would never hurt me, Garek."

Without another breath, he descended, catching her lips on his. His right hand curled around her neck under her braid, his fingers gently tilting her head, angling her so he could deepen the kiss.

Every nerve exploding, Lily could not help but lean into him. Lean into this man—this rock—that had held her hand

and wiped her tears late at night when she had broken, time and again, in desperation.

This man that had shown nothing but tenderness when he touched Brianna. This man that had listened to every word she had prattled on—recalling minute details that she had spoken. This man that was handsome beyond belief, strong and capable, smart.

Garek had become such a constant to her that his lips on hers were instinctive. Not to be questioned. Not to be denied.

His mouth parted, nudging her lips apart, and Lily's legs almost buckled.

Chaste kisses she had had before from suitors, but not this. Nothing like this.

This was raw desire, not yielding, not pulling back. Raw desire demanding she react. Raw power that Garek always kept bridled—but power that vibrated underneath every step he took, every flick of his finger, every look. Raw power she had always recognized was there, waiting for the smallest crack when it could be unleashed.

Unable to move under her own will, Lily could only accept him into her mouth, tasting his power, reveling in his exploration. His hand at the small of her back pressed her body into his, her flesh hitting the hard muscles of his chest, his belly.

Sinking, her breath gone, Lily clutched his shoulders, desperate for the kiss to not end.

Garek's lips left her.

It took long seconds for her eyes to open, and she found him looking down at her, mirth twinkling in the blue flecks in his eyes.

"I am going to let you go now, so we do not reach unseemly spectacle status," Garek said, the usual smoothness of his voice turned to gravel. "Even with the lack of servants around here, I imagine there are eyes that should not see this, and the horse blocks very little. Are you ready? You will not fall?"

"Fall? Of course I will not—"

Garek's hand left her back and Lily promptly stumbled forward, hands slipping from his shoulders and flailing until she awkwardly fell into his chest for balance.

"Fall?" he said, smirk curling up the left side of his face.

"Unfair." Her cheeks flushing, she untangled herself from his body, laughing through her frown. "What did you say about not becoming a spectacle?"

"I think you can still recover." He swept his hand in front of them. "Let us go in. I want to check on your sister directly. And then I want you to grab a cloak so you can be warm when I take you to the gardens."

"The gardens, why? Only the evergreens give color right now. There is nothing in bloom."

"Nothing?"

Her eyes crinkled at him. "Aah. Sly."

He nodded once, slowly, his eyes focused on her lips.

"Should I be concerned that you look like you could eat me right now?"

Garek chuckled, his palms flying up in defense. "An innocent walk, that is all I ask. It will be a novelty to talk with you in the fresh air instead of in Brianna's room. But I may still look at you like this."

"Am I wanton if I do not mind your look? No—do not answer. I do not care if I am." Her eyes went to the heavens as she shook her head at her own lack of modesty. "Tie your horse to the post, and I will round up a stable boy while you look in upon Bree."

~ ~ ~

Muffled voices floating to her, Lily walked down the corridor that intersected with the hallway leading to Brianna's room. She turned the corner to find Garek talking to Mr. Sneedly outside of Brianna's room.

A heated conversation—at least on Garek's part. Even before she could make out words, she could hear the usual pompous whine in Mr. Sneedly's voice. Lily's eyes flickered to her sister's door. Thank goodness it was closed.

Three more steps, and the men finally realized she was in the hall and walking toward them.

Mr. Sneedly turned, stepping in front of Garek to intercept her first. "Lily, I understand your sister is now fully conscious. Wonderful news. Truly a delight. I was stopping by to check on her before Dr. Harrison shoved me out of the room."

Garek glared at the back of Mr. Sneedly's greased hair. "If I had bothered to shove you, Sneedly, you would not be standing on two feet right now."

Lily's eyes snapped to Garek—even though his voice was even, those were the harshest words she had ever heard him speak.

Mr. Sneedly waved his fingers over his shoulder, his nose scrunched as he dismissed Garek's words behind him like the smell of bad fish. "As your sister has now recovered, Lily, I was just informing Dr. Harrison that his services in this house will no longer be needed."

Lily pulled her eyes off of Garek, forcing herself to look at Mr. Sneedly. "What?"

"Dr. Harrison is not needed. His time with us is done."

"You are wrong, Mr. Sneedly. Very wrong." She took a step towards Sneedly, instant anger flushing her cheeks—the man had absolutely no right. "Garek is here at my request. Not yours. I am his employer and will decide when we no longer need him. Brianna is far from well, and we are still dependent upon his services."

Mr. Sneedly's mouth stretched into a tight line. "Be that as it may, he is staying here at Weadly Hall by the generosity of the viscount. You may still use his services, Lily, but the viscount's generosity of room and meals will not extend another night for Dr. Harrison."

Lily's eyes went wide. "You are kicking Garek out of Weadly Hall?"

"I am."

"The viscount—he himself requested that directly of you, Mr. Sneedly?"

"It does not matter." Mr. Sneedly's chin tilted upward. He was short, the same height as Lily, so she had to stare up his thin nose. "I make the decisions regarding the management of Weadly Hall. Do I need to remind you of that?"

"No. No you do not, Mr. Sneedly." Lily couldn't keep disgust from curling her lip. "But Garek—"

"Step lightly, Lily." Sneedly's voice slipped from a whiny wheeze into sharpness. "Lest you and your sister find yourselves also at the end of the viscount's generosity. Do you think your sister would fare well out in the frozen land?"

Lily bowed her head, taking a step backward as she hid her fists in her skirts. She recognized very well his tone of voice. The tone and what came after it.

She swallowed a seething breath. She knew how to do it now—or at least how to try and clamp down on her rage in front of Mr. Sneedly so the back of his hand wouldn't fly at her face.

Sometimes she was successful. Sometimes not. Damn her stubborn tongue.

But submitting to Mr. Sneedly's temper was the price she needed to pay to keep Brianna here. Here and safe until her sister was well enough to travel—well enough to tell Lily what to do, where to go.

But this—kicking Garek out of Weadly Hall. Threatening Brianna. This went too far.

The rage in her chest swelled upward.

Mr. Sneedly was ruthlessly overstepping his bounds—going farther than he had ever dared.

Her mouth opened. She wasn't about to let Mr. Sneedly do this to her sister, to Garek. It was time Mr. Sneedly was put properly back into the rat's nest he had crawled from, come what may. She ventured her eyes, but not her head upward, sneaking a glance over Mr. Sneedly's shoulder to Garek.

The second her eyes met Garek's, he shook his head at her. A clear warning. Even though his wide shoulders swallowed the hallway behind Mr. Sneedly. Even though Garek could easily crush the man. Garek was warning her not to fight this battle.

Lily didn't want to acknowledge it. Didn't want to silence herself. For once, she didn't want to have to back down from Mr. Sneedly.

Garek's jaw flexed into hardness, his look turning from warning, to commanding. He gave her one last simple shake of his head. Simple, but she could feel the force of it cut across her tongue, stilling her voice.

Gritting her teeth, her eyes dropped and she exhaled, the rage balling in her chest.

"Mr. Sneedly, I will be gone by nightfall," Garek said, his voice a calm echo in the hall. "But Lily, know that I will come daily to check on Brianna and make sure she is progressing as she should."

Mr. Sneedly whipped around to Garek, his mouth sputtering against the plan. "No, that will not—"

"Surely you cannot think to deny Brianna medical care, Mr. Sneedly? I am quite certain that would be frowned upon by your cousin, the viscount, since he was the one that extended the invitation for Lily to keep Brianna here until she was well. Have I misunderstood—is that not true?"

Mr. Sneedly's look skittered back and forth between Garek and Lily. "That may be, but—"

"I will be happy to draft a missive to the viscount to ensure the invitation to stay here with proper medical care is still valid, Mr. Sneedly," Lily said.

"The viscount does not want to be bothered by matters at Weadly Hall, Lily," Mr. Sneedly said.

Lily fought down the rage in her chest and smiled her sweetest smile, forcing her voice extra light. "I am sure he will be willing to take five minutes to read my letter and answer me. I do not want you to have to worry on what the viscount thinks is proper in this situation, Mr. Sneedly." She started to turn from him. "I will go right now to draft it, so you may take it with you to town, Garek."

"That is—that is not necessary, Lily," Sneedly said, his boney fingers straining as they clasped in front of him. "Of course Dr. Harrison is welcome here at Weadly Hall to see his patient."

Lily spun back to Sneedly and Garek. "Wonderful, Mr. Sneedly. That will save me time spent writing the letter. Time that is better spent with my sister." Lily looked to Garek. "Will you accompany me to my father's study, Garek? There is the matter of your payment, which you will need to rent a place nearby. I have a cottage already in mind as an option, if it is still vacant."

"Do give my regards to the viscount for his hospitality during the past weeks, Mr. Sneedly," Garek said as he pushed past Sneedly, his wide frame making Sneedly shuffle backward and bump into the wall.

Lily ducked her eyes, hiding a smirk as she turned, leading Garek down the hall.

They walked in silence to her father's study, and once inside, Lily paused, facing the door with her fingers gripping the knob as she clicked it closed.

She leaned forward, her forehead resting on the door.

"What is it?" Garek asked.

She shook her head, not leaving the door. "I am just saying a quick prayer that the retribution for that fuss does not come back to haunt me." She turned to Garek, a bright smile on her face. "But it was worth it just to see his trapped little sniveling face of rat's arse attempting to scurry."

Garek did not answer her, the frown deepening on his face as he stood by her father's desk.

Her eyes immediately dropped to the brown and white Persian rug filling the room, fixating on the white area by the edge, stained purple long ago when her little fingers had dropped a half-eaten wild blackberry on it. Her father had not gotten even the slightest bit peeved. He had just cleaned it up and told her he would always think of her when he saw it.

She took a deep breath. Her father had not raised her to be petty. To put others to shame.

She looked up to Garek. "I apologize, that was not a generous thing to say. You must think me a shrew."

"I never want you to curb what you need to say to me, Lily. And no, I do not think you a shrew. But I do think you are very angry."

She shrugged, moving past him as she went behind her father's desk to pull open the middle left drawer.

Garek followed her, setting himself at her side, his chest just a sliver away from touching her upper arm. "What has Mr. Sneedly done to you?"

"Nothing I have not been able to suffer, Garek."

"And nothing you should ever have been put in the position to have to suffer?" He leaned slightly toward her, his breath reaching her temple. "Every time I see you look at him, Lily, your mouth curdles—your eyes, they go dark."

"I have lasted long enough with him that Brianna is improving. That is what is important." She bent, fishing her hand in the back of the drawer.

"I am only imagining the worst, Lily."

Pulling out a wide box from the drawer, she set it on top of the walnut inlaid desk. Her hands clutching the top edges of the box, she shook her head, her eyes downward. "Just words, Garek. Words. Threats. Do not bother to imagine what is in the past. The worst has been an occasional misplaced hand, an occasional slap. That is all."

She glanced up at him. Hard jaw. Fingers curling into fists. Murder in his eyes.

"Stop, Garek, stop. This is exactly what I did not want to happen. I have survived intact, and he is not worth your anger."

"Nor is he worth yours."

She turned to him, grabbing his left wrist and gently wedging her fingers into his fist, loosening the ball. "True, but I do not hold my anger nearly as well as you. I let it fly out of me in sometimes nasty ways. And then it rebuilds so quickly within me. But you. I have not seen you act upon anger once since you arrived here."

Her head tilted, contemplating. "Which makes me wonder what does happen when your anger is unleashed. I do not think I want to witness it. Witness you pummel another man, even if that man is Sneedly."

"That he has ever dared to touch you, Lily…"

She clasped his flattened hand between hers. "Please, leave it be. You were very right to stop me earlier. Stop me from saying something I would regret. Until Brianna is well enough to be moved, I cannot chance Mr. Sneedly doing something drastic. Until we can leave I need to submit to Sneedly's little game of power."

Garek's shoulders relaxed, if only slightly. "I abhor that you have been put in this position with that man. That I will have to leave you in his presence."

Her fingers trailing off his hand, Lily turned back to the box, fiddling with the latch. "Then do not think on it. Tell me how Brianna is, how she was when you checked on her. Tell me when she will be well enough to move. And then we can leave this place and never have to think of Mr. Sneedly again."

"You were right. Brianna does appear better. She awoke while I was with her, checking on her leg and setting fresh salve in place. She asked me who I was, which was awkward without you there. She asked for Dr. Rugbert."

"That makes sense since he was our physician for years—but we rarely used him. I had never imagined he would do so much damage to Bree. But I told her of you this morning—I am surprised she did not remember."

"Her mind is foggy," Garek said. "I am sure she will have trouble distinguishing reality from whatever world she was in, for some time."

She glanced up from the box to Garek. "Is this real? Bree waking up? Does it truly mean she will get better?"

Garek sighed.

Lily had come to hate it when he sighed after a question about Brianna. It meant he wasn't telling her something. Hiding some truth from her. But she let the sigh slide past without question. She probably didn't want to hear what Garek was truly thinking.

"It means Brianna is still improving." His words were slow, careful. Not promising too much. Never promising too much.

Lily nodded, looking down at the box as the latch opened. "Papa kept his coins in here." She lifted the cover of the box.

Empty.

"What? They were in here." Her bottom lip jutted out as her eyes swept the study, perplexed. "I do not know what happened..." She dropped to her knees, yanking open the other drawers in the desk, rummaging quickly through the contents.

"There were more coins in there—I know there were. I pulled some for Dr. Rugbert and the apothecary, but not nearly all—not even half. Sneedly." She exhaled a growl.

"And I am sure he had more in here. Bree would know. She knew where Papa kept everything. Anytime I was in the study I was reading, or working on my music, or doing needlepoint, or doing something that, apparently, did not matter at all. I was never paying attention to what Papa taught Bree."

She slammed a drawer shut. "She knows so damn much and I know so damn little and she cannot even tell me—at least not right now."

Garek's hand slid onto her shoulder, his fingers tightening. "You did not know what the future held, Lily—that your world would desert you. Do not worry on the coins. I did not want to take them from you anyway. I will go into town and find a way.

I have some money. And there may be other patients in the area that I can be of use to. Or other work available."

"I just…" Her shoulders slumped. "I just do not want you to leave."

"It will only be for the nights. I will be here during the days."

Her fingers went to her forehead, rubbing it. "The Franklin cottage was the vacant home I was thinking of for you to rent. It is small, room for only you, but it is close to Weadly Hall. But I wish you did not have to go." Still on her knees, she looked up to him. "I do not worry when you are here, Garek. I do not worry on Bree, and I do not worry for myself."

He dropped a hand in front of her, waiting until she reluctantly grabbed it. He pulled her to her feet, his hands settling on her shoulders, pulling her close to him. "And I do not worry about you when I am here. But this is as it has to be right now. That does not negate the fact that I hate that you are under the same roof with Sneedly."

Her fingers came up, wrapping around his wrists. Strength. So much strength in his arms, his hands. If only she could steal some it. "Even if Bree were well enough to move, I do not know where we would go. How I could go about moving us. I cannot even find a few coins in here. Bree would know, though."

Garek's eyes left Lily's face to scan the study above her head. "Do not yet bring up the topic of moving to Brianna. It would only alarm her—the possibility of suddenly leaving Weadly Hall. I do not think she remembers anything of what happened, yet. But in the meantime, you can dig through your father's papers, find out where your father's holdings are, what you can afford to buy or rent."

His hands on her shoulders moved up to cup her neck. "When I get to town to ask about the Franklin cottage, I will also inquire about a larger place—learn if there is something suitable for you to rent in the area. At least for the short term until Brianna is well enough that you two can plan together where you would like to settle."

Lily's eyes closed, nodding. "Yes. A nice cottage home—it is winter, but if it has a place for flowers—Weadly has such nice gardens, and roses—Papa loved the rose bushes. Brianna too."

Garek chuckled. "I will inquire about that exact thing."

She met his eyes. "Thank you. I cannot leave here or prepare to on my own. I am afraid of Mr. Sneedly's retribution were he to find out I was planning on leaving."

"Make me a promise, Lily."

"What?"

"Do not push him. Avoid him at all costs. I do not want you in the fray of his maliciousness. If you see him coming down a hallway, you duck into a room, walk the other way. You stay in Brianna's bedroom. Eat there. Do not put yourself in his path. And when Brianna is no longer fragile, we will get the two of you out of here safely."

He pulled her to him, kissing her forehead.

Lily's eyes fell shut as she let the feel of him, the strength of him, wash over her. Everything would be good again. Her world would be righted. Garek would make it so. She knew it. She just had to wait a little longer.

She nodded against his lips. "I promise. I will avoid him."

{ CHAPTER 5 }

Lily tiptoed out of Brianna's room. Garek had been gone for hours, and the winter's early darkness had descended, lit only by the wispy glow of a half-moon.

Lily had waited. And waited. And waited. But Brianna had not opened her eyes again. Not since Garek had checked on her one last time before he left for the day. The only comfort was that Brianna's breathing was now even, not labored as it had been.

Standing from her chair at Brianna's bedside, Lily went to the window, pulling back the drapery to stare at the night sky. She had hoped Brianna would wake for at least a few minutes—long enough for Lily to ask her about their father's dealings. Where the money and investments were held. How she could access enough coin to at least pay Garek and make sure he had a place to sleep. Enough coin to move them out of Weadly Hall.

She looked back to her sister. Brianna was not waking anytime soon and Lily had to figure this out, and figure it out quickly. She needed to get them out of Weadly Hall. Away from Mr. Sneedly. Away from this place that surrounded her with memories of happiness that would never be hers again.

She had to get out, and her father's study was the place to start.

Leaving Brianna, Lily slipped along the darkened halls, ignoring the chill as her hand blocked the air in front of the flame from the candle she carried. She saw the light spilling from under the doorway before she reached her father's study.

Light that should not be there.

With each step, dread filled her chest and warred with sudden anger twisting her stomach into a rock.

Feet stopping, she paused at the doorway to the study, her hand hovering above the knob.

Avoid Mr. Sneedly at all cost.

The one request from Garek. But the only one who would dare to be in her father's study was Mr. Sneedly.

In her father's room. Going through her father's things.

Her anger won out.

Lily opened the door in one swift motion, stepping into the room.

With a yelp, Mr. Sneedly jumped at the intrusion, a pile of papers slipping off the desk, crashing and fluttering to the floor.

"Mr. Sneedly, what in the blazes are you doing in here?"

Mr. Sneedly rushed around the desk, moving in on her.

Close, too close.

Her neck craned backward, as she tried to avoid the smell of him. The man stunk of brandy. She hadn't known Mr. Sneedly drank, but at this moment, he reeked of it.

Then she saw it, her father's very best brandy sitting out on a sideboard by the window, nearly empty with a full glass next to it. Her chest tightened, the anger in her belly exploding.

"Lily, why are you not in bed?"

"Why are you in my father's study?" She straightened, not willing to let him, or his stench, intimidate her out of the room.

"Oh, I…" His hand flipped up over his shoulder, waving. "I was searching for something the viscount requested."

"Everything in this room belongs to my father, Mr. Sneedly. Not the viscount." Lily skirted around Mr. Sneedly, moving herself deeper into the room before she spun back to him. "And you are very well aware of that fact. You have no right to be in here."

"Your father is dead, Lily. Everything in this room is under the viscount's roof. I think he has every right to take anything and everything that exists in this place." He followed Lily further into the room, his boots almost touching the toes of her slippers. "As does his proxy."

Lily wedged her arms up, crossing them over her chest, but refusing to cower a step backward. "And you are his proxy, Mr.

Sneedly, so you have every right? You emptied the coin box, didn't you? You had no right."

"I have every right." Sneedly leaned in, bumping her arms, his face invading her space. "To everything. Everybody." The last word snaked out slowly, his black squinty eyes leering.

Her head jerked backward, her face crumpling in horror that he would dare threaten her directly. "Me?"

"Now you are beginning to understand the way of things." His hand came up, his fingers trailing along her arm, dragging rough against the black bombazine silk of her dress.

Fighting instant bile chasing up her throat, Lily took a step backward, only to ram into the desk. Her arm flicked up, trying to shake off his fingers. Fingers that leeched onto her arm. "No. I need you to leave this room this instant, Mr. Sneedly. I insist."

"You insist?"

"Yes. I insist, or may heaven help you."

"Heaven help me?" He sneered a laugh. "Heaven does not seem to favor you as of late, little chit. You are far too headstrong, my Lily." His hand dropped from her arm, only to reach up, his fingers wrapping into the hair on the side of her head. He twisted his hold, tearing hair.

Lily tried to jerk away, even though it ripped more hair from her scalp. "Do not call me Lily."

Mr. Sneedly's eyebrows slanted inward. "No? Dr. Harrison calls you Lily."

"And you are not Dr. Harrison, Mr. Sneedly. You are the furthest thing from that man. You are a sniveling coward—"

He yanked her head, cutting her words as his other hand reached out to grab her left breast, twisting and squeezing.

Lily yelped, grabbing his wrist and digging her nails into his skin, trying to break his hold.

Sneedly laughed, wrenching her breast again. "You will learn, little wench." He shoved his head close to her face, spittle collecting in the corner of his mouth. "You will learn to submit to me, Lily."

Without another word, he shoved her backward, releasing his hands from her, and Lily fell onto the desk, papers scattering from the force. Before she could catch her balance and look up, Mr. Sneedly was out the door, the click of his boots receding down the hall.

Gasping for breath, Lily stared at the door, the fear pounding through her veins morphing back into rage.

Helpless.

She had been utterly helpless—frozen in inaction since she walked into the damn abbey and found her father dead and Brianna near death.

And now she was shackled here until she could move Brianna. Shackled at the mercy of that rat.

Her fist cracked down on the desk.

She was so damn tired of being helpless.

So damn tired.

~ ~ ~

Garek tugged on his horse's reins, damning the clouds that had blocked most of the moonlight. Moving through the woods, the darkness had slowed him enough that he had needed to dismount, and now he contemplated just tying his horse to the nearest tree so he could make faster progress.

He was about to do that very thing—and chance not being able to find his horse again until morning light—when the woods thinned and he heard a crack. He broke into a run over the brush, tossing the reins over the nearest branch as he reached the clearing.

He found Lily instantly in the sliver of moonlight, just as she swung her whole body into a whack of the hammer. Stone from the abbey shattered, pieces flying as the weight of the hammer sent her stumbling.

"Good god, Lily—I was frantic." Garek sped across the clearing, capturing her before her feet had resettled on the ground, wrapping her into his body.

She wedged her head up. "Garek? What are you doing out here?"

His arms clamped harder around her. "What am I doing? What are you doing? I could not find you at the house—only Sneedly passed out on the floor in the drawing room. No you. You scared me half to my grave, Lily."

"You were at Weadly Hall tonight?"

"Yes. I could not let it rest—leaving you—I had thought to only ride by, but then I had to go in and check on you." His right hand moved from her back to cup the rear of her head. "I was worried."

"About?"

"Sneedly. And now I find you here." He motioned with his head to the abbey. "Why are you out here, Lily?"

She shrugged in his arms. "I am mad."

"Why?"

Her eyes dropped to stare at his chest. "I will not tell you."

"No. Do not hide from me, Lily. Are you mad at me? Mad that I left?"

Her eyes went wide, her head shaking as she looked up. "No—no, of course not. I am furious that you were forced to leave, but I am not mad at you."

Garek's arm tightened around her. "Then what did Sneedly do to you?"

She ducked her head, her arms wiggling under his clamp. "Nothing."

He stopped her from escaping, then slid his hand from the back of her head to the line of her jaw. Thumb under her chin, Garek tilted her face upward, but she averted her eyes. "You are out here for a reason, Lily. You are mad for a reason. Something happened. What did he do to you?"

"I will not tell you. It was not dire. I am whole. Uncompromised. It was nothing I could not handle. Nothing of consequence."

"You are lying."

She met his eyes. "You do not know that."

"I do. Have you come out here to the abbey once since I went with you to Weadly Hall?"

"No."

"So what sent you here? Only anger that you have no place for would bring you here, Lily. I know that much of you."

Her bottom lip jutted out, stubborn as she shook her head. But Garek could see it in her moonlit eyes. See that Sneedly had done something very vile to her. See the shame. The helplessness.

Rage exploding through his body, Garek set her free from his hold, whipping around to stalk back toward the woods. "I will kill him."

Lily was on him in an instant, both hands wrapping around his left arm, her heels digging into the ground. "Dammit, Garek. No you will not."

She yanked hard against his movement, her grip slipping and sending her sprawling.

Her grunt as she hit the cold ground, landing hard on her side, stopped him.

Garek turned back to see her holding her shoulder as she tried to scramble to her feet, the dead grass slippery with frost.

A pang cut through his chest at the sight, landing in his throat. It was just as much him that had sent her to the ground— just caused her pain.

He sucked in a breath, trying to calm himself as he stepped to her and reached down, threading his arm along her waist. Righting her, he set her as gently to her feet as his rage allowed.

Dammit to hell, he wanted to protect her.

Protect her and take her and her sister away from Weadly Hall so she never had to worry. Protect her so badly he was willing to go and crush a man.

Something he swore he would never do again.

But he had no money. He had no home to bring Lily to—to bring her sister to. No way to get them out of Weadly Hall. He couldn't very well bring them to that cramped room above the tavern he had landed in.

He had never planned for any of this—hell—he had never planned to leave London. Never planned to let his surgical tools into the light again. Never planned on travelling through this area, on staying here. Never planned on complicating his life with a hammer-swinging woman, much less having to protect her.

He had gotten involved when he had known from the start it was doomed.

Hell—he only had enough coins to stay at the tavern for a week the way it was. Not to mention Brianna's reaction to his presence by her bedside. Never had he been eyed with such suspicion as he had been by Lily's sister.

Stuck. Utterly stuck. He wasn't about to leave Lily—not when the very thought twisted his heart. He was very near in love with her. In love with a woman he couldn't protect.

And he knew damn well he would do anything for her—including wiping the earth of Sneedly if that's what needed to happen to keep her safe.

Her feet under her, Lily jerked away from his hold, her arm swinging in a wide arc. "Do not listen to me, then." She stomped over to the building, picking up the hammer she had dropped. "Go. Ruin your life over a sniveling vulture." She swung the hammer, stone smashing.

"Ruin my life. Ruin my sister's. Just go." She swung again, shards flying.

"Lily—"

A smash of stone sent sparks flying, interrupting him. "What the hell do you think is going to happen to you, to all of us if you injure Sneedly, Garek? Or kill him? How will that help anyone?" She refused to turn to him, her yell echoing through the woods.

"It will keep you safe."

She swung, a long, vicious grunt unfurling. "I am safe. As safe as can be managed. You know I cannot leave Weadly Hall until Brianna is well."

Her right arm dropped, the hammerhead swinging above the ground as she leaned forward, her left hand landing on the ripped stone in the wall before her. He watched her shoulders, the black dress covering her back rise and fall with heavy breaths.

Garek moved toward her, stopping an arm's length away from her backside. His hands stayed solidly at his sides, even though he wanted to grab her, hold her—banish every horrible thing weighing upon her that he knew he couldn't.

His fingers spread wide on his forehead, rubbing his eyebrows. "Lily…I know you will do anything for your sister. Suffer anything, and it scares me to no end. I have known men like Sneedly, they prey upon the fragile, take advantage of situations that only call for humanity, for mercy. I cannot allow him to hurt you, Lily. To lay a hand upon you."

She pushed off from the wall, her face tipping up to the sky, yet she still did not turn to him. "Mr. Sneedly is manageable, Garek. He is better than the viscount. That man. That man is just evil. I do not want him to come back here. I do not want the viscount near Brianna. He had demanded I take my 'bloody, raggedy hobgoblin sister' out of Weadly Hall after I found her. He did not want the blood to sully his floors. I had to keep her in the barn until I managed to convince him to let us stay—but he only relented because he was very, very drunk. The barn, Garek. The damn barn."

Her chin dropped to her chest as her arm shifted, swinging the hammer half-heartedly at the corner of the abbey.

"Just leave me, Garek. Leave me to my stones." Her voice escaped in a puff of cold air, a cracked whisper.

Her arm drifted to a standstill at her side, the handle of the hammer nearly slipping from her grasp.

"Smash them all you want, Lily. I am waiting right here for you." Garek took a step forward, his hands setting softly on her shoulders. "You will not be alone. I was not about to desert you that first night I saw you, and I am not about to leave you alone now. It kills me that I cannot make right everything in your world. But I will. One day, I will. I swear it, Lils."

It took a very long moment, then Lily swayed slightly, finally releasing her body backward. Backward to lean into him. To let him slip his arms around her.

Garek's throat clenched, halting his breath.

This moment. This moment of safety he could give her. If nothing more, this he could give her.

A shiver ran through her body, and the hammer slid from her fingers, thumping to the cold ground.

"You are freezing." Garek tightened his hold around her belly, trying to heat the chill from her body.

"And you are warm."

His head dropped, his chin resting on her hair. "This is all I want, Lils. To heat you. Comfort you. Let me do that, if I can do nothing else."

Garek stared at the beaten stone in front of them, the holes that had been ripped open into the interior.

A mess. A ramshackle mess.

{ CHAPTER 6 }

Garek stepped along the garden path outside of Weadly Hall, crunching the frost clinging to the blades of dead grass. He had checked on Brianna, but not finding Lily in her room, he had gone searching.

Her absence troubled him, as they had fallen into a reliable routine during the past weeks—Garek would arrive late in the morning and stay until just before nightfall unless there was a new patient in town to visit.

Dread building, he knew the formal gardens were the last place to check before he headed on to the abbey. If she was there, it most likely meant Sneedly had overstepped his bounds again.

The sound reached him softly at first, louder with each step, until he fully heard it.

His footsteps stilled.

The most hauntingly beautiful singing voice he had ever heard curled through the air along the evergreen hedges lining the pathway.

To pine on the stem;
Since the lovely are sleeping,
Go, sleep thou with them.
Thus kindly I scatter,
Thy leaves o'er the bed,
Where thy mates of the garden
Lie scentless and dead.

Stepping lightly, Garek followed the sound to find Lily sitting on a black iron bench in an evergreen garden room.

Transfixed, he stared at her profile from afar. Huddled under her dark cloak, her fingers plucked at the tightly wrapped petals of a dried rose, pain echoing in every word from her lips.

So soon may I follow,
When friendships decay,
And from Love's shining circle
The gems drop away.
When true hearts lie withered,
And fond ones are flown,
Oh, who would inhabit
This bleak world alone?

The last red petal, lined with dark decay, crumbled under her fingers, falling to the cold ground by her feet. She stared at her fingers, rubbing the remnants slowly from her skin.

It gutted him.

Garek thought for a moment to escape, to leave her to her pain. At least for the moment. At least until he could conjure words against the suffering that weighed upon her soul. He knew how to deal with her anger, but this—this he was at a loss with.

Instead of escape, he stepped forward into the small space.

Lily jumped, her blue eyes flashing to him. "Garek. I—I thought I was alone."

He shook his head, walking silently to her, stopping before her feet, but careful to not crush any of the petals on the ground.

She held up the barren stem of the rose. "I found it. The last one. Hidden deep. It held on for so long. I do not know how…" Her voice trailed off.

His chest tightening, Garek watched her face closely, the sorrow crinkling the edges of her eyes. "The ones that hold on, fight, are always the most beautiful, Lily."

She dropped the stem to the ground. "Dead now."

Staring at it on the bed of petals for a long moment, her chin finally lifted to look up at Garek. "These were Papa's—he loved the roses—loved watching softness blossom from the thorns. He always chuckled when he pricked a finger—angry stems reward with the most beauty, he would say. I used to sing to him out here. That song was one of his favorites."

"I knew your voice was pure, Lily, but I had no idea you could break my heart with so few notes."

An achingly sad smile crossed her face. "Our nursemaid—she had a very sad soul—used to sing that to us when we were tiny."

"Tell me you do not feel that," Garek said, his voice rough.

"What?"

"Alone."

Her head tilted, contemplating as she looked up at him. "No. And yes. When you are not here, I do. Bree still is not awake for very long stretches, so I only have my thoughts to keep me company. Have you seen her already? I did not see you come up from the stables, or I would have accompanied you."

Garek pointed to the empty space on the bench, and Lily nodded. He sat next to her, leaning on the back of elaborate iron scrollwork. "I did check on her. She was sleeping, but she is holding steady, Lily. Gaining her strength back. We should be able to move her in a few days as long as there are no set-backs."

Lily nodded, staring at the dried petals on the ground. "I had to tell her today—about father, about how I found her."

"That is what has put the sadness into your eyes." His arm went along her shoulders, pulling her into him. "Why today?"

"She has been asking, pestering me every time she awakens. She is still so confused about what happened and why."

Lily picked up a crispy petal that had fallen onto her lap and attached to her cloak. She stared at it, turning it around in her fingers. "I had hoped she would be the one with answers for me. Instead, I have only confused her because I have no answers as to why this happened. I only know what I saw. Papa dead. Her cuts. But I could delay her no longer. She wants to visit the abbey, see it for herself, the spot where Papa died. She says she only sees snippets in her mind. Flashes of what happened."

"That is good. It means her mind is coming back to her."

Lily's head tilted back, resting on his arm as her eyes went to the grey sky. "I do not want to bring her there, Garek. I do not want to remember. I do not want to watch her face when she remembers."

"Then I will bring her."

Her look fell to him. "You would do that for me?"

His hold tightened along her shoulders. "I would do anything to ease your burden, Lils."

Taking a deep breath, her eyes closed. "I do not believe you are here, sometimes. Believe you are real." The vibrant blue of her eyes opened to him. "How did you get here, Garek? Why did you leave London? You never speak of it."

Garek had to stop his arm from noticeably tightening around her shoulders. "Dr. Halowell is a genius, making impressive advancements with what a surgeon, what medicine can achieve. Astounding research. It was why I was training under him. But his tutelage was also expensive and my funding for that privilege ran out."

"That is all? I have seen your skill, Garek, your knowledge of herbs, of treating wounds—I am sure you were useful to him. Why could he not keep you on?"

"It was not Dr. Halowell's decision. His son runs his practice along with the finances. Dr. Halowell does not want to be bothered by details. He wants to devote his time solely to his work and research. So his son controls the details, and I was given a choice when my funding expired. I could perform some duties for the practice as payment for my training, my room and meals, or I could leave."

Her head tilted. "Duties? What duties?"

Garek shrugged. "Something I thought I could stomach, but as it happened, I discovered I am morally opposed to what he asked of me. So I was forced to leave."

Lily turned under his arm to more fully face him. "What did Dr. Halowell's son ask of you?"

"You do not need to know the details of my departure, Lily," Garek said, cautious. He had not intended to ever have to tell Lily any of this, much less tell her at this very moment.

"Possibly not." Her hands curled together on her lap. "But the devil always lurks in the details, Garek. I think I need to know."

He sighed, shaking his head. It was very possible Lily would eventually discover this very detail from another source, and that would not do. She needed to hear it from him. "Cadavers. Dr. Halowell's son wanted me to dig up cadavers."

Lily yanked away from him, mouth agape, her face etched in horror. "He wanted you to rob graves?"

"Yes." Garek's arm dropped to his lap, meeting her eyes. He could not hide his past from her. And he wasn't about to lie about it. "Dr. Halowell is advancing the field of surgery—brilliant—but it comes at a cost. He needs bodies—lots of bodies to dissect. A cost I had never thought about until I was asked to produce the bodies for the research."

"So you refused?"

"No. Not immediately. I was at a gravesite, shovel in hand. I had dug three shovelfuls of dirt before the war in my head finished—respecting the dead versus the need for knowledge. And I could not do it. The dead should be given the respect to remain dead."

Garek cleared his throat, flattening the fist his hand had balled into on his thigh. "So I stopped, much to the dismay of the three other grave robbers I was there with. There was…an altercation. And I left. I was done. Done with everything. I had thought never to practice medicine again."

Lily stared at him, the horror melting from her forehead. Her mouth closed with a deep breath, her chest visibly lifting under her dark cloak. "But then you met me."

He nodded. "I met you."

"I am glad."

"You are?"

"You are very good, Garek. I never thought you looked it—
you are too large, a force—people should naturally cower from
you. But you have such control—you are so gentle." Her blue
eyes centered on him. "The most compassionate man I have ever
met. It would be wrong if you were not doing this work that so
very clearly suits you."

Garek's jaw dropped slightly.

This he had not expected. Of all the words she could have
spewed at him, just this—genuine acceptance. No condemnation
of poor choices from his past.

Not that he had told her the whole story. He never intended
to.

"You do not care?"

"I have far more important things to care about, Garek.
Or have you not noticed?" A clear twinkle sprang into her eyes.
"Whatever it took to put you in my path, I am grateful for it—
however insidious it may have begun. And now…now I feel as
though I have known you my whole life, that you are a constant
in my world, and I have no patience for the past that clearly still
disturbs you—sets your eyes to regret."

His hands flew up, capturing her face.

"I am going to kiss you, Lils." The words burned from his
chest, full of intention.

She blinked, startled for a moment, and then nodded.

Garek paused, stuck in that very moment. Hell. How he
needed to make her his.

The last two weeks had been torture. Stolen kisses in the
shadows of Weadly Hall. Watching her move about Brianna's
room, wanting to touch her, hold her. Every moment wishing
they were far from this place. Far from Sneedly's leering eyes. Far
past Brianna's sickness.

He needed quite desperately to take her and leave no mistake
that she was his now—would always be his.

Garek leaned forward, pulling her to him, his warm lips meeting her cool ones. She offered no hesitation, taking his attack, meeting it with purpose.

His right hand slipped along her jaw, wrapping along the back of her neck as he parted her mouth. He could feel her smile against him as his tongue ran along her teeth, the very sensation sending his body into hardness.

Garek knew he needed to pull back. Stop the madness he was slipping into before restraint abandoned him.

Ignoring reason, his left hand slipped down, moving under Lily's cloak. Finding her wrist, his fingers danced up her forearm, past her elbow, and landed on the edge of her shoulder. His thumb dove inward, tracing the outer curve of her breast.

She gasped into his mouth. But held. Did not pull away.

No. Lily leaned into his hand, the softest murmur coming from the back of her throat.

Garek could not keep his palm from slipping downward, taking the full weight of her breast in his hand, gently cupping it, teasing the nipple through the layers of fabric.

Again, Lily only leaned into his touch, her breath quickening under his lips.

Damn. His last snippets of restraint wavered.

With a groan, Garek pulled away from her. Her lips had gone raw, her skin pink from his stubble. She looked thoroughly sated. Sated and fully ready for hours of his hands on her body.

He pulled his hand free from under her cloak.

Her blue eyes fluttered open to him.

"You are stopping?"

"If I do not, I will not be able to walk for days."

Her eyebrows cocked with curious innocence at his comment, just as a snowflake landed on her forehead.

"It is no matter." He smiled, resigned, and wiped the fat snowflake from her forehead with his thumb. "It is beginning to snow. You should go inside."

"Are you gone for the rest of the day? I have started to gather much of my father's papers, his ledgers. I know we will need them when we leave Weadly Hall, but they are in such disarray. The bound ledgers are fine, but the papers—they are a mess and I am making no sense of them. I think some guide me to a bank in London and others to the bank in Annadale, but I am not sure."

"Why are they in such a mess?"

Lily's nose scrunched. "Mr. Sneedly. Do you have somewhere to keep them safe at the tavern? I have some of the piles in several satchels. Will you look at them for me? I no longer trust leaving anything in this house, so I am trying to move everything of importance I can find to Bree's room."

"Including yourself?"

She smiled, her head tilting as her eyes went upward. "Yes. Including myself. I have made myself near invisible within the house."

Garek's jaw tightened. She tried to make light of the situation, but he could still see the angry fear veiled in her eyes. "Good. Keep it so. Brianna should be well enough to leave in a few days. I have found several homes that are possibilities for you two."

"You have?"

He nodded.

She shook her head slowly, her blue eyes turning serious, pinning him. "I do not know what made you follow the sounds to the abbey those many weeks ago, what made you appear to me. But whatever it was, I owe it my heart, Garek. I had nothing left—nothing when you found me. But now Bree...You..." Her voice broke, words evaporating.

"Fate." His hand went to the side of her face. "Fate put me in your path. It is the only explanation, and I am not inclined to believe in fate."

"Maybe you should start." She chuckled. "Fate it is, then. It is fate I owe."

~ ~ ~

Lily softly cracked open the door to her father's study, peeking her head into the room.

Empty, thank goodness.

After Garek had left, she had waited all day in Brianna's room until late into the darkness, hoping that Mr. Sneedly had retired or drunk himself into a stupor, then made her way to her father's study.

Dropping the four burlap satchels she had scrounged up from the kitchens onto the desk, she set the one candle she had brought far across the room from the doorway to hide the light. She didn't want Mr. Sneedly passing by and stopping to investigate.

Pulling a stack of her father's papers onto her lap, she began sifting through them, squinting at his tiny scrawl in the low light, trying to decide what was needed and what wasn't.

Hours passed in silence, only the slight crinkle of paper disturbing the stillness. Mr. Sneedly hadn't interrupted her, which Lily was grateful for, though she continued to jump at every odd creak of the house. The wind had picked up with the snow, and the house was groaning against the cold.

The last thing she wanted was a repeat of the scene in the study with Mr. Sneedly from weeks ago. Not when she was so close to leaving this place for good.

Two satchels filled with her father's papers, Lily shifted the balance of them in her arms, clutching them to her chest as she stepped out into the corridor. She quickly moved through the dark hallways to Brianna's room.

The door closing behind her, it took Lily a moment to realize something was very wrong in Brianna's room. Drastically wrong.

Brianna was gone.

Not in her bed. Not in the room.

Her sister had been improving, but for her to get out of bed on her own, walk somewhere—that was still beyond Brianna's capabilities. Lily dropped the heavy satchels to the floor, racing to the adjoining dressing room. No Brianna.

Hand on her chest, her heart out of control, Lily rushed to the door, swinging it wide open.

"Bree?" she whispered loudly. "Bree?"

Her head swiveled up and down the corridor, searching the darkness for some movement.

A hand gripped her arm.

Then the rush of half-digested alcohol smacked her nose. Sneedly.

After a second of disbelief, Lily realized Mr. Sneedly was dragging her down the hall away from Brianna's room. She jerked, swiveling, but his clamp on her upper arm was too hard, too vicious. He wasn't letting her escape.

"You thought you could hide it, you twit." His slurred words tripped over one another.

"What?" She hit his arm with her free hand, twisting. "Where is my sister, Mr. Sneedly? Where is Brianna?"

"You will find out, you little whore."

"Whore?" Lily's feet froze and she stumbled.

He ruthlessly jerked her upright, tearing her shoulder. She yelped, pain burning down her arm.

Mr. Sneedly shoved her against the wall, his putrid breath invading her face, stinging her eyes. "You ruined everything, you little bitch. Whore. Filthy, nasty whore. I was giving you time, waiting for your sister to die before we married. Time I should not have allotted you."

"M-married? What—"

"Did you truly believe I would want you after that man touched you?" He turned, wrenching her from the wall as he stomped down the dark hall, yanking her along.

"Touched me?" Her feet slipping, she tried to keep his pace while being jerked with every one of Sneedly's words.

"I saw you in the garden, Lily. Saw the bastard paw you. Soil you. You were perfect. Mine. And now you are just rubbish. Filthy."

He swung her wide around the corner at the top of the stairs and dragged her down the steps. Halfway down, he shoved her and she fell, tumbling over the last five stairs.

The sharp edge of a step cracked against her temple, and for seconds, Lily was blinded, bright stars in her eyes. She landed in a heap, motionless. But the reprieve lasted only a moment before she was yanked upward, her toes only partially finding ground to carry her weight.

Mr. Sneedly was dragging her again. Dragging her to the front door.

She tore at his arm, her nails ripping into his jacket. "Where is Bree? Bree. Where is she?"

"Out with the filth, slut." Sneedly's steps didn't slow.

"Stop, Sneedly, stop. Where is my sister? Stop." Lily tried to dig her heels into the marble floor, only to lose her grip on his arm.

Mr. Sneedly slapped her across the temple and then reached for the front door to Weadly Hall.

He flung the door wide and a blast of freezing wind whipped into the house.

Lily found footing, pulling from his grasp. "Dammit, Sneedly, where the hell is my sister?"

"Here." He jerked her through the doorway, shoving her past him and down the front step.

Lily landed, her knees and hands crunching into the frozen gravel. It took a quick breath to gain her bearings and balance.

And then she saw it.

Brianna sitting in her robe, propped up against the outside wall by the door.

She wasn't moving. Her head fallen over. Limbs limp. Still. Snow collecting on top of her hair.

Lily rushed to her, screaming, her hands grabbing Brianna's face. Cold. Too cold. "No. No. No. What did you do to her, Sneedly?"

"Extra laudanum. That is all."

Lily tore her eyes off of Brianna to look up to him, her jaw hanging. He stood in the doorway, his arms crossed, a satisfied sneer on his face.

Her wide eyes dropped to Brianna.

The world slowed, froze.

Wind swirled, whipping snowflakes into her eyes.

In the next breath, everything in Lily broke, anger consuming her body, setting the world around her on fire.

"You damn bastard." She lunged at Mr. Sneedly, barreling into him, fists swinging. It sent him flying backward, his backside crashing onto the entryway floor.

"Sniveling, ugly little rat bastard. The devil himself, you are—the shaggiest, rotting rubbish of a sheep's arse." She continued the attack, fists beating at his body on the ground, one making hard contact on his cheek.

Several more blows landed on his body before Mr. Sneedly gained space to shove her shoulder up.

He kicked, his boot ramming brutally into her stomach. It sent her sprawling to the floor, seized in pain, gasping for breath that would not come.

Rolling her, he kicked her ribcage, shoving her out over the threshold of the door once more. Lily dropped off the step to the gravel drive, still fighting for breath.

She craned her neck upward, only to see a malicious sneer fill his face. It froze her, terror racing down her spine. He wiped his bloody cheek with the butt of his palm.

"You are done here, Miss Silverton. You and your half-dead sister."

Lily snatched onto the slightest breath, forcing it from her throat into a shallow whisper. "But—possessions—my father's—"

"I do not give a damn about your possessions, bitch." His hand went to the doorknob, starting to pull it closed. He paused. "Do not bother pounding at the door—begging. It will do you no good and will only interrupt my sleep. I will, frankly, be happy to send you to blackness if I have to look at you once more."

The door slammed shut.

Lily's head dropped, her temple crunching cold gravel. Minutes passed, and she could only lie there, fighting for air, gasping again and again for breath that refused to reach her lungs.

The cold invaded her body before her breathing came back to her. Already, the freezing air had snaked around her arms, the cold seeping into her bones. Her simple black woolen dress held no defense against the cold.

Lily tried to sit up, only half succeeding. She could finally force shallow air into her lungs, and it would have to suffice.

Using her hands to turn around, her knees dragging along the gravel, her eyes found Brianna in the little light that shone from the window beside the front door. Lily's eyes swept over her sister. Brianna's body jerked.

Thank the heavens.

She was alive, breathing, but for how long?

Lily dragged herself over to her sister. Thank goodness she had put boots on earlier to keep her feet warm in her father's study. But on Bree's feet—only slippers.

Dammit. Dammit to hades and back again.

How in the hell had this happened? And what in the hell was she going to do now?

She didn't have the slightest clue.

Lily stared at her sister. The snowy wind whipped around Brianna's head, snatching her hair and sending it flying around her face.

What was she going to do? Brianna was going to die, freeze to death right in front of her if she didn't do something.

Lily searched her mind. What would Brianna do?

She mentally kicked herself. Brianna wouldn't have gotten booted from the only home they'd ever known in the first place. And she most certainly wouldn't have attacked Mr. Sneedly, sealing their fate. No, Brianna would have stared Mr. Sneedly down and used irrefutable logic to make him bend to her will.

Even at this juncture, Brianna would come up with something to save them—Lily knew she would. But what?

A gasp, and cold air reached a little further into Lily's chest. It surprised her. But it also gave her hope.

Her look dropped to Brianna's lap and she stared at her sister's bare hands, the fingers half-curled, not moving. What would her sister do?

Brianna would save both of them. That's what she would do.

Lily took another breath, forcing it further into her chest.

Wedging her feet under her, she gained her footing and shoved herself upwards. Reaching under her skirt, she pulled free the one wool petticoat she had on.

She dropped back down to her knees in front of Brianna and wrapped the petticoat around her sister's feet. Dragging the extra fabric of it up, she tucked it around Brianna the best she could.

Lily leaned forward, kissing Brianna's forehead. Snowflakes melted on her lips. She set her mouth next to Brianna's ear. "Do not dare to leave this earth on me, Bree. I will be gone for only a moment, and then I will be back for you."

Using the wall, Lily pushed herself to her feet, ignoring the shards of pain ripping into her body from too many places to count.

Her steps unsteady, she started off, stumbling to the stables.

{ CHAPTER 7 }

The pounding of a door echoed down the tiny hall, shaking the walls.

"Garek. Garek."

A yell. Desperate. More pounding.

Garek jolted upright, rubbing the deep sleep from his eyes with both palms. Had he just dreamt the bellowing?

"Garek." More banging.

He jumped out of bed, racing to the door. He was behind the last of the four doors in the hallway above the sole tavern in Annadale, and he hoped the other residents were well enough inebriated to not wake. Not that it was likely with the ruckus.

He flung the door open, poking his head into the hall.

"Lily?"

"Garek." She almost collapsed in relief, stumbling to his door. "Thank heavens."

His eyes ran over her. Her black dress clung to her, molding around her legs as she moved. "Lily, you are soaking wet."

Her hand flew in the air, both cutting him off and dismissing the comment. "I need you, Garek. Why are you hiding?"

"I am naked. I was sleeping. It is the middle of the night, Lily. How did you even find me?"

"You said this was where you were sleeping. Get dressed. I need you. Fast."

Her hand grabbed the doorknob, frantic, and Garek had to hold it so she didn't yank the door open.

"What in blazes is going on?" His set his free hand over hers on the doorknob. "Your hand is frozen, Lily."

"Get dressed, get outside and help me." The words were sharp, but then she took a breath, her eyes begging in the low light from a lantern at the far end of the hall. "Please. Bree is outside."

"In the snow? It is the middle of the night, Lily."

"I know."

Garek nodded, finally understanding her desperation. "Go down. I will be right behind."

Lily spun, running down the hall, and Garek fumbled in the darkness for his trousers, yanking them on as he followed Lily down the steep staircase.

The bitter wind slapped him the second he stepped outside, lashing across his bare chest.

"Garek, here." Lily jumped up into a curricle, landing next to Brianna. Her sister was slumped awkwardly in the corner, eyes closed, not moving.

Garek swore under his breath.

Her arms wedging behind Brianna, Lily dragged her on the seat to the edge of the carriage just as Garek set his bare foot on the mounting step.

"I had the stable boy help me drag her up into here, but I could not get her down—not without dropping her off the edge."

Garek shoved Lily's grip from her sister, and gained a solid hold on Brianna. Picking her up, he lifted her from the curricle as he stepped backward down to the ground. Fabric wrapped around Brianna's feet caught on the mounting step, ripping when he stepped away from the carriage. His arms under Brianna's back and legs, he stopped and shifted her as he looked up at Lily.

"What in the hell happened, Lily?"

Lily jumped from the curricle, untangling the cloth from the step and pushing him toward the building as she piled what looked like a petticoat onto Brianna's stomach. "Not now—inside. Bree—she is the most important thing, Garek. You have to help her."

Garek moved to the rear door of the tavern, letting Lily run ahead to hold the door for him. Carrying Brianna into the tavern and up the stairs to his room, he set her on his bed, his hands searching for a heartbeat along her neck.

"Lily, a light." He pointed at the candlestick on the one small table in the room. "Light it from the hall lantern."

Brianna was frozen. But then he found it. A pulse. Slight. Slow. But there.

Lily hurried into the room, her hand covering the flame of the sputtering tallow candle. She flipped the door closed with her foot.

"Laudanum. He gave her laudanum." Lily stood by the foot of the bed, holding the candle out for light. "I could not get her to wake up. Tell me she will be all right."

"She is near frozen, Lily. Why the hell did you move her—bring her here?"

"He kicked us out of Weadly Hall, Garek. He dumped her on the ground outside—left her unconscious—and shoved me out after her."

Garek stopped, looking up to Lily. "Sneedly?"

Lily nodded.

He turned from her, looking to Brianna. Rage exploded in his chest—rage so thick it smothered every word, every blasphemy he wanted to utter.

His head shaking, it took him a long moment to move again. He picked up the petticoat from Brianna's belly, pulling it from her feet, and then pointed at the small fireplace by the door. "There should still be hot coals there. Rip this cloth and wrap two separate bundles of them. One for her feet and one for her chest. Then go down to the main room of the tavern—it should be empty, and bring up more coal, wood—whatever they are burning down there. We need a fire in here to stop her from sinking too deep into the cold."

"And her leg, Garek. I tore it when I was trying to get her into the carriage. It is bloody again."

Garek nodded, swearing to himself. A quick glance under Brianna's robe told him at least two, maybe three of the gashes had split open again, bleeding. But the blood appeared to have already stalled, no doubt from the cold.

Lily set the candlestick down, quickly making the warm bundles. She handed one to Garek and tucked the other around Brianna's feet.

Garek waited until Lily silently slipped from the room and then gently slapped Brianna's cheeks, trying to rouse her. Nothing. His hands went to her shoulders, shaking her. Still nothing. He slapped her right cheek again, harder.

A sudden moan, and her head moved.

Good. He had no idea how much laudanum Sneedly had given Brianna, but he knew the laudanum would have killed her already if it had been too great a quantity. So now it was just the cold in her body to contend with, and whatever would be borne from that. And her bloody leg.

He pulled free the lone blanket on the bed. Setting the hot bundle of coal on top of her ribcage, he layered the blanket heavily over her body.

Lily came into the room, juggling several split logs as she clanked hot coals in a small tin brazier to the floor next to the fireplace. She dropped to her knees and set the wood in the fireplace, stoking the coal embers for a blaze.

Garek checked Brianna's fingers, rubbing the blue-tinged skin, trying to force blood back into the flesh.

It wasn't until the fire crackled bright that Garek noticed the sound. A low chattering.

Teeth chattering.

His head swiveled to the sound—to Lily. Huddled and facing the fire, Lily sat on her legs, her arms wrapped around her waist. Garek squinted at her back. She was shaking. She was trying to hold hard against it, but she was shaking.

He tucked Brianna's hand under the covers next to the warmth of the wrapped coal and went over to Lily.

His feet stopping next to her black skirt puddling on the floor, he looked down at the top of her wet head. "Lily."

Her face snapped upward, her blue eyes reflecting the warm of the blaze. Her chin quaked, attempting to hold back the clatter of her teeth as she tried to speak. "What are you doing? Bree—"

"Brianna needs to warm. It was not an overage of laudanum. As long as her body warms, she will survive. The coal is already working on that. The blood looks to have stopped on her leg, but I cannot deal with it until she is warm."

Lily nodded, her face sinking back to the fire.

Garek bent, balancing on heels. He reached out, touching her upper arm, the cold dampness of her dress seeping into his palm. She flinched at the touch. Pain?

"You are freezing wet, Lily."

She didn't look to him. "I will dry."

"What the hell happened, Lily?"

Her head shook. "I forced it—he threw me out, and when I saw Bree outside in the cold…I…I… He was drunk and I could have reasoned with him, but I attacked him. I could not help myself."

"You what? You attacked him?"

"I did. I lost my mind, Garek. We will never be allowed at Weadly Hall again."

"But why did he do it—put Brianna outside?"

"He saw us, Garek." She looked to him, her eyes huge. "He saw us in the gardens. He thought I was his, Garek—his—I never said or did anything to make him think…" She shuddered. "And he saw us and he was scary—crazy."

Her arms wrapped tighter around body. "And I did not know what to do. Where to go. So I stole the curricle and a horse from the stables and came here. I knew you could save her."

"I did not do anything, Lily. You are the one that saved her. Much longer in the freezing air, and she would have died."

"Do not speak of her death, Garek." Her head swung back and forth, voice vehement. "Sneedly said he had been waiting for her to die—to die, Garek. My sister…"

His hand slid up from her arm to the back of her neck, squeezing. "She is alive, Lily. Do not think on it. You managed to get her here and she is alive and safe. You are alive and safe."

Her body twisted around as she looked from him to Brianna on the small bed.

Garek stilled.

He hadn't seen this side of her face in the dark. But now the light of the fire clearly lit her.

"Lils, your head."

She glanced back to him, her eyebrows furrowed in confusion.

"Dammit, Lily, your temple." Garek reached up, his fingertips gentle on the gash across her temple. He held up his bloody fingers in front of her.

Confusion still crinkling her eyes, she touched her temple, feeling the cut. "I...I did not know...I could not breathe for so long—"

He grabbed both of her shoulders, forcing her attention to him. "What do you mean you could not breathe?"

"When I attacked him at the door. He kicked me, right here." Her blood stained fingers ran across her belly, just below her ribcage. "I could not breathe. This is the first that I have taken a half normal breath."

Garek dropped his hold on Lily, shooting to his feet. With a growl, he flew across the room, his fist hitting the wall.

Plaster shattered. It wasn't enough.

He punched the wall again.

His fist busted through the outside wall, thrusting into the frozen night air.

Loosening his fist, Garek withdrew it from the hole.

Still not enough.

His elbow drew back, cocking to punch a new hole when two hands clamped onto his high arm.

He tried to shake her loose. She refused to let go.

"Garek. No."

He spun, ripping his arm from her grasp as he stomped to the chair. "I failed you, Lily. I failed you and your sister. I said I would keep you safe and I failed." He uncurled his fists and grabbed his linen shirt from the chair. Jerking it over his head, he bent, tugging on his right boot before the fabric of the shirt fell around his waist.

"Stop. Garek, stop. Where are you going?"

"This. This was too vile, Lily." He glanced up at her as he hopped onto his right foot to pull on his left boot. "Tossing you from the house was despicable, but that he dared to hit you. Kick you. He is a dead man."

"No. You cannot." Her voice pitched into a yell.

Garek stood straight, his fists digging into his thighs. "I am."

"No. I need you here." She jumped in front of the door, blocking his path, her hands behind her, gripping the knob. Her voice notched louder. "I need you, Garek."

Garek stepped to her, stopping just before his body touched hers. He stared down at her. "Move, Lily. Sneedly needs to suffer."

"No. Sneedly needs to be forgotten." Her glare up at him hardened. "Do you not think I want you to go to Weadly and crush him? Crush him for what he did to Brianna, to me. But now—right now—I need you here, dammit."

She pulled one hand from behind, wedging it up between them, her palm thumping onto her chest. Her voice lost its edge, faltering. "I need you. I need to curl up into you. That is what I need. I cannot stand more worry—Brianna has already taken all I can stand. I just need you, Garek. Your arms around me."

Her crystalline blue eyes begging, her hand flipped, going to his chest, her fingers curling into him. "Please. Please do not leave me, Garek. Not now."

Her eyes closed as a shiver ran through her.

It halted him, the tremble of her body.

He knew it—in that instant, it hit him. Every last drop of rage drained from Garek. This was what he needed to do to keep her safe. He had not failed her yet.

But if he walked out that door, he would.

He grabbed her, pulling her from the door and wrapping her in his arms. She tightened against him, her stance shifting, ready to physically fight him to stop him from leaving.

Garek tightened his hold, his lips settling onto her damp hair. "I am here, Lils. I am not going to leave you."

With a choked exhale, her body went limp, folding into him, all fight dissipating.

She was cold, still far too cold.

He picked her up, her toes dragging on the floor as he took three steps to position them in front of the fire. Sliding to the floor, Garek propped his back against the wooden rail at the foot of the bed, not letting his hold on Lily loosen.

Minutes passed, and Lily's stillness, her even breathing told him she had fallen asleep.

Garek concentrated on the serene weight of her rising and falling on his chest with every one of his breaths. It calmed the remnants of fury that reignited, again and again, ebbing into his gut with every thought of what had happened to her and Brianna.

Her sudden soft words, sleepy, startled him. "What next, Garek?"

His hand went to her head, stroking down her loose hair, the braid from earlier in the day long since disheveled. "Do not worry on it, Lily."

"I can think of nothing else." Her fingers twitched against his shirt, but her nose did not leave the nook on his chest. "We have nothing. Nothing but the clothes we arrived with."

"That is not true. You have your possessions at the house, whatever your father left you. I will go to Weadly in the morning—"

"I will accompany you."

A chuckle rumbled from his chest. "By myself. I am not letting you within thirty paces of Sneedly."

"I am not afraid of him, Garek. I know he can hurt me, but I am not afraid of him."

"That has already been proven, Lils. Too much so." His lips dropped to her head and he smiled into her hair. "But no. I will go alone. Just tell me what I should gather from Weadly Hall. What you need."

"Our father's papers. One dress for me, two for Brianna, since she only has the night rail and robe she has on. We are the same size, just go to her dressing room."

"That is all?"

Lily shrugged. "Everything else—they are just things, things I do not care about. But I need father's papers. I still have not had time to decipher any of his holdings. So that is what is important. That is what we have to rebuild our lives with. I do not even have a place for us to go to in the morning."

"You do."

She lifted her head to look at him, her eyebrows high. "We do?"

"I was going to tell you tomorrow—it was why I left early in the day. I found a cottage for you and Brianna. I did not think you would need it so soon, and it is not up to your current standard of surroundings, but it should suffice until Brianna is well."

"How did you find a cottage?"

"I met Widow Thompson. Her son-in-law was at the tavern yesterday and asked me to look at her gout. She just moved in with her daughter and son-in-law, so her cottage is vacant."

"But how did you manage this? You have no money."

"I appealed to her sense of compassion. She knew your father and has kind memories of him—many people do, Lily. He was a friend to a number of people here in Annadale."

"And that worked—appealing for compassion?"

"Yes, until you can set your affairs in order, she is happy to lend you the home."

"And what else?" Lily's eyes pinned him. "I can tell there is more you are not fessing to."

Garek tilted his head with a sigh, sliding his fingers into Lily's hair and pressing her back against his chest. He kissed the top of her head. "I also promised her free care. She apparently has a certain dislike for Dr. Rugbert."

Lily chuckled, and Garek was pleased with the warmth of her breath on his neck. She was finally drying off, heat returning to her body.

"If you leverage yourself on that matter alone, you will soon own this town, Garek. I do not think anyone cares for him, or ever has."

"Which is good, since I do not plan on leaving this place— not as long as you are here," Garek said, his gaze going to the fire. "You should know, Lily, there are quite a few people in this town that regarded your father in the highest esteem. He has assisted many of them, donated his time to their affairs. Everywhere I turn, I meet someone who has been very worried about you and Brianna. Sneedly had cut you two off from the world, they said, once he dismissed all the servants. They have been concerned that you have been captives at Weadly Hall."

She nodded, her hair catching on the unshaven stubble under his chin.

"Garek—" her voice caught, cutting her words.

He stayed silent, waiting for her to take a deep breath and continue.

"You have never failed me, Garek. Never. Know that." Her hand slipped up over his shoulder and she burrowed further into him. "All I can do is worry on tomorrow and the next day, but you have already taken care of it all. All my worries."

Garek set his hand on the crown of her head, tucking her further under his chin. "So sleep. Sleep. Wait for tomorrow. All will right itself."

She nodded, silent.

Within minutes, she was asleep. And this time, her soft snoring was clear evidence.

Two hours later, Garek bent the soreness out of his legs as he lifted Lily and laid her on the bed next to Brianna, wedging her against the wall. He checked Brianna's leg, assuring himself the blood flow had stopped. It had, and he could wait until Lily was awake again to clean it.

He stoked the fire, looking out the hole he had made in the wall. Dawn approached. Snow still whipped through the air, but the darkness was lifting.

Going to the corner of the room, he rummaged through his bag, pulling free a handkerchief and going to the wall to stuff it into the opening.

It was time to pay Sneedly a visit.

~ ~ ~

A door slammed, jarring Lily awake. She had been lost in such sweet blackness that it took a muddled moment to realize she was in bed with Brianna. That was not new, but the wall behind her back was.

Her eyes opened, and the blinding rush of reality made her eyes squeeze shut. Sneedly. Brianna slumped on the ground. The cold. Making her way in the dark. Fingers that could barely move. The empty tavern.

And then the instant relief the moment she found Garek.

Garek. Her eyes flew open, scanning the room. It was well into daylight, and aside from her and Brianna in bed, the room was empty except for a wooden chair, small wooden table, and Garek's leather satchel in the corner of the room.

Lily swung her leg over Brianna, trying not to flatten her sister as she untangled herself from the blanket.

Feet on the floor, Lily leaned over Brianna's face, smoothing back the light brown hair that had matted onto her sister's forehead.

"Bree. Bree."

Brianna's head turned, a grumbling moan coming from her chest.

"Bree." Lily shook her shoulder.

Ever so slowly, her sister's eyes cracked open. "Lils?"

Lily hovered, her face directly above Brianna's eyes so her sister could easily focus on her. "Bree, do not be alarmed. You are in a different room, a different bed. But I am right here and we are safe."

"Safe?" Brianna's forehead scrunched slightly.

"Do not fret." Lily forced what she hoped was an easy smile. "All is well. I just have to leave the room for a moment, and I will return in a minute. I did not want you to worry if you awoke and I was gone. Just go back to sleep."

Brianna started to nod, her eyes drifting closed before the jostle of her head finished.

Lily stepped away from the bed, smoothing the wool of her black dress the best she could. The wetness had combined with her odd sleeping position and had set creases deep into the fabric that there was no recovery from.

Running her hands through her hair, she slapped sections into a quick braid, knowing it would fall apart soon if she didn't find a ribbon to secure the bottom of it.

A quick glance over her shoulder at Brianna, now returned to a deep sleep, and Lily opened the door, stepping out into the hall. She immediately tripped over legs angled across the doorway and stumbled into an awkward fall.

One knee hit the floorboards as she caught herself on the opposite wall.

"Sorry, dovey." A plump lady in a grey dress with a brown-stained apron pushed herself up to her feet from the chair she sat in. "I be catchin' a few winks while I be waitin'."

"Hello," Lily said slowly, drawn out with tentativeness as she smoothed her skirt again. "I am—"

"Lily. I know. Miss Silverton."

Lily's head cocked, her words stilted in confusion. "And you are sitting outside the room because…"

"Because 'e asked. Dr. Harrison. This be 'is room, but 'e didn't want no one besmirchin' ye or yer sister's reputations. 'e woke me husband and asked me to guard the room. 'e told me how ye got yerself booted from Weadly Hall and that yer sister be waverin'. Shame, that. Shame 'bout yer papa—'e be a fine man. Helped me mister out a number o' times on some papers." She winked at Lily, her forefinger wagging down the hallway. "Besides, I don't rightly trust a few of these 'ooligans currently in residence, neither."

Lily glanced down the hall. "Oh. Thank you. I had no idea." She looked to the woman. "I do not believe I have made your acquaintance?"

"Mrs. Fulgton. This be me and me 'usband's tavern. The Twisted Tin." Mrs. Fulgton opened the door to Garek's room, peeking in.

Nosy, but Lily could care less. She was just happy Garek had the foresight to enlist Mrs. Fulgton's help.

Mrs. Fulgton closed the door quietly. "Yer sister. She well now?"

"She is. Last night scared me, but she has been enormously better than she had been. Ever since Dr. Harrison started tending to her at Weadly Hall."

"Yea? 'e's got some admirers 'bout town, too. Me included. No one with a right head likes that mangy ole Dr. Rugbert. But Dr. Harrison—that one is a fine man—endearin'." She elbowed Lily with a sweet cackle. "And 'andsome like the devil, too, eh?"

Lily's mouth spiked in a half smile, chuckling to herself. "Yes. He is all of those things. I am very grateful for his skill with my sister. He saved her life." Lily pointed to the floor. "Is he here? Down in the tavern? I was hoping to get some tea, maybe some broth for Brianna, but I did not want to leave her for long. Her mind is still very muddled."

"Course, child. You stay right here." Mrs. Fulgton moved past her in the hall. "Don't worry a wallop. I'll bring ye up some porridge and tea." She waved her hand. "Get ye back in. Dr. Harrison said 'e would be back soon."

The gratefulness that swept through Lily threatened to send her to her knees. She managed a smile for Mrs. Fulgton, her voice choking. "Thank you. Thank you for your generosity."

"Not a fret, dovey." Mrs. Fulgton's thick hand went to Lily's shoulder, patting hard. "Ye got a bounty o' kindness to be repaid from yer papa and Dr. Harrison. Ye'll be sparklin' once more, dovey."

Lily nodded, moving back into the room. She leaned against the door, staring at her sister.

Sparkling once more.

Lily couldn't even dare dream the thought. But for the first time in forever, she felt hope that wasn't faked. The true possibility of it.

Maybe she could sparkle again. Both her and Brianna.

{ CHAPTER 8 }

The moment she heard footsteps in the hallway, Lily was out the door.

Garek stopped in the hallway, his eyebrows cocked. "So you were waiting for me?"

"I was watching for you out the window. Bree is asleep again, and I did not want to wake her."

"She was awake?"

"Yes. And she sat up, had some broth. The wounds that I tore open last night have stopped bleeding."

Garek flinched at her words. "It was unavoidable, Lily."

Lily shrugged. She didn't particularly want to rehash how she had set all of the current mess into action. "I cleaned the wounds and set the linen as you showed me." Stepping closer to him in the hallway, her eyes searched his face. "What happened at Weadly Hall?"

"I have your father's papers. Most of them, at least. And some clothes for you and Brianna." His face stayed stoic with the words.

"Thank you. But beyond that. What happened?"

"Nothing of concern."

"No?" She took another step forward, leaving only a sliver between them, and looked up at him. "It is of concern, Garek. I am not sure what exactly it is, but your face—your eyes—they have darkened."

He closed his eyes, shaking his head. "Now is not the time, Lily."

Her voice went to a low whisper. "What happened?"

His eyes opened, the green flecks in the hazel taking over the blue. His jaw flexed visibly as he rubbed the back of his neck.

"Lily, no. Right now I have a borrowed wagon waiting for us to take you and Brianna to Widow Thompson's cottage."

The warning in his voice offered no room to argue.

Lily ignored it.

"Garek, if something—"

"No. Lily. We are moving you right now." His hands went to her arms, shifting her so he could slide past her in the skinny hallway. He opened the door. "Do you think Brianna will be able to sit upright for fifteen minutes, or should I make a place for her to lie in the back of the wagon? Mrs. Fulgton said we could take whatever blankets we needed."

Lily sighed to herself, following Garek into the room. "I think she will be fine to sit upright in front, as long as she can lean on the backboard."

"Good." He looked back over his shoulder at her. "Not another word, Lily."

She stared at the back of Garek's rumpled dark jacket, a shiver of fear running down her spine.

What the hell had happened at Weadly Hall?

~ ~ ~

"She is settled." Arms crossed over her belly, Lily stepped out into the last of the grey day, a swathe of hair whipping into her eyes. The snow had ceased, but the wind had become angrier.

Lily dragged the loose tendril from her face, tucking it behind her ear. Three steps forward and she stopped next to Garek, her shoulder touching his. She followed his stare down the rolling hill in front of the cottage to the snow-covered mounds where Widow Thompson had been growing potatoes and beans in neat rows.

His eyes glassy, he didn't say a word to her.

She set her gaze forward, watching the dried rushes along the hill crackle in the wind. "I am settled, Garek. Brianna is settled. All of that is thanks to you."

"You should have a cloak on Lily. I grabbed a cloak for you from Weadly Hall, did you not see it?"

"I need the air."

"I will not have you catch your death out here, Lily," he said softly, not looking to her.

"Now is the time, Garek." She looked up at him, her arms tightening around her ribcage. "Tell me what happened at Weadly Hall."

She let the silence between them thicken, offering no more questions. Hair flew into her face, but she ignored it, staying still, frozen in place. She would wait like this all day if she had to.

A sigh—a heavy sigh—slipped from Garek's lips. "I went dark, Lily. Dark. My hands were around Sneedly's neck. His eyeballs bulging."

She swallowed down panic at the words, forcing herself not to jump in front of him. Not to grab him and shake him. It took several breaths before she could speak. "Did you kill him? Tell me you did not kill him, Garek."

It was only seconds, but an agonizing lifetime passed in Lily's mind before Garek answered her.

"I did not." His eyes swung to her. "But I wanted to, Lils—I truly did. I have never wanted to see another person dead. Not until Sneedly. I choked him—watched as the life almost left his eyes. "

Lily's fingertips relaxed from sharply digging into her ribcage. Garek's soul was darkened, but his hands were clean. "But you let him go."

He nodded. "I let him go."

She moved around to the front of him, letting his body block her from the snapping wind. "Is it that you let him live or that you believe you should have killed him that has sent shadows into your eyes?"

"Shadows in my eyes? What do you mean?"

"That something in you has changed, Garek. I can see it. I do not know how to explain it. Last night you were the same as

I have always known you, but you came back from Weadly Hall with darkness weighing you down."

He swallowed, turning his head as his eyes found far-off woods. Lily's heart started to thump hard in her chest. He wasn't going to tell her—wasn't going speak to what was in his mind. Hide from her.

Just when she opened her mouth, his hazel eyes slid down to her.

"It is darkness, Lily, but not because of Sneedly."

"No? Then what has changed?"

"You." His voice went low—dangerously low. "I was willing to kill a man, give up my whole life, just to make this world a safe place for you, Lily."

"Garek—"

"One reason—there is only one reason for that." Garek's hand came up, his knuckles brushing across her cheek. "I am desperately and unequivocally in love with you, Lily Silverton. So much so I was going to kill a man because he dared to hurt you."

Her eyes dropped to his chest as she blinked hard. He was saying this—this very thing that she had only dared hope for in her deepest dreams—but at the very same time, he was admitting it darkened his life.

Her look met his. "You...you love me? But why does this weigh upon your soul, Garek? You tell me this but you cannot smile? Hold me?"

His hand dropped from her face, holding fast to his side. "I cannot give you the life you deserve, Lily. Not now. I have no money. No home. Responsibilities from the past that weigh upon me, that must be dealt with. You have your sister to worry on. A life to recreate. I have no right to love you at this moment in time."

"No. You have every right, Garek." She unfolded her arms, grabbing his shoulders, shaking him what little she could with her strength against his mass. "I do not care on any of that—anything you try to use to convince yourself you should not love me. You should."

"I should?"

"Yes. You should love me. That is exactly what you should do. That is exactly what you have been doing. Every moment that you have been in my life. My life is right because of you. I was in shambles—everything in shambles, and then you. For as much turmoil as there is around me, I have been happy. Happiness I did not want to admit to because everything else is in such a sorry state. It was the wrong time and I had no right to it. But there it was—is—happiness because of you."

Her hands slipped up his neck to cup his jawline, the prickle of his dark stubble rubbing along her palms. "I love you, Garek. I do. It is the one true thing that has come out of the monstrosity that has become my life. You. For all that I have lost—you—you are the salvation in all of it."

"Hell, Lily." He grabbed her face, capturing her lips with barely restrained power nudging her senses. His breath warmed her face as his fingertips curled along her neck and under her hair, sending shivers down her arms.

The wind, the cold, fell away as he enclosed her in a cocoon of warmth, his body hard against her softness. His mouth opened, tasting her, and Lily pressed into him, wanting to disappear into the safe haven of him, the space where her body began to tingle, throb at the smallest brush of his muscles moving against her. Disappear into him, into the wonder of it, if only for a moment.

His hand slipped down her singular braid, wrapping the hair around his forefinger. "You found the ribbons." The words against her mouth were low, his breath tickling her skin.

"I did." She kept her eyes closed, not wanting his kiss, his command of her senses to be over. "But they were not necessary."

His face edged away from hers, and Lily opened her eyes to see him smiling, his warm hazel eyes taking her in.

"It is a small thing, the ribbons, but they are the one thing that has been on your body that has not been black in the time I have known you." His hand went to her cheek, his palm replacing the heat his kiss had offered. "They were something I could not leave behind."

"I happily leave everything at Weadly Hall, Garek." She brought her hands down from his shoulders, slipping them under the front edge of his great coat. "I have Bree. I have you. That is all that is important."

A horse neighed, pulling a cart and cresting into view along the road that ran along Widow Thompson's property. Lily glanced over her shoulder to it, and then her gaze swung back to Garek.

The shadows had returned to his eyes and he straightened, his hand drifting from her face. "You are freezing."

"I do not feel it."

"I feel it on you. You need to go back inside, Lily." He took a step backward, grabbing her hands and pulling them from his chest. "I cannot stay here any longer without setting the town ablaze with gossip. This road is too well-travelled."

"I do not care what the townsfolk think of me."

He gave her a rational smile. "Yes, but not caring is something we cannot afford just yet. For now we are beholden to the kindness of these people, to the reputation of your father. Until we can determine where you can access the Silverton funds, I will give no one a reason to revoke your current residence."

Lily nodded. She didn't like the logic, but she couldn't argue against it. She would stroll upon whatever fine line the townsfolk wanted her to, as long as Brianna was somewhere warm and fed.

"I will go in. But you will be back tomorrow?"

A smile lifted his right cheek high. "First thing in the morning, Lils. First thing."

{ CHAPTER 9 }

"What are you doing?"

Garek jumped, the paper in his hand crinkling as he set it onto the stack of documents in front of him. He turned in the wooden chair to see Brianna standing in the doorway to the bedroom, a robe stretched tight around her withered frame. Her fingers clutched the doorknob as she swayed slightly.

He sprung to his feet, rushing across the room to her just in case she started to fall. "Brianna, you should be in bed."

His words were met with an instant glare. "I cannot bear to be in bed another moment."

With a nod, Garek grabbed her elbow, helping her hobble into the room. He gently set her on the chair he had occupied. "Are you feeling well—you must have more energy?"

Brianna looked up to him, the glare not easing. "Where is Lily?"

"She went to the Plawton's cottage. She was hoping their youngest, Mable, had not left the area after Mr. Sneedly dismissed all of the servants. Lily hoped she could convince the girl to help here. But she did not want to leave you alone, so she asked me to stay."

Brianna nodded, and then her eyes swept over the mess of papers strewn across the square table.

"These—these are all my father's documents." She leaned forward, fingers lifting up a few papers to see further into the piles. "What are you doing with my father's papers?"

Garek pulled out the wooden chair closest to him and sat. "Lily asked me to help her go through them. They were in complete disarray, and she is having trouble piecing it all back together."

Picking up the paper closest to her, she scanned the writing. "But these are all his finances." She quickly picked up two more pieces, eyes whipping across them. "All about the Silverton estate."

"Yes?"

Her blue eyes, an exact match with Lily's, narrowed on him. "So what do you mean to do with them?"

"Do with them?" Garek shrugged. "Nothing. Lily is not sure where to access funds so that she can pay Widow Thompson for this place. Pay for food."

"Pay you?"

Garek's head tilted, his brow furrowed. "Pay me? Is that what you are worried on?"

"Of course it is." Brianna leaned forward, her lips set in a hard line. "You do not think I have seen how you have wormed your way into our lives? Seen how you have entranced my sister?"

"Entranced—"

"Is it our money you are after? You have the look about you—the look of desperation."

"Money?" Garek shook his head. "No. Lily was the one that asked for my help—both originally with you, and then with this." His hand swept over the papers on the table.

"And what did you make her promise you for your help? Money? Her body?" She coughed, having to stop and take a deep breath. Both of her palms went to the table to steady herself. Her head down, her eyes came up to him. "Have you compromised my sister, Dr. Harrison?"

Garek stood.

His conversations with Brianna had been very limited, as she was usually sleeping, and he had truly only talked to her about her leg and the infection. But he had never expected any of this from her. She had been most docile until now.

"I do not think I will stand for these accusations, Miss Silverton."

Her glare deepened. "Then leave."

"I told your sister I would stay and watch over you. I am only here, apparently, for her peace of mind."

"Is that not sweet—sweet and convenient." Brianna's lip went into a snarl. "You will get nothing of the Silverton estate, Dr. Harrison."

Garek sighed, his hand tightening on the top bar of the wooden chair. "Again, I have asked for nothing from Lily."

"No? How did you even get into our house, Dr. Harrison? How did she even find you? What was wrong with Dr. Rugbert?"

A sarcastic chuckle escaped before Garek could stop it. "You would be dead right now if you were still in the hands of Dr. Rugbert—that was what was wrong with him. Lily saved your life by bringing me here, Miss Silverton."

"Did she? Or is that what you have convinced her of?"

Garek took a deep breath. "I think this is a conversation better had with Lily present."

Brianna pushed herself to standing. "I am having it with you, Dr. Harrison. How in the hell did you swindle your way into our lives?"

Her hands were shaking, the muscles on her neck straining. Garek could see the immense effort it took for Brianna to stand.

His lips pursed. "I do think I will take your suggestion and leave you for the moment, Miss Silverton. Lily should arrive soon. Please tell her I will return to check on you, on your leg, when she is present."

"You need not bother Dr. Harrison."

"Be that as it may, Lily will still want me to check in. Please tell her I will be back later in the day." He walked to the outside door and paused, turning back to her, his voice genuine. "It is encouraging to see you upright, Miss Silverton. To see you with more…spirit."

Her scowl worsened. "Leave. Dr. Harrison. Just leave. You are needed here no more."

~~~

Turning into the space behind Widow Thompson's barn, Lily tugged on the leather reins, slowing the white speckled horse pulling the curricle.

She slipped the reins around the hook at the front of the curricle, and her fingernail caught her eye. Spreading her fingers wide, she sighed. Three fingertips popped out of the top seams of the leather gloves Mrs. Plawton had offered to her. Generous, even if they were half falling apart. Partially warm hands were better than fully freezing ones.

At least young Mable was still available and would be coming by daily until Lily could move with Brianna to a permanent home where Mable could have her own quarters. That the girl was just as relieved to see her, as Lily was to find her unemployed, was evidence of the turmoil Mr. Sneedly had caused not only with her and Brianna, but also with so many of the displaced servants.

Lily turned, stepping backward and down from the curricle. A hand suddenly on the small of her back sent an instant smile onto her face. Garek.

She found her footing on the ground, spinning around, and choked, falling backward into the carriage step.

Mr. Sneedly was smiling at her.

The metal step dug into her backside as her hands went out wide, guiding her along the curricle as she tried to dodge around him.

He sidestepped to remain directly in front of her.

Grabbing her forearm, he continued to offer what she presumed he thought was a charming smile. "Please, Lily, there is no need to escape me."

Lily's feet froze as she met his eyes, challenging. "What are you doing here, Mr. Sneedly?"

"I came to retrieve what you stole from the estate."

"What I stole? I did no such thing."

"The curricle. The horse." His head inclined toward the horse as though she was a simpleton.

"Take it. Take it and leave here, Mr. Sneedly." She twisted the arm he held, flipping her wrist as she tried to free herself. No success.

"Garek," she screamed, hoping he could hear her from the cottage.

"He is not here. He left an hour ago. Do you truly think I would approach you with him nearby? The man is a monster."

Lily shook her head, the first shivers of fear shooting down her spine.

"I am sorry, Lily."

She stopped squirming, shock crossing her face. "You are what?"

"I have said it once." The pasted smile slipped from his face. "I will not say it again. I may have acted hastily the other night. Asking you to leave Weadly Hall was not what I had intended."

"Asking? Not what you intended?" She blinked hard, dumbstruck. "Mr. Sneedly, you kicked us out of Weadly Hall in the middle of the night. In a snowstorm."

"A mere blunder," he said flippantly, the repulsive smile reappearing. "I did not think you would leave."

"You did not think we would leave? What did you think I would do?" She glanced down at his hand wrapping her arm, her words pointed and eyes harsh as she looked back at him. "You drugged my sister, Mr. Sneedly. Brianna almost died. She nearly froze to death. And you call it a blunder?"

"Come, now, Lily, there is no need to be so dramatic." His fingers tightened around her arm, his too-long nails digging through the wool dress into her muscle.

"Dramatic—you kicked me in the gut—stole my breath, Mr. Sneedly, and you dare to call me dramatic?" Lily yanked her arm, freeing it.

But before she could move away, he snatched her left arm in the same hold. "Be still, Lily. If you will recall, you attacked me first. Did you not expect there would be retribution?" He recaptured her right arm, his face now close—far too close to hers.

How to get away? The image of kicking him flashed through her mind, of slamming her knee up at his gut. Her right foot lifted, tensed, but then she stamped it to the ground.

Attacking him had done her no favors the other night. Words. She needed to get out of this with words. "I did not expect to be thrown from Weadly Hall in the first place, Mr. Sneedly. I did not expect to see Brianna abandoned to the frozen ground outside."

"And I did not expect to find you fornicating with that doctor." His thin lips pulled back, almost disappearing as he leaned in, his breath breaching her pores. "You must understand, Lily, it was jarring for me to see my future wife with another man. But I do not imagine you will make that mistake again after this lesson."

"All this was a lesson for your future wife—me?" Her voice incredulous, she wedged her hands up, fingers stretching backward to gain a grip on his arms and trying to push his body from hers. "You are mad, Mr. Sneedly. Truly and utterly mad if you think I want anything to do with you. Now kindly remove your hands from my body."

A grunt escaped her as she used the carriage to flatten herself against and then shoved at him with all her strength.

He only fell one small step backward. A step he reclaimed instantly, closer than ever.

"You need time to forgive my transgression, Lily? I understand." The words casual, he set his cheek next to hers, his voice in her ear. She cringed away as the grease from his brown hair smeared against her temple. "In the meantime, you may do so in comfort. Come back to Weadly Hall, Lily. You and your sister."

She craned her head to the side, trying to avoid his breath as she lost control of her voice. "What? Why do you insist, Mr. Sneedly? Do you not understand the simple words I say? Of course we will not come back to Weadly Hall. Of course I will never—ever—be your wife. Of course I never want to see your face again."

His hand whipped up, grabbing a fistful of her hair, stilling her head. His mouth went to her ear. "Do not say such things, Lily."

She shoved again, one hand now free as she started to kick at him. But he was too close now to make hard contact, his body shoving her up against the curricle. "Take your damn horse and curricle and go, Mr. Sneedly."

"Or what? You will attack me again? I think you know how that ends, Lily."

Sneedly twisted the hair on her head, shoving the side of her face onto the black wood of the carriage. "This only ends one way, Lily. You are mine. And I tried to be kind. But no more. No more waiting for your sister to die. Waiting for you to come to me broken." His hand holding her arm captive shifted to snatch her wrist, twisting it behind her back as his tongue went into her ear.

Repulsion swept through her, curdling her body and sending bile into her throat. She swung as hard as possible with her free hand, but the awkward angle negated all her power, her fist landing harmlessly, again and again on his shoulder, his head.

His tongue went deeper into her ear.

"Yes. Fight me, Lily." He pulled away, but only to smack her head into the carriage. "Fight it."

Pain shot through her skull, her eyes cringing closed, but she welcomed it. Anything that would take his tongue off of her body. Anything.

She swung again, only hitting air.

Hitting air because Sneedly was gone. His hands off her body.

Slumping against the curricle, her eyes opened to see Sneedly flying through the air, slamming into the grey weathered timbers of the barn.

Garek's hand clamped around Sneedly's neck, pinning him high to the wall, his legs flopping in futile kicks.

"I let you escape death once, Sneedly, and that was my mistake. A mistake I will not repeat." The growl that came from Garek was so savage, so brutal, it petrified Lily.

A gurgle escaped from Sneedly, his body flailing.

It was just enough horror to break Lily from her shock.

"Garek." Her scream echoed across the surrounding fields as she pushed off from the carriage.

A second before she touched him, she saw Garek's body tense, then shudder.

She reached Garek's back, her hands grasping onto his shoulders just as his hold on Sneedly loosened. She could feel the rage straining his muscles, along with the immense jolt of restraint that coursed through him as he let Sneedly drop from his crushing grip.

Clutching his neck, Sneedly slid down the wall, falling to the ground.

"Get the hell out of here before I come to my senses and destroy you, Sneedly." Garek said the words calmly, belittling the anger Lily still felt surging along his shoulders.

His boots slipping in the hay until he gained footing, Mr. Sneedly finally found his way to stand, and he ran away from the barn without a glance at Garek or Lily.

Heaving, Lily's forehead dropped onto Garek's back. She couldn't move for long seconds—she could only clutch Garek's shoulders, using his strength to hold onto so she wouldn't fall, wouldn't crumble into a sobbing heap.

She was fine. Fine. No harm.

No harm except Sneedly's tongue in her ear.

Bile rose to her throat as the feel of his tongue flooded her mind, and Lily ran from Garek, stumbling into the barn, aiming for the wooden bucket by the front stall.

No matter that the water was putrid and stale. It would do. She skidded onto her knees, ripping off her gloves as she set her head above the bucket and splashed freezing water up into her ear, cleaning, scrubbing it, again and again.

Garek followed her, his feet stopping next to the bucket. He stood silent, watching her, waiting.

The water sloshed over the edge of the bucket, splashing onto his dark boots. But Lily couldn't stop. Couldn't stop the scrubbing, the water rinsing and rinsing and not quite able to clean the filth of Sneedly off her skin.

"Lily, stop."

She heard the words, calm through the maniacal need in her mind to rid herself of Sneedly.

Garek knelt, balancing on his heels so she could see his face. His hand went to her wet neck, trying to still her. "You need to stop, Lily. Your cheek and ear are red. They will be bloody soon."

Her hand on her ear, scrubbing, made her jerk against Garek's slippery hold. She wanted to stop. But every second that passed and she thought she could, her hand kept going down for more water, splashing it into her right ear and rubbing.

One more rinse, and it would be clean. One more. One more.

Garek's other hand went around her neck. He had her captive, and he gently tugged her forward, away from the bucket.

Her hand fumbled behind her into the bucket for one last splash of water, bringing it to her ear, her palm forcing the liquid into the cavity.

His clamp around her neck lifted her upright, still clutching her ear. She met Garek's dark hazel eyes, knowing she looked ridiculous, her head half sopping, clutching her ear. A madwoman. But it was still on her, Sneedly's breath, his spit.

Slowly, Garek slid his left hand from the back of her neck upward. His fingers slipped under her palm pressed against her ear, the warmth of his hand enveloping her skin, her ear. Silent, his gaze stayed on her, his eyes flickering when she first flinched at the invasion.

Lily's fingers curled around his hand, her eyes closing as she pressed her head into his palm. He let her stay there for minutes, on her knees, motionless, while his hand calmed her mind, calmed her breath.

Her eyes slid open. Garek was still watching her, the green flecks in his eyes bright. His overwhelming concern was evident without a word.

She tugged his left hand downward from her ear, holding it between her palms in front of her chest. "How do you do that?"

"Do what?" His fingers still on her neck tightened, sending shivers along her spine.

"You touch me, Garek, and everything is right. All the wrong, gone—banished."

His head shook softly. "I do not know, Lily. But you do the same for me. Make me forget everything but looking at you. Wanting you."

His head bowed.

Staring at the crown of his head, his dark hair, sudden panic enveloped Lily's chest. Had Sneedly so soiled her that Garek had to avoid her? What if he couldn't look at her anymore?

Garek's chin rose, unmistakable heat in his eyes as they trailed up her body. Forever moments passed before his gaze met her eyes.

"Marry me, Lily. I love you. I want you. I need to protect you—and marrying you would make that a hell of a lot easier."

Stunned, Lily dropped backward, pulling Garek's hand with her as she landed on her calves. "W-what?"

His right hand stayed wrapped around her neck as his shins went flat to the ground, mirroring Lily's. His knees met with hers on the hay as he leaned forward, his forehead collapsing onto hers. "Marry me, Lily Silverton. Marry me."

Her eyes closed. "Garek, I...I do not want it like this. I do not want to be a problem that you have to solve by marrying me."

"Look at me, Lily."

She opened her eyelids.

"Lily, solving this problem—protecting you—is merely a bonus to marrying you—an excuse I can use to ask you today, this very moment, when I know I have no right to. I have nothing to offer you, Lils, except me. But know that I would have asked you a week ago, a month ago instead of today if I thought I could have. Or I will ask you tomorrow, and the next day, and the next day, and every day until you say yes."

"But I fear with Bree—we have no home, our lives are in shambles. I am afraid…"

"Afraid of what?"

Lily bit her tongue. She couldn't let him know this. But then her mouth opened, words tumbling. "Afraid you are confusing pity with love."

An instant chuckle left his lips. "Pity you? The woman that dismantles an abbey? Chances a complete stranger to save her sister? Attacks the man trying to freeze her and her family to death? You are a fighter, Lils. So no—pity has never even entered my mind when I look at you. Lots of things have entered my mind." His hand on her neck moved forward, his thumb catching her lip, tracing the lower edge of it as his voice turned heated. "Far too many things. But not that. Not pity."

Lily's breath caught. "You are certain?"

"I have been certain for weeks, Lily. But I have been holding back, waiting for the right time for this—for us. But the right moment in time has conspired against us, never appeared. Between your sister, Sneedly, moving you, all of it."

His thumb slipped downward, dragging along her jawline as he cupped her face. "But I am done being afraid of timing. Of feeling guilty for wanting you in the midst of all the turmoil, for not being able to offer you the world. I want you Lily. I have since the moment we met. And that need has only intensified. Intensified because I have fallen so deeply in love with you, there is no other option than to make you mine. You are my heart, Lily. And I am done waiting for the right time."

He stopped, clearing his throat as thick words he clearly did not want to utter came forth. "Unless you do not want me?"

"No. Never think that. Ever." She dropped his hand at her chest, her hands moving up to clamp his face, her palms running across the dark stubble. "I love you, Garek. And if you are done waiting, then I am done, as well." A smile broke wide on her face, her words breathless. "Yes. Yes. Yes."

His lips were on hers in an instant, his hand under her cloak and around her waist, dragging her to his body.

From her knees on the ground to her chest, her body molded into his, the width of him taking her over, heating her. His mouth opened, demanding more from her, demanding she open to him, let him in.

Lily lost herself. Lost herself in the muscles of his chest pressing against her breasts, lost herself in his breath on her face, his tongue exploring. Garek's hand slipped forward around her neck, unlatching her cloak, and the heavy fabric dropped from her shoulders.

His fingers stayed on the front of her neck, his thumb sliding downward, edging below the trim of her black dress, her chemise, and the top of her stays.

More. The only thought in Lily's head at the invasion of his fingers onto her skin. More.

Toes curling in her boots, her hands went up, fingers wrapping into his hair as she tilted her head, opening herself more to him.

More.

Cheeks throbbing, her heart wild, she angled her chest so he could reach deeper, go farther. "You make—"

His hand came up, fingers along her jaw shifting her head upward so he had access to her neck. His lips, his teeth went along her skin, stealing her words.

"Make you, what, Lily?" he asked, his voice a low rumble.

She couldn't help her hips from pressing forward, pressing into him, the large bulge in his trousers digging into her belly.

"I did not know this existed in my body. Bree told me of the motions, the specifics, but not this. Not what is happening in my body right now."

Gasping, his lips on her neck sending fire to chase along her spine, she slid her fingers downward, digging into his shoulders, the muscles along his arms. She grabbed his hand under her chin, dragging it down her body.

"This, what this is doing to me." She pressed his hand into her skirts between her legs. "Here."

His hand jerked from her hold. "Hell, Lily."

She pulled back, confused. "I—was that wrong?"

"No. Hell no, Lils. There is no shame in any of this—not between us. I was not expecting it. But it is right—too right." His hand went behind her neck, not letting her pull away with his next words. "But this should not lead to where we want to go. Not yet."

"Why? You make me feel this, yet you cannot touch me?"

"There is nothing I want to do more in the world right now than to feel you, my hands on your body, on your skin."

She stared into his eyes, the green shards in the hazel vibrating with hunger, reading his every intention. This man would never harm her, never let her feel anything less than cherished, wanted, loved.

She knew it—knew it in her soul. "No hesitation. I am not denying you, Garek."

His head dropped, hiding his face from her for a moment. With a deep breath he looked up to her, searching her face. "We can wait, Lily. We can post bans tomorrow—then only two weeks to wait. A proper marriage. A proper bed."

"You were the one that said you no longer feared timing, Garek. And I am not afraid. I want this. I want you. I do not want to wait." Her fingers on his shoulders moved to clasp behind his neck. "Two weeks from now, maybe there will be a bed. Maybe there will not. Either way, it has no consequence on this very moment. This moment when you can kiss me."

Her left fingers fell from his neck to trail along his arm, landing on the back of his hand on her shoulder. "This moment when you can touch me."

Achingly slow, she dragged his hand downward, setting his fingers over her left breast. He flinched, but she held his hand in place, squeezing it.

She moved her face closer to his, her lips only a breath away from his skin. "This moment when you can make me yours."

His muscles strained against her, his voice the gravel of a tortured man. "Once done, Lils, we cannot go back."

Pressing forward, she kissed him softly, opening her mouth to him with a whisper. "I am feeling something very real for the first time in a very long time, Garek. Real in my soul. Real in my skin. You holding me. Touching me. Do not take it away. Not in this moment."

"I would give up my life for you, Lils, but I have to ask again. This cannot be undone. Ever. Once you are mine. You are mine always."

She gave a slight shake of her head, her lips moving down along his jaw. The prickle of his stubble tickled her lips, roughed her skin. "I do not want to go back, Garek. There is nothing for me in the past. Only the future. The future with you."

With a growl rumbling from deep in his chest, Garek found her lips, kissing her hard. Hard with purpose. His hand on her breast needed no prodding, cupping then rolling the nipple through the cloth until it was taut, straining for him.

Wrapping an arm around her, he wedged a foot up, grabbing her cloak as he stood, lifting her. Five steps backward into the stall piled high with hay, and Garek flung her cloak down, spreading it wide.

He spun them, setting free a low laugh from Lily's chest, and then she was sinking into the hay, Garek on top of her, looking down. All doubt had disappeared from his eyes, only sheer, heart-pounding desire left.

Unbuttoning his waistcoat, Lily wedged her hands under his dark jacket, and shoved both pieces off his shoulders, stripping him free of them.

He descended, his mouth on her neck, and it took her a moment to realize Garek had tugged down the top of her dress, freeing her breasts to the air. The chilliness shocked her skin as Garek paused to take her in, hungry. He sank to her chest, his mouth enveloping her right nipple as his hand went to her other one.

"Heaven help me, Lils, I want every bit of your skin bared to me, but it is cold."

Lightning from his tongue ricocheted down her body to collect, boiling in her core. Her hands folded into the back of his head, holding him tight to her breast, as her hips writhed under him on their own accord. "As long as you are on me, Garek, I am warm—hot."

He groaned, taking one breath to lift from her and yank off his linen shirt.

His bare chest hovered above her, and Lily almost choked. "The devil in hades, Garek."

Her hands ran down the front of him, over his chest, down the lines of muscles along his belly. "I knew you were large—strong—but you are beautiful."

He smirked down at her. "You only know beauty if you are seeing what I am seeing, Lils." He dove, attacking her nipples once more.

Her hips instantly reacted to the onslaught, twisting under him, silently imploring him to touch her, to soothe the pounding blood in her core that had only boiled hotter.

Eyes closed, her head arched backward, Lily didn't recognize her own voice as it left her. "Please, Garek, please," she moaned, not even knowing what she was begging for.

At her words, his hand dipped down, moving under her skirts, dragging them upward as his fingers trailed along her leg, up to her inner thigh. At the first touch of his thumb in her folds, she jerked, gasping with a yelp, and gripping him harder to her chest.

She felt Garek shift, look up at her face, but she couldn't talk, couldn't move for fear his hand would leave her. It was exactly what she had been begging for, and not even known it. But he knew. He knew full well.

A chuckle vibrated from his chest as he circled his thumb, teasing her to arch upward, fully into him. In the moment that her hands shifted past his shoulders, fingernails digging into his back, demanding he drop onto her, Garek eased away for a second.

Too far from her. Too long. And she yanked on his shoulders.

In the next instant his face was above hers, questioning, and Lily could feel him poised, the head of him pressing into her entrance.

She glanced down, unable to see anything past her bunched up skirt.

"It cannot be undone, Lils. You are mine."

A statement, a question, she wasn't sure. But his thumb circled in her folds, made her strain upward, and she could only bear one answer.

With the slightest gasp, she nodded. Needing this. Needing him.

A grimace etched his face, and he slid into her. Slow, bit by tiny bit, letting her body stretch open to him. He held her eyes the entire time, but Lily gave him no reason to stop, even when her membrane tore, her legs only tightened around him, pulling him deeper.

His hips met hers, his shaft embedded deep, and he exhaled with a shudder. A shudder that ran along his back, vibrating under her fingers.

"Lils? Pain? Tell me there is no pain."

She gasped for air, meeting his eyes. "No. Only you. I…"

Her words fell away as Garek withdrew, his thumb rotating in her folds, bringing her body back to the agony that had yet to be sated. When she was writhing once more, he slid into her again, back and forth, bringing her to a peak, then easing the grind away.

Desperate. Making her desperate. Gasps with every breath.

"Garek. Gar—"

"Open it. Let it go, Lils."

The words in her throat turned into a scream as her body clenched around him. She lost all feeling in her arms and feet as explosions ripped through her core, consuming her.

Garek sped, the sound of his breath filling her head as he strained, his hips sending him ever deeper. With a growl, he expanded into her body, filling her.

His body throbbing, muscles twitching to match her own, Garek collapsed on her, pressing her deep into the hay. It took several long breaths before he moved, flipping them, holding Lily tight to him.

She flattened herself on top of his body, her head on his chest, the blood pounding in her ears matching the thundering of his heart.

Garek's hand went into her hair, still wet from the bucket, taking strands and smoothing them as he untangled them from bits of straw.

"Heaven help me, Lils, your voice—even in screams, has to be descended from Odysseus's sirens."

Lily smiled into his chest. "I have taken a weary traveler and kept him captive?"

"Something akin to that." His fingers clenched into her hair. "Tell me you do not regret this, Lils." His voice was thick, rumbling from deep in his chest.

Without lifting her head, Lily looked up to him, her heart welling so hard it stole her breath. She managed a whisper. "No. Never."

He kissed her forehead, his arm clamping hard around her body. "I give you everything I am, Lils."

Grabbing her hand, he flattened it to his chest. "You are mine. You are already my wife here." He brought her fingers to his forehead. "And here."

Curling her fingers around his hand, he brought them to his lips, setting the softest kiss on them. "And in my soul. Never question this."

Her heart clenching with wonder, with love, she smiled, meeting his gaze. "Never."

{ CHAPTER 10 }

"I need to go to the abbey."

Walking into the bedroom of the cottage, Lily found Brianna sitting on the bed, her knee touching her cheek as she laced her left boot.

Lily's heart skipped a beat. Brianna was in one of the black dresses Garek had brought from Weadly Hall, the top of the back gaping with undone buttons.

Dressed—Brianna was actually dressed in proper clothes for the first time since she was attacked.

Lily moved around the bed to Brianna's side, smoothing stray strands of her hair into the haphazard braid she had quickly weaved in the barn. The end of a piece of hay jabbed into her scalp. Hopefully, Garek had swept off all the hay from the back of her dress. Brianna had always been observant and would be sure to question it if any pieces of hay fell from Lily.

"The abbey, Bree? Why? Why now?"

Brianna looked up from the boot. "The memories are coming back of what happened there. But I need to see it. Need to see what is real and what I…what I may be imagining."

"What have you remembered?"

Brianna's mouth clamped shut, her head shaking. She went back to lacing her boot.

Stifling a sigh, Lily set her knee on the bed. Brianna was still refusing to tell her anything of what happened. She worked the black glass buttons up the back of Brianna's wool dress. "Fine. We will go to the abbey. But are you positive you are not too tired?"

"I will be fine."

Dress buttoned, Lily stepped away from the bed. "I will fetch the horse and curricle and bring it to the door so you do not have to walk far. Mr. Sneedly did not take them with him. But we will have to return them to Weadly Hall eventually."

Brianna's head shot up. "Mr. Sneedly was here?"

"Yes." Lily forced a smile. "But he is gone now."

Brianna stared at her, waiting for more.

Lily ducked her face, moving to the door before her smile faded. "It should only take a moment. Be sure to put a cloak on, and I will bring a warm blanket."

A half hour later, Lily eased the horse to a halt, stilling the curricle in front of the abbey. She glanced to Brianna. Her sister stared at the building, transfixed, her jaw line twitching.

"Bree, you do not have to do this. Are you certain you would like to go in?" Lily asked.

Brianna nodded silently, seeming to gather strength. Before Lily could ask one more time, Brianna pushed herself up, stepping down from the carriage.

Lily hustled down, sidling Brianna closely, ready to catch her if she swayed. But to her sister's credit, Brianna's steps were rock solid. Steady and even as she moved to the high arched doors at the front of the abbey.

"What happened to the corners? Is someone taking it down?" Brianna's head inclined to the right, toward the corner of the building. The wrecked stones still sat in random piles of rubble.

"Interesting." Lily coughed, pulling open the heavy ancient door. She put her hand on the small of Brianna's back and ushered her into the building. "It does look that way."

Dim light through the stained glass windows high on the walls greeted them. Stale air hit Lily's nostrils as dust floated into the air with their steps. She didn't want to be in this place. Didn't want to retrace her steps from that night.

"Is this far enough?" Lily stopped, watching as Brianna moved deeper into the wide room. Elegant stone arches repeated on the tall outer walls, framing the stained glass, though the gold gilded lanterns had long been stripped from the walls.

Brianna didn't stop. "No. This is not where it happened. I know that. I think I know that. It was down below."

Lily swallowed hard. Of course Brianna would want to go below. Lily picked up her left foot to follow, ignoring how very heavy her legs had become. What Brianna did not yet recall, Lily had no problem remembering—remembering too well. "It has been cleaned. That was what I was told. It was cleaned."

Brianna nodded, moving to the opening on the side of the room where the stairs descended in a tight spiral.

Her hand going onto the cold stone wall at the entrance to the stairs, Lily braced herself, fighting the wave of nausea that swirled through her body. The last time that she had gone down these stairs...Brianna...Papa...

Brianna's heels clicked on the stairs, echoing up to Lily, then suddenly stopped. Lily's eyes squeezed shut as she gulped air. She couldn't let Brianna do this alone. She had to go down into the hell below.

Her feet moving quickly down the spiral stone stairs, she bumped into the back of Brianna as she rounded the last curve. Brianna stumbled forward with a yelp, dropping off the last stair she stood on.

Quick to follow, Lily caught Brianna's shoulders before she fell to the ancient stone floor. She pulled her sister upright, realizing that Brianna was already shaking violently.

Lily kept her eyes solely on her sister, refusing to look around the cellar. Refusing to let the bloody scene resurface in her mind. "Bree, we should go. You are shaking. I do not think you can handle this—not yet."

Brianna jerked from Lily's hands, stepping to the middle of the room. Her voice came out solid, but soft. "I can handle this, Lils. I need to."

Folding her arms across her belly, Lily watched as her sister spun in a slow circle, her eyes flickering over every inch of the room.

"Not you. No. Not you." The cracking whisper slipped from Brianna's lips, the words crumbling in the stale air. And then Brianna's mouth started to move, silent words forming on her lips—fast—yelling—but no sound came from her mouth. Again and again Brianna spun, her eyes glazed, her mouth moving, her forehead crumpled in horror.

The sight sent Lily's skin crawling, so she lifted her eyes up, focusing on the two small openings high on the wall across from her that jutted down from the ceiling. The glass long gone from the windows, they offered just enough light to see in the dank cellar.

Lily stared. Stared at the frozen brown grass along the bottom edge of the opening where the snow couldn't reach. Stared at the tops of the barren trees.

As long as she didn't look down, she could do this. Didn't look down at the spot where her father was dead, his throat cut wide, blood thick and warm. Didn't look down at the spot where Brianna sat tied in a chair, bloody, near death.

No. She shook her head. Eyes up. Eyes up and she could be here for Brianna.

It was moments before Lily realized Brianna had stopped spinning. Her gaze dropped to find her sister staring at her, fear deep in her eyes. A terror so deep that Lily could see Brianna's skin quivering.

"We can go, Lils." The words slipped from Brianna's mouth in a raw whisper.

Lily reached her hand out, and Brianna stumbled forward, taking it, squeezing it so hard Lily thought the bones in her fingers would snap.

She dragged Brianna up the stairs, not letting her slip from her grasp. Not that Brianna was about to let her go.

Without a word, they walked out of the abbey.

The fresh air enveloped them, and Brianna dropped Lily's hand and stumbled to the edge of the clearing where the woods started.

Following, Lily reached for her sister's shoulders to steady her, but Brianna jerked away. "No. Do not touch me. I need…I need to sit."

Her sister slid to the snowy ground, her back ramrod straight, staring at the building. No tears fell from her face. Lily watched as the terror on Brianna's face morphed, descending into anger. Silent, bitter, ground-shaking anger.

Lily's gut tightened, fear pooling at what Brianna would do next. She let a few more minutes pass before she went forward, dropping to her knees in front of her sister.

"You remember everything, Bree. I can see it."

Brianna's blue eyes drifted from the abbey to Lily. "I do."

"What happened to you, Bree?" Lily snatched her sister's hands, clutching them. "You have told me nothing. What happened to you in there? Who did this?"

"You do not need to know, Lily." Brianna's voice was unnaturally wooden. Even and calm against the anger swallowing her face. "You need to forget it. Forget everything. Forget anything and everything in our lives before this moment. I need you to do that."

"But—no. I cannot do that. Why would you even ask that of me?"

"It is important, Lily. Forget everything. We must move on from here. From this place."

"No." The shout escaped loud from her chest, surprising Lily, but it didn't stop her from continuing, her pitch rising. "No, Bree. I lost him too. I was the one that found Papa dead. Found you. My hands were on his warm body turning cold—not yours. Mine. It is not fair that you know how…" Her words choked off, but she swallowed hard, forcing air past the rock in her throat. "That you know how he died, but you will not tell me."

Brianna's lips pulled inward, disappearing, her eyes closing as her head fell back. "Do not do this, Lils."

"I am demanding this, Bree."

Brianna's eyes flew open, pinning Lily. "It was brutal, Lily. Is that what you want to hear? It was brutal and his blade cut into my flesh and blood flew. Is that what you need to hear?"

Lily's head snapped back, stung, but her hands tightened on Brianna's. "Yes. If it will help you to tell me, to share this burden—whatever has blackened your eyes to where I do not even recognize them—then yes, yes I want to hear."

"And I will not subject you to that." Brianna tugged her hands free from Lily's grasp and got to her feet. "Papa died trying to save me, Lils. He died because he loved me. That is all you need to know."

"But—" Lily scrambled to her feet, following Brianna to the carriage.

"No. No more, Lily. We will never speak of it again." Reaching the side of the carriage, Brianna spun back to Lily. "Do you understand? Never again."

Lily's head shook. "It is not fair that you ask this of me, Bree."

"I do not care if it is fair or not. I only care that you adhere to my wishes." Brianna turned back to the carriage, hoisting herself up the iron step and onto the bench cushion.

At a loss, Lily stared up at Brianna. Her sister had huddled herself into the corner of the curricle, dragging the blanket over her lap, staring at the twitching horse's tail.

She looked tiny. Lost. Her older sister—the one she had always depended on, always looked to for strength, for guidance, for everything—shrinking from the world.

Lily exhaled, her heart sinking. What had she imagined letting Brianna come here would do? Fix everything? Fix her sister? Fix the past? Fix the fact that their father was murdered?

Silly. A silly hope. She saw that now.

She should have been more diligent about destroying the abbey.

Lily stepped up into the carriage, unwrapping the reins from the hook. Without a sideways glance at the abbey, she set the horse forward.

Halfway back to Widow Thompson's cottage, Lily looked over to her sister. Brianna had sat in silence, rigid against the carriage bouncing along the rutted road.

"Bree, I am to marry."

Her sister jerked upright, grabbing Lily's arm. "Marry? Who? What?"

Lily smiled, trying to calm Brianna's instant panic. "Garek. We are to have the bans posted tomorrow."

"No, Lils. What? No. You cannot. No, no, no."

"I realize the timing of it is not desirable, he does too, but—"

"No." Brianna screamed the word, shaking Lily's arm. "You cannot marry him, Lily. We cannot trust him, he will hurt you. You cannot let him into our home, into our lives."

"What? Bree, you are being ridiculous." Lily's head cocked to the side as she looked at her sister, trying to decipher the sudden madwoman sitting beside her. "Garek has been with us for months—he is already well ingrained into our lives. He has given up his life to help us, to help you. He saved you from death, Bree—from death."

"What he has done has no consequence on today. He cannot be trusted, Lily. No. He is a man and cannot be trusted. You must break anything you have with him."

"No, Bree. You are absolutely wrong. I love him. Love him like I never thought I could love—completely—every part of me. I trust him unequivocally. And you should too."

The shaking of Lily's arm grew manic. "No, Lily, do not say that. You cannot marry him. I absolutely forbid it."

Lily yanked on the reins, stopping the horse and turning fully to her sister. "You cannot forbid anything, Bree. I love Garek, and I will be marrying him as soon as the bans are sufficed. I thought you would be happy for me."

"You know nothing of love, Lily." Her fingers dug into Lily's arm with more strength than Lily imagined Brianna had. "You are so wrong about this. That man does not love you—he cannot."

Lily blinked hard. "Why would you even say that, Bree? This is not you."

"You are young and besotted and stupid about this and have no idea what love is, Lily."

"And you do? I am the stupid one?" Lily jerked her arm from Brianna's grasp. "What would you know of love, Bree? Your fiancé disappeared on you—he did not stay to see you well—he did not even attend Papa's burial."

The slap across Lily's face was instant, the sheer shock of the action delaying the sting of it.

Brianna's hand clamped over her mouth. "Lily—I am so sorry." She grabbed Lily's shoulders, shaking them, desperate. "Lils—please, I did not mean to—I am so sorry."

Her cheekbone throbbing, Lily smacked Brianna's hands away, turning forward. She flicked the reins, sending the horse forward, her voice hissing. "Do not speak to me, Bree. I cannot imagine what you have been through, so I forgive you. But do not dare to speak to me. Do not. Not now."

Brianna slumped into the corner of the carriage, silent.

Lily tried to quell her heaving breath, quell the fury she wanted to spew at her sister.

Not marry Garek. Ridiculous. Brianna had no idea what she talked of.

And in that moment, Lily had no patience to explain to Brianna why she was so incredibly, absolutely wrong.

{ CHAPTER 11 }

Wiping the bleariness from his eyes, Garek stood outside the door to his room at the Twisted Tin Tavern, looking down at the letter he had partially crumpled in his hand.

He had been woken early the night before to tend to the babe of the blacksmith.

The wee boy had been on fire with a hacking cough, not giving him room to breathe. Precarious hours had passed before Garek had finally found a way to curb the cough enough for the babe to breathe and bring his fever down. And now it was midday, and Garek was exhausted.

All he wanted to do was collapse onto his lumpy bed for a few hours and then get to Lily before nightfall, as he hadn't seen her since yesterday.

But now this.

He scanned the letter that had been waiting for him a fifth time, assuring himself the words were true, and not just his drained mind playing tricks on him.

Garek—

I write this bluntly, as the situation deems it a necessity. Your uncle is fading. I fear he will be dead within months if his conditions are not improved. He did inquire as to your well-being. I reassured him that you would return soon.

—Joseph Tangert

Garek looked back to the date. Joseph had posted the letter two weeks ago.

Damn.

Rubbing his eyes, he stepped into his room, setting his surgical wallet on the table by the door before his fingers left his face.

With a sigh, he opened his eyes only to find a figure in a black cloak standing in the middle of the room. Lily. His spirit lightened, but then the figure turned to him.

"Brianna? What are you doing here?"

Her hands clasped in front of her. "Forgive me for surprising you, but I needed to speak with you in private, Dr. Harrison."

Garek's eyes flickered to his leather satchel in the corner. The top flap was flipped back, the bag wide open to the world. Not how he had left it.

He looked to Brianna. "Have you been rifling through my bag?"

She shrugged. "You rifle through my business. I rifle through yours."

"Is this about your father's papers, again, Miss Silverton? I told you, Lily asked me—"

"Stop." Her mouth pulled back tightly. "I do not want you to hide behind my sister any longer, Dr. Harrison."

Garek's hand ran through his hair. Lily's sister was the one thing standing between him and the bed. But he would get no sleep until he dealt with her. "You are here to insult me, then? What do you want, Miss Silverton?"

"You are wanted for grave robbing in London."

"What?" Shock cut through Garek and he staggered a step backward. Sure, he had not left on the best of terms with Dr. Halowell's son. But he had been the one to walk away from what they were doing. To not dig up the body. And now he was wanted for robbing a grave?

His head bowed, Garek turned to close the door behind him. He slowly spun to Brianna, his words careful. "Those are false accusations, Miss Silverton."

"Are they? Lily told me you were in a graveyard, shovel in-hand, digging."

"She would not have told you that."

"She did."

"And did she also tell you I walked away from it? The whole despicableness of it?"

Brianna shrugged, her head tilted and mouth half pulled up, disregarding his words. "It would seem the family of that particular…corpse…wields considerable power and is demanding retribution."

"They could not know I was there that night."

"There were witnesses."

Blast it. Of course there were. Especially when Garek had almost killed one of Halowell's men. There had been four of them there that night. And the other three had taken exception to his abandonment of the business. It had been the first time Garek had so completely lost himself in rage, he had not even recognized himself. Not until he saw the man writhing in front of him, struggling for breath.

Garek took a step toward Brianna. "Lily knows exactly what I have done—and what I did not do. The accusations have no merit."

Brianna's forefinger tapped on her arm. "You did not know you were wanted for grave robbing, did you? Or that you will be thrown into Newgate if you set foot near London?"

"How did you learn of this?"

"Mr. Sneedly. He had sent an inquiry about you to The London Hospital when you first appeared at Weadly Hall. He just received a reply."

"So why are you here, Miss Silverton? What do you want?"

Her hands dropped to her sides, her shoulders pulling back as her posture went taut. "I want you out of Lily's life. Gone. Never to speak to her again."

"That is not going to happen, Brianna." Garek had to consciously unclench the instant fists at his sides.

"No, it is going to happen, Dr. Harrison. You truly have only one option, and that is to leave. I will give you enough money to disappear, to escape to a different land. Or I can have you delivered directly to Newgate." Her hand reached under her cloak, pulling free a piece of crisp vellum that she unfolded. She held it up to him.

A bank note. A note with an incredibly large number on it. Her eyebrows cocked at him, and she stepped to the side, setting the note on the bed.

She moved back to the middle of the room, her gaze penetrating him. "I am offering you a sizeable sum, Dr. Harrison."

Garek's eyes drifted down to the paper on the bed. There it was in front of him. The whole reason he had left London—the reason he'd gotten drawn into digging up that grave in the first place.

Money.

He needed that money, needed it desperately if he was going save the one person that meant more to him than his own life. The one person up until Lily.

His gaze shifted to Brianna. "Or I can take this, find Lily, and leave with her. She will come with me."

His words didn't faze Brianna—not even a flicker of concern. If anything, her head tilted slightly, her eyes pitying. "There, you are wrong. She does not want you, Dr. Harrison. She is disgusted that you lied to her."

Garek's hand twitched at his side. "I did not lie to her and I will not leave her, Brianna."

"You will leave her—leave this land. Why do you think I am here—in the weakened state I am in—instead of Lily? She could not even face you."

Brianna gathered a big sigh into her lungs, her head shaking. "I may as well tell you, they are coming for you right now, the Bow Street runners the family sent from London. And this is money enough to run. To disappear. But you only get it if you leave Lily alone. She does not want to see you again. She recognizes the liar you are and does not want a criminal for a husband."

"No."

"She could not have been more emphatic with me about that fact, Dr. Harrison."

"I do not believe you." Garek's head shook. "Lily would not have said that—she will not stand for this."

"No? Why do you think she sent me? Whose idea do you think it was to give you money to disappear? To escape?" She forced a strained chuckle. "The idea was most certainly not mine. I would rather see you rot in the hole you dug in that graveyard. But Lily has a much different heart—for all that she hates you now, she still did not want to see you end up in a cell at Newgate."

"I refuse to believe it—refuse to believe she hates me. Not until I talk to her." Garek spun, going to the door.

"Believe it or not, but she did not hide the fact that seeing you would sicken her." Brianna's words cut sharply into the room. "And I do not think you will put her through that torture. She is already distraught, grieving for the man she thought you were, but are not. And if you stay to find her and verify what I say—and make no mistake, she will refuse to see you—you will be caught. The men from London are at Weadly Hall at this very moment and will be here within the hour."

Garek froze, the doorknob half turned. "You did not."

"Mr. Sneedly did. He told them exactly where to find you. And he would not have shared that information with me had he known I would warn you."

Brianna pointed to the note on the bed. "So you can take the money and disappear, Dr. Harrison, or you can chase a dead dream and make Lily not only refuse you to your face—but also make her watch you get dragged off to prison. Do you know what that would do to her? She loved you before this. She is already inconsolable."

His head turned to the side, Garek refused to look at Brianna, refused to believe her blasphemies. "Then I will get to Lily before they come, and she will leave with me. I know she will."

"No. She will not. I think you recognize that, underneath your anger." Brianna gave him a sad smile. "Even if you were able to convince her to listen to you, convince her that this was a horrible misunderstanding—and that would be a paramount feat in itself—we both know she will refuse to leave me here alone. Not in my weakened state. Be assured I will do anything—anything, no matter how insidious, to protect her from you. And if you stay here for her, you will be arrested in front of her. Transported for at least seven years for robbing graves. She does not want you, Dr. Harrison. Not anymore."

His heart thundering, Garek's hand dropped from the door, his eyes going over his shoulder to rest on the bank note on the bed.

Two choices.

He could stay, stubborn, fighting for Lily when she had already discarded him, and soon find himself in Newgate. Or he could take the note and save the one person he owed his life to.

This was it. All that he had wrought, finally come for him. His reckoning.

His eyes pinned Brianna, cold, abhorring the words he was about to speak. The words he had to drag from the pit of his belly. "Take care of Lily."

Brianna gave him a pinched smile. "Do not insult me."

Garek bit back a tirade, his head shaking. "Just keep Sneedly away from her. Please."

The smile disappeared, and Brianna's blue eyes went serious with an earnest nod of her head. "I will do so."

Grabbing his surgical wallet, he took two heavy steps forward and snatched his satchel from the corner. Moving around Brianna, he picked up the bank note from the bed.

He looked down at it, the elaborate words and numbers blurring.

His eyes focused on the signatures at the bottom. Brianna's, and then right below it, Miss Lily Silverton in a heavy scrawl.

She had signed the note.

Services rendered.

Garek's gut dropped. Pain cut across his chest, severing his breath as the last of his disbelief of Brianna's words disintegrated.

Lily did not want him. Could not stomach the sight of him. The message was quite clear.

And he held in his hand exactly what he had needed when he had stumbled upon Lily in the middle of the night months ago.

She had altered him from his course, from his purpose.

But now it was time to pay his debts.

Garek shoved the bank note into his bag, sickened at his own actions.

Without another word, he walked out the door.

~ ~ ~

Lily tightened the cloak across her chest, her eyes scanning the winding dirt path up from the main road. Beyond the rushes and gardens, fields and pastures lined the road in front of Widow Thompson's cottage, and Lily could see a long distance in every direction.

She looked up to the sky at the cover of grey clouds that slid slowly past. Much slower than her quick steps across the cold ground.

"Lily, you have been pacing for hours. What are you doing out here?"

Lily's feet stopped, looking to Brianna in the front doorway. "I am waiting for Garek. He said he would be by in the morning, and we are now not far from nightfall."

"Come inside." Brianna motioned backward with her head. "You have not eaten today. Mable made a mince pie."

Lily shook her head. "I will wait out here."

"Lily, please. It is cold and I do not want you to catch your death. I have Papa's papers in order, so we can start planning on where we want to move. Mable has already agreed to come with us."

Lily offered her sister a smile to cover her pang of jealousy. Brianna had already planned in one morning what Lily could not accomplish in a month. "We can discuss it later—after Garek arrives."

Brianna stepped out of the doorway, pulling the door closed behind her. She came to Lily, slipping her arm within the folds of the cloak and into the crook of Lily's arm.

"He is gone, Lils. I had hoped to delay telling you."

"What do you mean, gone?" Lily looked to the south along the road, not noting her sister's words. "You are not talking about Garek."

"Lils, look at me. I am talking about Dr. Harrison. He is gone." Brianna hugged Lily's arm to her body, her voice low. "I discovered some things about his past—this is so hard to tell you, Lily—Garek is a grave robber."

Lily jerked away from Brianna, untangling her arm to step backward. "No. How do you know about that—and no—no, you are mistaken. Garek never unearthed a body. He was in a cemetery, going to assist with that very thing, but he could not go through with it. He left before anything happened."

"I do not know if that is true, Lily, but I do know that Garek is wanted for grave robbery. He will go to prison. So he left Annadale."

Lily gripped Brianna's upper arm, panic flushing her body. "No—that is not right. He did nothing." Her eyes flew out to the fields and then back to Brianna. "You are lying. You do not want me to marry him, so you are lying, creating falsehoods about him."

Brianna shook her head softly. "I am not, Lils. If Dr. Harrison were to stay here, he would be arrested and brought to prison."

"No. You are wrong. He would not have left. Not without me." Lily dropped her hand from Brianna, spinning from her. "Not without seeing me, talking to me. Impossible—he would never—"

"I gave him money." Brianna rounded Lily, capturing her shoulders and shaking them. "Money to leave here. Leave you."

Lily froze, her eyelids fluttering as her head jerked back. A whisper left her mouth with a long exhale. "You paid him off?"

"I did."

"To leave me?"

"Yes."

Lily's head started to shake uncontrollably. "No. He would not have taken it. He would not have left me. I do not believe you."

"He did take the money, Lils. He is gone. I will take you to the tavern to prove it."

Lily slapped her sister's hands from her shoulders, backing from her. "No. You are lying, Bree—lying, I know it. He did not leave me."

"Get the curricle, Lily. We are going to the tavern."

Lily's jaw set hard, her eyes narrowing on her sister. "Yes. Yes we are. And I will prove to you Garek would never leave me. Never."

Lily pushed the horse hard on the painfully silent ride to Annadale. Into the middle of the village, Lily stopped the horse, flying down from the carriage and running into the Twisted Tin Tavern. Her feet racing, she bumped past several empty wooden chairs, knocking them down as she dodged around the round tables in the common area to get to the back stairs.

Up the steps three at a time, she was to Garek's room in seconds, flinging open the door.

All was still. Quiet.

She stepped into the room, her eyes desperately scanning the space. Seeking out the tiniest corners, searching for something—anything of Garek's. Anything to prove he wasn't gone.

The bed had no sheets, just lumpy stuffing open to the air. No satchel. No boots. No shirt drying by the fireplace. No coals simmering.

Nothing. Emptiness. Silence.

Not a trace that Garek had ever set foot into this room.

Clomping heels came up behind her.

"Do you see, Lily?" Brianna moved into the room with the words. "Do you see now? He is gone."

Lily's head shook, disbelief numbing her body. Her eyes still searched for the slightest piece of him. Something. Something to hold onto. The slightest remnant that he had been here. Been in her life. Loved her.

From behind, Brianna's hand settled lightly on Lily's shoulder. Her sister was wheezing, probably from running after her. Lily knew she should turn to her, check on her—Brianna still was not fully well—but Lily could not do it. Not look at her.

"He took the money and left, Lily. I am sorry he was not what you thought he was."

Lily's legs slipped from her at that moment. Turned to jelly, all support lost. She crumbled to the floor, the shock vibrating through her body turning into heaving breaths. The heaving breaths turning into sobs.

He couldn't have left her. He couldn't have.

But all she had to do was wipe her tears and look around the room for reality.

Garek was gone.

"You...you spoke with him, Bree." Lily looked over her shoulder up to her sister. "Did he say anything—any message for me—something?"

"He did not." Brianna's fingers squeezed Lily's shoulder.

She swatted Brianna's hand away. "How could you do this to me, Bree?"

"It was the only way I could make you see what he was—what he was truly after, Lily."

"But he would not have…not have taken the money and left. Left me."

Her sister's hand landed back on her shoulder. "He did, Lily. He took the money. That was all he wanted."

Lily looked up to Brianna. "And he said nothing? Nothing for me? Nothing to explain?"

"As hard as it is to hear, Lils, I think his choice explains everything."

Her head dropped as her arms wrapped around her belly, rocking back and forth. "I will never forgive you for this, Bree."

Brianna's hand left her shoulder, her voice turning cool. "Lily, take a moment here, collect yourself. I have to visit with Mr. Turner up the road for a few minutes about father's estate. I will be back shortly, and we can leave. You will never have to look at this place again."

Without waiting for an answer, Brianna left the room, her footsteps disappearing down the hall.

Lily crumpled further into herself, heaped into a sobbing mess for an eternity.

She stayed balled up in the barren room, until the cruel reality of his leaving hit her, truly hit her.

Garek had chosen money over her.

The thought flipped her stomach, and she had to swallow bile chasing up her throat.

She had loved him with everything she had, trusted him with everything, and he had chosen money over her.

Money.

Her fingers uncurling from her body, she made her limbs go straight, and she pushed herself to standing.

Without another look around the room, she staggered into the hall and down the narrow stairs.

In the common room, she landed on the closest chair, sitting, numb.

"Why the red face, dovey? Wot ye need?" Mrs. Fulgton stopped across the table from Lily.

The words invaded her brain slowly, pulling Lily from the stupor that had taken over her mind.

She looked up. "Sherry. Do you have sherry?"

"I do, dovey."

{ CHAPTER 12 }

Salvation came in the form of a liveried footman.

Desperately needed salvation.

Salvation delivered by a footman bearing a wide, silver platter filled with flutes of bubbling, sparkling champagne.

He paused in front of Lily, and she took the fullest glass she could reasonably reach. The sherry that she had consumed at the Duke of Letson's townhouse was already waning. She had thought she had imbibed enough to calm her nerves, but it had taken far longer than she had anticipated to arrive at Lady Palton's home, and even longer to be introduced and make it through the throng of the crush.

Tipping her head back, she let the golden liquid slide down her throat, the bubbles tickling her tongue. A forearm slipped under the crook of her elbow.

"Are you ready? Have you noticed the eyes already fixated on you?" Wynne Lockton, the Duchess of Letson, smiled. Lily looked to Wynne, noting how very prettily her blond hair had been weaved into an elegant upsweep. So very different from the Wynne she was accustomed to at Notlund Castle, as Wynne's hair was usually in a simple braid and paint was most often smeared somewhere across her face, if not covering her fingers. But in this ballroom, she looked every spec the duchess that she was.

A deep breath, and Lily returned Wynne's smile, comforted that her new friend was at her side. For as difficult as the last year had been for her, the duke and duchess were the one bright happening. They had brought Brianna and Lily into their home at Notlund and offered to serve as their guardians, much to Brianna's chagrin. But Lily had been entirely grateful their father had long ago asked the Duke's father to care for them in the event of his death.

And not only had the duke and duchess welcomed Lily and Brianna into their home, they had offered to present them to London society. Brianna had bristled at the thought, claiming herself a spinster, but had conceded to at least attend events as Lily's chaperone.

Lily sucked the last drop of liquid from the glass, already eyeing the next champagne-balancing footman making his way around the perimeter of the ballroom. She glanced to Wynne. "Eyes are fixated?"

"You do not look happy on that fact."

Lily forced a bright smile onto her lips. The footman stepped in front of them, and she traded her empty flute for a full one. "I...I just did not expect it. I did not know what to expect."

Wynne squeezed her arm. "Well, I expected it. I am positive any eligible man here would be delighted to make your acquaintance. This was the best idea, to come down from the cold castle to London for the season. As much as Rowen and I adore having you and Brianna to ourselves, it is only fair that you meet new people, a suitor or two. Or three, or four, or five. And then Brianna will see how much fun this can be, and maybe allow herself to proffer the slightest smile for a gentleman."

Lily scoffed at Wynne's last words, shaking her head. But instant guilt made her stop, and she fixed the smile back onto her face. "You sound as if you have already filled my dance card?"

"Yes. I do have options for you. And did you see Rowen?" She pointed across the brightly-lit room. "See the gentleman already edging their way to him?"

Lily nodded, taking a long sip of the champagne as she found the duke in the kaleidoscope of shifting, brightly-colored gowns.

"The lot of those gentlemen are already angling for an introduction."

Lily noted several men jostling to get a step in front of one another. Almost comical, if that was what was truly happening across the room. Almost.

Her gaze slipped to the right and her breath caught.

Garek.

A head above the men around him, his dark hair glistened in the candlelight as he turned. Lily's eyes swept along his profile.

Not Garek.

Not Garek in the ballroom. Or on Percy Street. Or in the Notlund Castle stables. Or at the market. Not Garek.

He wasn't there in the ballroom, and she needed to stop seeing him every place she looked. Needed to stop searching for him in every crowd. Needed to put him out of her mind, out of her heart.

That was why she was here. To move on. To stop torturing herself every single day. To not see him around every turn. To stop thinking of his lips on her skin, his breath in her ear.

To stop everything. To stop being a shell.

The hollow emptiness in her chest threatened to swallow her. Lily's head dropped, her eyes fixating on the sparkling crystals sewn into the edging along her bodice. They shimmered against the deep blue of her dress. Bright. Happy. Radiant as they hid the vast hollowness beneath.

Damn. She just wanted to feel again. Feel something— anything. Even if she doubted it was possible to truly do so.

"Lily, you have gone pale. What is it?" Wynne's hand went onto Lily's gloved forearm, rubbing.

Lily's eyes rose to the duchess. "Nothing." She tried to reclaim her earlier smile. "Just a moment of being overwhelmed. Again, I had not expected this. I thought we would just slip into this world…quietly, somehow. Not cause a clamor."

Lily brought the glass to her lips, draining the champagne as Wynne's gaze slid across the crowd.

"Your dowry alone swept that possibility aside quite neatly. And now they have seen the loveliness of you. But I cannot imagine they are all rakehells and rogues, even if I have heard a number of stories." She looked at Lily with a wink. "Which is why you have me. And the duke. And Brianna. Just for a gentleman to get by the three of us will be a feat in and of itself."

"Yes." The smallest smile, genuine crossed Lily's face. She had to remember, at the very least, she had Wynne and the duke and Brianna.

"Are you ready?"

Lily paused for a moment, busying herself with watching the masses of swirling colors on the gowns. A footman was nearing them, and if she stalled for another second, she could snatch one more flute of champagne before being devoured by what was in front of her.

She raised her glass, and the footman stopped for her to exchange her empty flute. Lily could see Wynne watch her movements, but the duchess did not say a word. Not like Brianna would have.

Lily turned to Wynne, clutching the full champagne flute, her voice solid. "I am ready, come what may."

~ ~ ~

NEWGATE PRISON, LONDON, ENGLAND
MARCH, 1822

Salvation came in the form of a duke.

Unexpected. Unwanted salvation.

Salvation delivered by one Devin Williams Stephenson, twelfth Duke of Dunway.

A boot nudged Garek's belly.

His eyes crept open, and a strand of dirty hay trapped in his eyelashes cut into his eye. Garek blinked several times, trying to dislodge it as he looked at the shiny black boot in front of his face.

Far too fancy for these wretched guards.

He turned his head, the hay poking into his neck. A tall man. Finely dressed. Cane, beaver hat, all the accoutrements of wealth. A sliver of morning light hit the man across his cheekbone.

What now? What, after more than a year in this rat hole, could this man possibly be standing over him for? Garek knew the executioner preferred black clothes—absolutely everything black. If you were to be transported, it was usually a few sailors that came for you. Quite possibly, the delayed and delayed and delayed trial had finally happened without him even knowing.

At this juncture, nothing would surprise him.

But no. This man had none of the business of criminals about him.

"You are awake, man?"

Garek nodded. He hadn't had anything to drink in days and couldn't afford to try and make words, create saliva that wasn't there.

"Good. Then gain your feet. Your fortune is about to change."

Garek stared far up to the face, trying to see the structure of it. Did he know this man?

The man bent, slipping a hand under Garek's upper arm. His eyes squinted, running over Garek's face until he nodded, satisfied with whatever he saw. "Once I knew it was you, Harrison, I volunteered to deliver the news and deal with this matter myself." His gloved finger pointed upward, swirling about the stone cell. "And none too soon, I can see."

The voice. The face Garek couldn't place, but the voice. The voice he could. Far, far back. The continent. The war. Dunway. The Duke of Dunway.

"You saved a number of my men on the continent, Harrison. Had I known you were in here, I would have come regardless of the current matter—and sooner." Dunway pulled up on Garek's arm, bringing him to standing.

Garek's eyes didn't leave Dunway's face. He opened his mouth, stretching for words. Three tries before his tongue made a sound. "Why?"

"As much as the Worthington family would like to continue to put off your trial and let you suffer in here, they waited a pinch too long," Dunway said. "Fate now has a very different end for you, my old friend, than to have you wither to death in this hell hole."

Dunway slung his arm across Garek's back, supporting him as they walked out of the cell.

{ CHAPTER 13 }

Garek watched the Earl of Luhaunt walk down the hill from the small structure—a painting studio of some sort, from what he could surmise earlier when he had passed it.

The earl's low voice a murmur in the clear night, his hands were animated as he talked to Mr. Flemming, the Bow Street runner Garek had been shadowing for weeks. The two men disappeared into the stable furthest away from where Garek stood watching the scene from the deep shadows of the forest behind the painting studio.

After lurking for a day, Garek finally had a handle on the many buildings surrounding Notlund Castle, the Duke of Letson's estate in Yorkshire. Garek knew the duke and duchess had assumed the role of unofficial guardians to Lily and Brianna within the last year. And after launching Lily successfully into London society during the season, the sisters had been living at the castle for the past four months.

Garek had heard the majority of the conversation taking place within the studio. None of it was news to him, but, he imagined, devastating to Brianna. And now he only had mere moments to talk with Brianna in private before her new husband returned from the stable.

Pulling the hood of the black cloak lower about his face, Garek slid along the side of the building. He stepped lightly, silencing his boots on the wooden porch as he opened the front door and slipped into the painting studio, closing the door behind him.

Brianna sat slumped back in a chair, holding herself with her eyes glazed over, staring into the light of the lantern on a table. In shock—much as he suspected she would be after hearing what she just did.

The sight of her again, up close, jarred him for a moment.

Healthy, her cheeks were no longer sunken, her eyes no longer dead. Her light brown hair was pulled into an elegant upsweep. No longer fragile, with delicate bones barely propping her up, Brianna looked strong and even more like Lily than he remembered.

A few seconds passed and Brianna's head turned, her eyes lifting from the light to him.

Garek took one deep breath, pulling the hood from his head.

Instant fear crossed her face, but then her eyes widened and she leaned forward, recognizing him.

Garek smiled at her, giving her a long second to digest his presence.

"So what will it be, Brianna? The devil you know, or the devil you don't?"

Her jaw dropped as her hand flattened on the table to push herself to her feet. She looked a force, instantly ready to battle, but Garek could see her fingers straining against the table, holding her steady.

"Dr. Harrison," she said, her voice solid. "So you know Lily is to marry tomorrow?"

Garek inclined his head. "I do. And it seems as if you have a decision to make."

"You know?" She stared at him, her eyes narrowing. "So I am to decide—a grave robber or a lecher?"

The blow came out of the darkness, ramming into Garek, tackling him. Flying through the air, Garek and the mass wrapped around his chest slammed into a wall of shelves, sending glass jars of paint plummeting, breaking everywhere as Garek crashed to the floor.

A grunt rang in Garek's ear as the mass of a man landed on him, crushing him. Garek's fist already in motion, it made contact on skull just as Brianna's scream filled the room.

"Seb. Stop. Stop. Stop." Brianna's words froze the man on top of him.

Garek kicked up, flipping the man off of him as he sat up.

So this was Brianna's husband, Lord Luhaunt. The man was ready to pummel Garek, already to his feet with his fists drawing back to strike. But then he paused, his eyes not veering from Garek.

"An explanation, wife," Luhaunt growled.

"Seb." Brianna ran to him, her hands wrapping around his upper arms, tugging at him. "This is the man that saved me—saved me from my leg wounds. The physician—the surgeon. The man Lily loved."

Lord Luhaunt relaxed slightly, looking to his wife as she moved to his side, her left hand staying on his arm.

Her eyebrows arched as she tilted her head down toward Garek, her blue eyes pinning her husband. "The man I paid to leave Lily alone. Garek Harrison. This is him."

Luhaunt shook his head, his arms relaxing as he looked from his wife to Garek. "I apologize. I could only think the worst."

He offered his hand down to Garek. "A cloaked man cornering my wife in the dark is just not done, man. Not done at all. I am sure you can imagine, and sympathize."

"No harm suffered." Garek grabbed Luhaunt's hand, letting Brianna's husband pull him to his feet. "You were right to have tackled me. I would have done the same."

Luhaunt slapped him on the back, sending a shard of glass deep into his shoulder. Garek hid a cringe. He could feel all sorts of shards needling into his back, as he had been on the bottom side of that pile, grinding into the broken jars.

"So, with my apologies, please also accept my gratitude for saving my wife." Luhaunt's eyes swung to Brianna, smirk on his face. "I do appreciate the effort, and most notably, the end result."

Luhaunt stepped away from his wife, muttering as he brushed glass debris off the front of his jacket. "First that Sneedly character and now this—I need to have a serious conversation with Rowe about the safety here at Notlund—far too many ways in." He moved back to Brianna and tucked her under his arm, seemingly oblivious to the blue paint on his jacket that smeared into the side of her peach gown.

Garek's ears perked, his look whipping to Brianna. "Sneedly? What the hell was he doing here?"

Brianna waved her hand. "It was nothing. Mr. Sneedly recently had a change in fortune. The viscount's holdings have been seized, and Mr. Sneedly has found himself a pauper. He appeared here yesterday to cause trouble. No harm was done. The duchess intercepted him—she is very protective of Lily—and then the duke had him removed far from the premises."

The earl looked to Garek, his jaw going tight as his eyes hardened. "Which brings up the current point—what the hell were you doing with my wife, Dr. Harrison?"

"I am here for Lily's sake." Garek's eyes stayed on Brianna as he blindly picked at a sliver of glass embedded in his palm. "I know about her fiancé, Lord Newdale."

"You know of Newdale's activities? How?" Lord Luhaunt asked.

Garek shrugged. "I have been following your runner, Mr. Flemming, for weeks, ever since I discovered he was investigating Lord Newdale. I am well aware that Lily's betrothed is keen on buying virgins from brothels. It is why I am here. I do not intend to let her marry a demon such as that." His look went solely to Lord Luhaunt. "I also knew I needed to approach Brianna first, in order to gain access to Lily, as Lily may not welcome me or what I have to say. She can be stubborn."

"Yes. You remember," Brianna said.

Garek's gaze swung to her. "I do."

Brianna's eyes narrowed at Garek. "But why? Why now? Why not five months ago? A month ago? Why appear on the eve before her wedding?"

A yank, and Garek freed the glass sliver from his palm. He glanced down as he flicked the bloody glass to the floor, his hands falling to his sides. He met Brianna's stare. "I did not have a reason five months ago to interfere. I do now. I also have the means. You are aware of my change in fortune and that I have been cleared of any misdoings? I was assured the bank note was delivered to you."

"Yes, I did receive it, and I am aware of your new status."

"But you have not told Lily?"

Brianna squirmed, glancing up to her husband, then looked to Garek. "I could not tell her. She has been happy, Dr. Harrison. I did not want to send her life into a tumble."

Garek bit his tongue but managed a curt nod. Brianna was being much more accommodating than he imagined she would be, and he could not let slip what he truly thought of Lily's sister. He still needed her help. "I understand. But I can give her the life I could not before. That is why I am here."

"You still want her? After all this time?" Brianna asked. "She is to marry another tomorrow, Dr. Harrison."

"Do not play the innocent, Brianna." A wry smile lined Garek's lips. "Every one of us in this room knows you will not let Lily marry Lord Newdale on the morrow."

Brianna's arms came up, curling around her waist. She exhaled with a nod, conceding the fact. "It will be hard to convince Lily to see you—to give you a proper chance."

"That is where I must ask for your assistance," Garek said. "I do not want her ruined by this—do not want scandal to touch her because of Lord Newdale. If any word of his actions were bared to the light, it would ruin him, and everyone attached to him—his family, his fiancé—all innocents."

Brianna's lips sucked tightly inward, nodding. "I agree. It is messy beyond belief—purchasing virgins, for heaven's sake.

While Lord Newdale deserves whatever he would get, his mother, his sisters, and most certainly, Lily, do not deserve the same fate because of his ill actions."

"Exactly." Garek cleared his throat, glancing from Lord Luhaunt to Brianna. "I will be forthright. I am thinking an elopement."

Brianna gasped. "An elopement?"

"It will extract Lily from the situation. There is scandal attached to an elopement, of course."

"But elopement scandals tend to be forgiven when love is involved." The smallest smile crossed Brianna's face as she nodded, her eyes lighting up.

"Exactly."

"But that means she will go with you. She is not prepared for this. She has not seen you in a year and a half. She thinks she is marrying Lord Newdale tomorrow. She is happy."

Garek's forehead crinkled. "Is her current happiness going to continue in any fashion after tonight?"

Brianna's eyes dropped to the floor. "No. It is gone, and she does not even know it yet." She paused, her fingers tapping her arm. Her eyes came slowly up to Garek. "I cannot—I cannot make this decision for her. I have played God once too many times in her life, and I cannot chance another mistake with her."

Garek suffocated a growl. Now Brianna had a conscience?

His words came slowly, holding himself in check. "So what will you do?"

"I will have to tell her everything," Brianna said. "Everything I know—about Lord Newdale buying virgins, about you. It is her decision on how we proceed. Will you wait in...in the stables? Stall eighty-nine? It is in the third stable from the left."

Garek gave a curt nod. He had hoped for more. So much more. But this would have to suffice. He could always take more drastic measures if Brianna's conversation with Lily didn't work.

Brianna looked up to her husband. "We should make our way to the castle. There is no use in delaying this."

"Brianna."

She looked to Garek. "Yes?"

"Do not tell her about the title—not yet."

Brianna's eyebrow cocked. "You wish to begin this with a lie?"

"I do not want something so trivial to factor into Lily's decision."

"Trivial?" Her hand flipped up in a wave, dismissing whatever she was about to say. "Do not make me regret this, Dr. Harrison."

She turned and they started to the door, the earl's arm still wrapped along his wife's shoulders.

At the door, Brianna stopped, turning back to Garek. "Before we leave…"

"Yes?" Garek's eyebrows arched, prompting her.

"I would like to apologize for my actions years ago. How I sent you away, Dr. Harrison. My only defense is that I was not in my right mind at that time. I had been hurt badly and was incapable of trusting anyone. What I did was unfair to you, to Lily. Know that I am earnest when I say I hope Lily will consider the possibility of you. This is a second chance that I thought I would never be able to give her."

The earl kissed the top of his wife's head, a smile crossing his face.

She glanced up at him, then back to Garek. "I thank you as well, Dr. Harrison, for saving me. I do not think I ever told you."

Garek inclined his head, his breath halted. All were words he thought never to hear from this woman.

"There is one last thing, Dr. Harrison," Brianna said. "I must warn you, Lily is not the same person you knew. She has drifted far from who she once was."

"Then I will lead her back, Brianna."

A frown creased Brianna's face. "It will not be that easy. She is calloused, Garek. She lost her innocence when you left. What I did to her."

Garek's eyes pinned Brianna. "I was the one that let her lose it, Lady Luhaunt. I will not disappoint her again."

A soft smile, hopeful, touched Brianna's face.

"We should hurry, Bree," Lord Luhaunt said.

She offered a nod and they turned, the earl ushering them out the door of the studio.

Garek stood still, his head shaking as his breath exhaled with a low whistle.

No. Not what he was expecting at all.

{ CHAPTER 14 }

Garek paced. Stall 89. That was where Brianna told him to wait.

This was ridiculous. Just how long did it take to break the news to Lily that the man she was to marry was a perverted beast?

For all he had suffered in the last eighteen months since leaving Lily, these moments—these moments waiting for her, waiting to learn her decision—were the only thing that truly cut through his chest and gripped his soul.

Spinning in the corner, he kicked hay, sending it flying into the air. Soft, fluffy hay. Not the filthy, matted hay that carried such a stench he could not sleep for the first three days in prison.

Damn the hay.

If Lily didn't choose him, then what? Charge through the castle? Kidnap her? He rolled his eyes. Did he need to get a sword and armor of old as well? He didn't want it to come to that, but if he needed to…

Garek stared at the black iron lantern hanging by the stall door, watching the flame flicker. This was all he had been dreaming about, planning for months. Ever since that late spring day on the London street when Lily's carriage had passed him by.

Ever since he had discovered what losing everything truly felt like.

He heard the sudden crunch of boots coming down the main walkway of the stable. Light, even steps. Garek braced himself. It could be Lily—or it could very well be Brianna, or some other random wedding guest.

The steps slowed as they drew closer.

A figure turned the corner, and Garek exhaled.

Lily.

Lily looking at him, eyes wide, her face ashen.

She swayed slightly and then grabbed the waist-high top of the stall door. Her fingertips wrapped around the rough wood, shaking as she tried to steady herself. Her other hand, clutching leather gloves, came to her belly, pressing onto her plum-colored riding habit.

Garek fought the instant urge to go to her, wrap her in his arms. Take away all the unsteadiness. That urge was not why he was here.

Far from it.

"It is you. Bree told me, she said…but I did not believe it… not truly…"

"Yes, Lily, it is me." Garek took one step toward her. "Brianna told you about your fiancé?"

She nodded, disbelief still ravaging her features. "I still cannot believe…believe that he would…"

"He did, Lily. Does. I verified it." He watched the reflection of the flame from the lamp flicker in her clear blue eyes. Eyes that had haunted him every single night since he had left her. "Which leaves you with a choice. Have you made it?"

Her hand still shaking, she lifted it from the stall door and managed to take one step forward, closing the distance between them. "I choose you, Garek."

His eyes fell closed, the few words reeling through his body. Her voice, even sweeter than he remembered it, seeped into his head, consuming him.

Damn.

He had no idea she would be able to do this to him. Make his body react like this.

Four small words from her, her eyes on him, and he felt himself growing hard. Felt the burning need for her explode in his belly. His hands itched they wanted so badly to touch her skin. Rip off her dress. He swallowed, his mouth salivating at the thought of her nipple full, plump between his teeth.

Exhaling, he opened his eyes to her. Grimacing against his body revolting against his brain, he offered one nod in response to her words.

"I have thought about it a thousand times, Garek—what if you appeared before me, returned to my life." Her words rambled. "What would I say? What could I say? What would you...but this...to be inside the castle and about to marry another and then he...then this...this I never imagined..."

She watched him, cutting off her own words at his silence, his lack of response.

She dragged a deep inhale after a moment, both of her hands gripping the gloves she held, wringing them. Her eyes possessed far more raw astuteness than he remembered.

"Garek, Brianna said that what she took from me, she wanted to give back."

His eyebrows arched in question.

"But it will not be that easy, will it?"

"No. No, Lily, it will not." He pointed to the horse in the next stall, sidesaddle already in place. "Are you ready to ride?"

Her head bobbed numbly, and she turned from him silently, going to the adjoining stall.

Garek followed, grabbing the reins of his own horse and leading it from the stable.

They needed to ride.

~ ~ ~

The hooves of Lily's horse clomped over the wooden bridge, snapping her from the stupor she had sunk into.

For three hours she had silently followed Garek in the moonlight. He had said very little—nothing except to tell her they were on their way to a coaching inn along the route to the Scottish border town, Coldstream, where they could marry.

"The inn is just up from this river. We can sleep here for a few hours, then move onward," Garek said, his voice low in the still of the night. He didn't turn back to her.

They were still half a night away from daylight, but Lily doubted she could sleep. Her mind was creeping out of the overwhelming numbness that had consumed her since talking with Brianna.

One minute she was laughing, reveling in the party on the eve before she was to marry, and in the next, she found out her soon-to-be husband was a virgin-buying lecher.

A cringing shiver shot through her body. She could not even think on that fact yet—that she had almost married a man with such perversions.

And then Garek had appeared—manifested out of the abyss of the past. Out of long past memories she had been determined to forget.

Lily stared at Garek's back, the dark jacket lining his shoulders, his mass shifting smoothly back and forth with the gait of the horse. The moonlight dappled by the trees danced across his dark hair.

She swallowed hard.

Hell. Garek had appeared, and it was instant. The very second she stepped into the stall and saw him. Even after all this time. Even after he had crushed her soul.

She wanted him.

Damn her body.

She wanted him. Her body had flushed hot and had not stopped pulsating since she saw him in the stall. She wanted him in her gut, in her core. She wanted his hands on her. Wanted him deep within her. Controlling her body. Wanted him in the quiet. Wanted his eyes on her, his comfort.

Wanted him.

Everything she had thought was gone far into the past.

Lily tore her eyes from his back, staring at the passing trees. She hated herself for wanting this man. This man that had abandoned her.

But there it was, undeniable. Her body still craved him.

The road turned and the coaching inn, lit brightly from within, came into view. Lily's hands tightened on the reins, the sight of the building removing any remnants of weariness from her shoulders.

Garek led them to the stable behind the inn, stopping and dismounting outside the wide entrance. He silently came back to Lily, holding his hand up to her. Taking it, she moved down from the horse, noting Garek's stiff arm kept a noticeable distance between them.

Without a word, he collected the reins of both horses, tugging them into the stable. He led his horse to one empty stall, then deposited her horse in an opposite stall.

Lily stood just inside the entry to the stable, peeling off her leather gloves as she waited for him under the glow of the lantern by the main opening. Garek stepped out of the stall, moving toward her until he stopped, his toes almost touching her boots.

Lily inhaled to steady herself, but his scent filled her head, doing more harm than good. This was the closest he had come to her, and she was woefully unprepared for it. For the heat of him. For his scent. For his breath tickling her forehead.

Garek looked down at her. Even in the dim light, she could see his eyes were hooded, letting no emotion break forth.

"I have only one question for you, Lily."

"Yes?" The word was meek, barely making sound.

"Do you still want me?"

Her eyes did not leave his. "Heaven help me, I do. I chose you, Garek. I would not be here were that not true."

His hand clamped around her neck, yanking her up to him, his lips meeting hers hard, angry.

Anger she had no trouble reciprocating.

No hesitation, she met him with her own fury unleashed, pouring into him as she grabbed him, her fingers deep into his hair, scraping his scalp. His mouth opened, his tongue invading, and Lily took it, nipping, her tongue attacking, fighting for control.

Not breaking the kiss, he lifted her, his movements rough, jarring. He grabbed her thigh and wrapped her leg around him, and then repeated with the other.

Striding into the closest empty stall, he pushed her onto the outside wall. Her back hard against the wooden slats, Garek lifted her higher, his hands sliding, pushing up her skirts, going under the back of her bare thighs, supporting her.

He pulled his face away from her mouth, his breath heavy, to look at her, but Lily would have none of it. She clasped her hands onto his head, his neck, forcing him close, forcing his lips to meet hers.

She opened her mouth, her teeth grabbing his tongue, pulling him inward, pulling him closer.

His hand dropped between their bodies, opening the front flap of his leather breeches. The instant she felt him stretch free from the cloth, she yanked her legs around his waist, forcing his hardness onto her body, forcing his chest to meet her breasts.

A grunt. A mess of hands, clawing. Another grunt. And then Garek was huge, the tip of him at her entrance. She bit his bottom lip.

A brutal thrust, and he was deep into her. Fast. Forceful. Leaving no quarter for her body to adjust to him. Just demanding. Demanding, thrust after thrust, that she come for him, unleashing every bit of his massive power into her.

She ripped her mouth from his, straining over his shoulder, gasping for breath on the edge. Losing all control. "I hate you. I hate you for leaving me, Garek."

Her words turned into a scream, and she came, fingers tearing at his back.

He slid up, pummeling into her hard, and her back slammed into the wall. A grunt, hot breath invading her ear. "And I hate you for forgetting me, Lily."

His body shuddered, filling her. Warmth flooding her deep within.

Their chests warred with each other, both panting for breath, for control.

Garek slid out of her, removing her legs from his waist and letting her slip down the wall to the floor.

Shock brewed with throbbing aftershocks. Her breath not returning, all Lily could do was duck her head and yank down her skirts.

Without a word, she stepped around Garek, rubbing him from her lips. The only hiccup in her steps came when she bent to pick up her gloves on the way out of the stable.

She walked, her vision blurry, toward the light of the tavern. Opening the front door under the Golden Pheasant Inn sign, she stepped into the warm glow of the common area to find a smattering of people dotting the room. Heads turned to her, but she ignored the stares, moving to the closest circular table and sinking into a rounded-back wooden seat.

The barmaid was quick from behind the counter of the bar to Lily, but before the woman could say a word, Lily cut her off.

"Sherry. Or Madeira. Or brandy. Whatever is closest."

Her hands wiping the front of her white apron, the barmaid nodded, backing away.

Lily watched the barmaid as she clenched her hands against the shake taking over them. She slid them onto her lap, hiding them under the table.

The barmaid had better be quick.

~ ~ ~

As hard as she fought against it, Lily's eyelids drooped. Maybe she shouldn't have had that last drink. Had that been her third or fourth? Either way, her empty belly had not been an asset to the alcohol in her stomach.

She focused in on the bearded man sitting in a tall booth across from her—on his long, scraggly grey beard that went down past his chest. The man took a drink from his mug, the liquid trickling down the wiry hairs off his chin. Drip. Drip. Drip. Was he watching her? Her look drifted upward, meeting his eyes. Yes. Watching her.

How long did it take to settle two horses? Garek should have made his way into the inn long ago.

The sudden thought that he had deserted her popped into her brain.

No. Garek could not have left her again. Not have come for her only to desert her once more.

She popped upright, turning to the front entrance. She had no coin on her person. Nothing except for that horse she had ridden here. A horse that could very well be gone—gone with Garek.

He did hate her. He said so.

She gave herself a shake. No. He wouldn't just leave her here. He couldn't be that cruel.

But then again, where in the hell was he?

"Bar lady. Bar lady." She spun slowly in her seat, watching as all eyes in the place swiveled to her. She had thought they were done looking at her an hour ago, so what now? "Bar lady. More. I need more. Another drink, please."

"Shut your mouth, Lily."

The hiss in her ear came with a clamp on her upper arm, and she was jerked up, chair falling as she stumbled to her feet.

Garek.

She tried to yank her arm away, but the clamp went tighter, pinching her skin. He dragged her, manhandling her through the tables to the rear of the large room. Before she even had a chance to get her feet about her, Garek flung her onto the bench of a booth with high wooden backs.

"You are embarrassing yourself," he said, his voice a low growl.

Hands flat on the bench, Lily shoved herself upright. She grabbed the table, trying to still her spinning head.

Garek stood at the end of the table, looking down at her and blocking her path from escaping. "Are you going to heave?"

She shook her head, not able to lift her face to him. "No. Maybe."

A heavy sigh fell from Garek. He moved a few steps from her. His voice seemed small, far, far away. "Bread. Meat. Anything you have. Tea. Only tea."

His thighs, clad in dark buckskin breeches, appeared next to the table again. He paused for a moment, his fingers tapping the table, then he moved, sitting across from her.

Good. She could look at him without having to tilt her head back and sending the spinning out of control.

Garek took a sip of something amber from the thick glass he held. Setting it on a wide plank of the wooden table, he ran his fingers through his dark hair. She could see his hazel eyes clearly with the light of the nearby fire. The green flecks shining, just as they always had indoors.

Except his eyes had gone hooded again. Hiding everything from her.

She had only been given that one moment in the barn. That one moment when she was against the wall and he was deep inside her. In that moment, the hood had been lifted. Anger. Lust. Hatred. Love. It had swirled in his eyes. Swirled into blackness, the whole of it directed at her. A darkness she never could have imagined coming from Garek.

What had she truly chosen back at Notlund—the man she had once loved, or someone she no longer recognized?

She was suddenly thankful for the hood on his eyes. She wasn't ready to face what she had seen in him—not yet. Not when she was only hours removed from abandoning her fiancé and hundreds of guests at Notlund to elope. But elope with what?

Her fingers edged toward the glass he had set onto the table.

Garek snatched the glass, setting it far away from her on the back edge of the table. "Embarrassing, Lily. Utterly embarrassing." His voice was low, oddly calm. "You are not the sane person I once knew—not the woman I would have moved heaven and earth for."

That was what he had to say? A year and a half, and that was it? He hated her. Was embarrassed by her. Thought she was crazy.

She scoffed loudly, leaning against the table toward him, her voice hissing. "Heaven and earth? When did you ever try to move those for me, Garek? And sanity? You took my sanity, Garek. You."

She pushed herself away from the table, the back of her head banging into the wooden back of the tall booth. "Do you know what I did for months after you left me, Garek? I tried to forget—I questioned every single second of the time we spent together. Over and over and over." Her head banged against the wood with every word.

"It would drive anyone insane—going over those moments again and again with no end. Tearing them apart, looking for anything—the slightest clue as to why you would leave me—how I could not have seen what was coming."

Her head shook slowly, bitterness easing from her words. "All of those seconds—those moments. I could not convince myself I was so very wrong about you—about you wanting me—wanting to marry me. But I was wrong."

He didn't answer her, offered no words of comfort, of explanation. He only stared at her with his hooded eyes, picking up the glass and taking another sip.

She watched, silently, as he set the glass carefully down. Specific in his movements, his eyes stayed on the glass.

"When you held me, Garek, I could lose myself in you." Her voice faltered. "And it was never your size. It was that my mind could curl up into you. Safe, protected. You made the world right for me."

Lily bowed her head, tears threatening. "But then you left me alone, Garek, alone. And I have not been able to find sanity since that day."

A metal plate of bread and meat clanked onto the table, making Lily jump. The barmaid set a steaming mug of tea directly in front of Lily, giving her something other than the pockmarked wood of the table to stare at. The barmaid's footsteps were long gone when Garek finally spoke.

"You want to talk about alone, Lily? Then let us talk about prison."

Her face whipped up to him, only to find his eyes, cold and harsh, burrowing into her.

"You were in prison? Garek—"

"Yes, for robbing graves. For falsehoods. So let us talk about the filth I sat in for more than a year—cold and starving—for something I did not do. That—where I was in a barren cell—that was alone, Lily. More alone than you will ever know in your life." He leaned forward, his chest hitting the table and sending the mug in front of her wobbling. She caught it before it tipped over.

"If you were alone, Lily, you chose it. You." Spite bled from his voice. "Look at all you had. You had your sister. Your season. Everyone in society at your feet."

She slapped him. Hard. Without warning.

"What do you know of it? I did not have you, Garek. So, yes—yes, I was alone. All that time. Do you not think that was where my soul was? In the filth? Cold? Starving? Dead?"

He offered no reaction from the slap. No reaction from her words. He merely sat back, leaning against the back of the booth, his words soft. "I saw you in London, Lily."

"What?" She blinked, dragging her wrist across the corner of her eye to clear wetness.

"Early in the morning. Late spring—the season was almost over. I was on a random street, walking from a graveyard, looking to cross, and an open-air carriage barreled at me, two matching white horses thundering. I stepped back, and as it passed, something flew onto my feet—vomit."

"Vomit?"

"I looked up, and it was you in the carriage, retching over the side. Your sister was behind you, holding you."

Lily jerked back from the table, horrified.

"I started after you, concerned, worried—even then I thought I could forgive you for what you did to me. I thought I still wanted you. But then you stood up in the carriage, spinning and laughing in your bright pink gown, pointing at me, heckling. And then you fell down out-of-sight, disappearing."

Her mouth agape, Lily's head swung back and forth, disbelief furrowing her brow. "I vomited on you? Then laughed? Garek, I...I would never have...I dreamed of you all the time—about loving you...about hating you. About how I needed to hate you. But I could never bring myself to do it. Not truly. I would never have laughed at you, Garek—never."

"You did." Malice hollowed his low voice. "And I realized you were drunk. Just as you are now. Embarrassingly, gutter drunk. Not the woman I knew. Not the woman I had loved."

"Garek, no—I—"

"Yes you, Lily." He cut her off, his voice turning brutal. "You ripped away everything from me on that day—the very last thing I had to hold onto. In that instant, I realized who you truly were—a selfish child with no regard for others. I realized our time together was a lie—you were merely an actress using me to get what she wanted. It was in that moment I realized you needed to feel my pain."

Lily gasped.

Garek's eyes didn't flinch. His jawline hard, he stared at her, his eyes still hooded, a mystery to her.

This couldn't be. Garek could not be this callous. Not the man that had been her life, her everything.

No. Impossible. She had drunk too much and she wasn't hearing his words correctly. He didn't possess this viciousness.

The air left her lungs, shaking as it slipped from her lips.

"You were the one that flippantly threw me away, threw away my love, Lily. But unlike what you did, I thought you at least deserved the courtesy of an explanation. A reason why."

"So you are here for revenge? Against me?" She said the words numbly, not believing they could possibly be true.

Garek offered one nod, leaning across the table to her. "I wanted there to be no chance this did not ruin you. Did not destroy your life. I want you to hurt, Lily. Hurt like I did that day on the street."

No. God no.

Her gut clenched, bile threatening, speeding up her throat. Frantic, she fumbled to the edge of the booth.

Garek's hand clamped her upper arm in an instant, dragging her toward the back door of the tavern. He flung open the door, spinning her to the outside wall of the tavern.

Just in time.

Her fingers clawed at the stone wall of the inn as she leaned over, retching all the liquid she had just consumed, trying to avoid her skirts.

Avoid your skirts. That was what Brianna had reminded her time and again in London. Avoid the skirts. It gave the maids extra work to clean them.

Lily concentrated on that one task as heave after heave racked her body.

Rain dripped onto the back of her head, the moisture reaching her scalp. Rain. When had that started? And heavy enough that the wetness had already soaked through the back of her tight-fitting jacket, cooling her skin.

Her body quivering, depleted, Lily tried to take a step away from the wall, but Garek's hold on her didn't loosen. He pulled her backward, dragging her back through the door, and then pushed the small of her back up the stairs adjacent to the door. His fingers stayed tight around her upper arm the entire time.

Moving her through two hallways, he finally stopped, opening the door to a room and sending her through.

"Get in the bed."

Lily couldn't take a step in any direction.

Not forward. Not backward.

Outside, behind the tavern, her body had understood immediately what her mind couldn't quite comprehend.

Garek wanted her destroyed.

The thought, his words, sat dull in her mind, unable to turn into belief, into reality.

Garek pushed her forward, turning her and setting her on the bed. Lily leaned, dropping to her side and curling into a ball.

Her head spinning, she watched him move about the room.

And then it hit her. Not what was past. But what was to come.

She tried, but could not lift her head, it had become so heavy. But she wasn't going to let that stop her from asking the question, her voice dull. "You do not intend to marry me, do you, Garek?"

Digging through a satchel sitting atop a bureau across the room, Garek stopped. It took a moment for him to turn to her. He walked across the room, stopping right before her head.

Staring at his thighs, Lily made a fist under her temple, angling her head far enough upward so she could see him staring down at her.

"Maybe I will marry you. Maybe I will not."

"No." Lily used her last reserve of strength, pushing herself half upright. "No. I will leave right now. I can still get back."

Garek only stepped away, grabbing a simple wooden chair and pulling it near the bed. He sat, leaning back in the chair, and threw his feet up upon the foot of the bed. Elbows bent, his hands clasped behind his head.

"Get back to what, Lily?" His eyes closed as he deepened his lean on the chair. "Besides, I cannot let you go back yet. Not yet."

Lily looked at the angle of him. He had effectively trapped her in the bed. There was no way she could get past him, escape him with the current state of her body.

She slumped back down in the bed, huddling into herself.

Garek was right. What was back at Notlund for her, anyway? A perverted lecher?

Her head spun into darkness.

No backward. No forward.

{ CHAPTER 15 }

Lily opened her eyes, ignoring the muck of thick cotton stuffed into her head. She had become quite adept at ignoring how her body truly felt after getting foxed.

Still on her side, still in her riding habit, Lily wiggled her toes. Her boots were gone. Rain still lashed at the window, sheets spraying across the glass in windy gales.

His back to her, Garek set down the fire poker and walked across the room, stopping by the bureau and pulling items from the bag.

In silence, she watched him rummage through the contents. All of his clothes were still intact, including his dark boots. Hessians, as far as she could tell from the angle and the dim light. All of his clothes, from his boots to his black jacket fit him well, crisply. She had not noticed that the night before. When had Garek come into money enough for such fine clothes?

He pulled free a white linen shirt, setting it on the top of the bureau.

"There are scones and tea on the side table," Garek said, not turning around to her.

Had she opened her eyes that loudly?

Lily tilted her head upward on the bed to see a plate of breads, a cup, and a teapot sitting atop a silver platter on a table by the wall. Her chin dropped back down, her eyes going to Garek's back.

He stripped off his jacket, his arms moving gingerly. Before she could wonder at it, the darkness of his jacket fell, and she could see his linen shirt beneath. Bloody spots scattered the white cloth.

Lily jerked upright, swinging her legs off the bed.

By the time she was across the room to Garek, he was already peeling the shirt up over his head. "Garek, your back. It is bloody."

He glanced over his shoulder at her, then looked down at the shirt in his hand. Bloody splotches marred the cloth, undeniable.

He spun to face her, removing his back from her sight. "It is nothing you should be concerned with, Lily."

She grabbed the shirt from his hands, holding it up. "Some of this is fresh blood, Garek, so yes, I am concerned. Why are you bleeding like this?"

He shrugged. "Glass shards."

"Glass that is still in your skin?"

"Possibly."

"How did you get glass embedded into your back?"

His mouth clamped shut, his lips drawing back into a hard line.

Eyes to the ceiling, Lily dropped the cloth, pushing him aside. She reached for his bag, starting to rummage through the contents.

Garek grabbed her wrist, stilling her. "What do you think you are doing?"

Her glare went straight to his eyes. "I am finding your surgical tools. They are in here, are they not?" She tried flicking his hold away from her wrist.

His hooded eyes pinning her, he dropped his fingers from her wrist without a word.

Her look slid downward, only to land on his bare chest.

The bare chest she had once strained against in sheer ecstasy. Once rested on in complete peace.

Damn her wandering eyes.

She swallowed hard. Even though she couldn't quite fully believe it, she had to remember Garek was out to destroy her in every sense of the word.

Yet she still wasn't going to let him walk around bleeding.

Lily turned back to the bag. "It is good to know you have not lost all good sense." Her words sank to a mumble as she dug further into the bag. She pushed aside clothes, finding the bottom of the bag. Smooth leather touched her finger. Down in the furthest corner, untouched.

She glanced at Garek. How long had it been since he had used these?

Pulling free the leather wallet, Lily set it down, setting free the latch holding the leather flaps together. She quickly found the fine-pointed tweezers among the silver instruments and pulled them free.

A quick glance to the window told her the dark downpour would offer little light, so she pointed to the fireplace. "Come. Sit down by the fire."

Garek's jaw flexed. "I do not need you to do this, Lily."

"No, you do not." She flashed him annoyed eyes. "Because it will be so much easier for you to pluck the glass out of your back by yourself."

She held the tweezers out to him. "Here. Go ahead. I will just watch."

His jaw shifted sideways before he let out a sigh and turned from her, moving to the fireplace.

"Sit on the floor," Lily said as she followed him, grabbing the wooden chair and dragging it across the room.

Garek sat, his legs stretching out straight before he propped up his knees, his forearms resting on them. Lily sat the chair behind him, then brought the wash basin and pitcher, along with a fresh cloth, over from the washstand. Setting the bowl on the floor, Lily perched herself on the edge of the chair, scooting forward until she was close to Garek's skin.

Dabbing away both dried and fresh blood with the wet cloth, Lily found six obvious wounds with glass in the skin, still trickling blood. Her fingers stretching his skin tight, she went after the first shard with the tweezers.

"When was the last time you used your medical instruments?"

"Your sister."

Lily yanked the first shard free and sat back, pausing for a moment. "Since Brianna?"

"Yes." The word snapped out, filling the room.

Lily blinked hard at Garek's reaction. Obviously a sore spot—as every word from her seemed to be. But then, he wasn't here for conversation. He was here for her pain, by his own admission.

She leaned forward, wiping clean the area she had just pulled a shard from, and then moved to the next spot. The edge of this piece of glass was harder to find, set just below the surface of his skin. Lily tugged and squeezed the skin around the glass sliver, trying to plump it out far enough to grasp. "Are we leaving today?"

"No. Not unless the rain ceases. Ouch." He jerked forward.

"Sorry. It slipped."

Garek eased back close to her. "One can hardly see through the rain to the stable from the tavern door."

Lily plucked. "So we are stuck here?"

"Yes, at least until the rain eases enough to travel."

She flicked the shard into the fire, then turned to him, dabbing at the next spot. "What happened to you, Garek?"

He shrugged. "It was minor. I was tackled in that little structure by the stables at Notlund—a painting studio? We hit the wall with paint jars stacked along it—they fell, and I landed on them."

"Who tackled you?"

"Brianna's husband. I had found Brianna in the studio by herself and went in to talk to her about you, and Lord Luhaunt decided to first attack, instead of ask, when he found us."

"Ahhh. He is not a man to trifle with, that one. Especially when it comes to Bree." Lily could not hold in a smile. At least

Brianna's life was right with Sebastian—never mind that her own had just been upended beyond comprehension.

"Do you like him?"

"I do. He understands my sister like no other. Better than even I do, if I have to admit."

"And you loathe to admit it, I imagine?"

She chuckled. "I do. Do not ever tell him I did."

"I would not dare."

Lily shifted on the edge of the chair, grabbing Garek's shoulders to angle him more to the light of the fire. This was so close to the easy conversation that she always remembered with him. So close to normal.

She wrung out the cloth, starting on the next sliver of glass. Maybe she could ask him now. Ask him what she had wondered all night, what had haunted her fitful dreams.

"Garek, what happened to you when you left Annadale?" she asked, her voice hesitant. "I know you mentioned the prison last night, but you have just…changed so much."

"Whatever you see in me now, you can thank your sister for, thank yourself for."

Lily squeezed his skin a little too hard, and she knew it, but Garek didn't flinch away. She looked up at the back of his head. "What Brianna did a year and a half ago does not matter, Garek. It never did."

"How can you even say that?" He looked over his shoulder at her. "It sure as hell does matter, Lily."

"No. I was the one most harmed by her actions, and I could care less what Brianna did. She was trying to protect me, in her own misguided way. Protect me because she loves me. But that day she offered you money to leave me, you had a choice, Garek—a choice. You. And you chose not to fight for me. You chose to take the money and leave. Money over me."

He twisted fully around, his hard eyes pinning her. "You blame me for that? I was the one that chose money over you? You are changing history, Lily. Changing it to ease your own conscience. You were the one that would not see me. You were the one that offered me the money to leave. And Brianna supported it, encouraged it. Made sure it happened. I had no hope of you, Lily, so what choice did I have except to leave?"

"What?" Lily's head shook, confusion creasing her brow. "Garek, I did not offer you the money to leave. Brianna did."

"You signed the note, Lily."

"What note?"

His eyes went impossibly hard, and then his look silently dropped from her, moving to the fire.

Seconds passed.

Lily sighed, annoyed she had allowed herself to be drawn into the memories that still, to this day, cut through her heart, paining her. Silently, she twirled her hand holding the tweezers, motioning him to turn around.

Garek grabbed her wrist, stilling the tweezers as his eyes came up to her face. "It was Brianna's idea?"

Lily shrugged, exhaling a long breath. "She paid you to leave me. That was what she said. And you took the money and left. Left me."

Her chest clenching, she twisted her wrist out of his grasp, her hand landing on her lap. "I did not believe her that day—did not believe you would leave me—not until we went to the tavern. Not until I went into your room and there was nothing. Nothing. Not the slightest remnant of you, Garek. Nothing to touch, to hold onto. I..." Her voice petered out.

"What?"

She shook her head, taking a deep breath as her spine straightened. "It was difficult."

"Difficult, Lily? How about being told you refused to see me? That you thought I was a liar. That you were giving me money to leave. That I was about to be arrested for robbing graves?"

Her eyes went wide. "I never said those things—and arrested? But Garek, you did no wrong. You left that graveyard—you did not do it."

"It did not matter." His jawline tightened, his voice dropping into a near growl. "Not when Halowell's son had several of his men to lie for him. My word was not enough. My word was not even heard."

"And you blame me for that? You blame Brianna for that?"

"She set this into motion, Lily. All of it."

Lily growled. "So what if she did, Garek? So what if she told you I did not want to see you? You believed her. You believed her, and did not believe in me—you took the money and what did it get you? You still went to prison. And then this is how you come back to me? Vengeful? Spiteful. Wanting to destroy me? That is most certainly not Brianna's fault, Garek."

Her anger threatening to overtake her, she grabbed his shoulder, twisting him until she could see his back again. She had to finish getting the glass shards out. Finish this, and she could stop touching him. Stop talking to him.

She plucked the next two shards in silence.

"I had to leave, Lily." His voice was soft. "I thought you were done, done with me. And without you, I had nothing. Nothing to stay for. I had to leave."

"No. I will have none of it." The words flew from her, bitter. "You took the money, Garek. You took it instead of me. I would have left with you in an instant. No questions. But you took the money. You left me. Without. A. Word."

She yanked, pulling the last shard from his back.

"And I am done." She set the tweezers down, rinsing her hands in the bowl of water.

Kicking the chair back, she stood and went over to the silver platter by the window. Picking up a scone, she tore into it with her teeth, chewing as she stared at the rain blanketing the window.

She could hear Garek moving behind her, silent, his boots clicking across the floor. The rustle of fabric.

The door opened and closed.

Lily did not even bother to turn around.

She knew Garek was gone. Again.

~~~

Garek scanned the common area of the inn. Lily hadn't been in their rented room when he had come in from the stable.

He had escaped to the horses after Lily had finished with his back, still reeling at what she had said.

If Lily had never wanted to rid herself of him, never refused to see him...

Hell.

All this time, he had believed her fickle, willing to toss him aside at the slightest lie cast his way. Believed she had never loved him. But if she never even knew the lies Brianna had told him to make him leave, then he very well did abandon her. Without a word.

Dammit to hell and back again.

Garek exhaled, slapping his gloves on his thigh. He had been in the stable most of the day, avoiding her. But now where the blast was she?

The rain had eased slightly, but darkness was falling and she wouldn't have been stupid enough to leave. Would she? He would have seen her in the stable coming for her horse. Unless she had just walked away.

His eyes a bit more frantic, Garek scanned the room again.

Then he caught a glimpse. The delicate toe of a boot flopped back and forth off the edge of a booth bench. He walked to the rear of the common room, stopping in front of the boot.

Lily sat, leaning against the inside wall, both her legs sprawled long onto the bench. Her elbow propped on the table, she held the side of her head in her hand, her fingernails curled into her loose chignon. Her free hand tapped out a melody only she could hear on the edge of the table.

Not exactly becoming of a lady. And the empty glass goblet next to her elbow was not an encouraging sign.

He sighed. "Have you eaten anything?"

Her eyes crept up to him, her face blank. "Yes. Earlier."

"How much have you had to drink?"

Her hand flipped down to the goblet, wrapping about the rim of it to lift it, swinging it back and forth as her eyes followed. "How much is enough?"

Garek bit his tongue, sitting down across from her. He grabbed the goblet from her, glancing at the contents. Empty. Not even a drop. Had she licked the bottom clean? He set it at the edge of the table. "What are you doing to yourself, Lily?"

The barmaid stopped at the edge of the booth, looking at Garek. "Wot can I getcha, luv?"

"Brandy, and whatever pie is handy."

The woman pointed at Lily, her eyebrows raised at Garek. He shook his head.

She nodded. "Be out right quick, luv. And ye be hearin' 'bout the bridge?"

"The bridge?" Garek shook his head.

"Me 'usband just got back from checkin'. The river done swelled again. Always does in these rains. Bridge won't be crossable 'till the morrow at the fastest. If it keeps sturdy, that is."

"I had not heard," Garek said. "I was waiting, so thank you for the news."

"Ye and yer bride will have to snug up another night upstairs." The lady winked, smirking.

Garek managed a flat smile. "Yes. I imagine we will. Thank you."

She ambled off.

"No bridge?" Lily looked at Garek, a lazy half smile below her dull blue eyes. "Then I will need another drink to make it through the night. Much as you would like me to resist."

She started to scoot forward on the bench. Garek leaned across the table to snatch her arm, holding it to the wood.

"You cannot stand to look at me sober, Lily?"

She shrugged. "Or I could go up the stairs and not look at you at all."

His head tilted as he stared at her, trying to find the woman he had fallen in love with. Trying to search under her anger. Under the sodden state she was determined to remain in. Trying to find the smallest glimmer of who she once was.

He had yet to see it, but he had felt it. The previous night when they were in the stable and he was deep in her—as angry as both of them had been—he had still felt it. The passion. The love. Even if her mind, her words were hateful, her body betrayed her. That he could feel.

The barmaid set down both a short glass of brandy and a silver mug of ale at the edge of the table. Garek gave her a nod, then set his eyes back on Lily as the woman stepped away.

"You are not the same person I left a year and a half ago, Lily."

"We both have changed, Garek."

"Yes, but I never believed you would have moved on from me. Through everything—prison, pain—you were the one thing I thought I would have at the end. What I held on for."

"And then I retched upon you and laughed at you. I understand—I destroyed your dream, so now you are here to destroy me."

She pulled her arm from his grasp as she leaned across the table, her voice a loud whisper. "Well, let me share a secret with you, Garek. You destroyed me long ago. When you left I was crushed—destroyed. I could not breathe for weeks—months. Every breath was short, never filling my chest."

Pausing, her hand flattened on the table, her eyes closing for a long moment. "You hate me for moving on from you, but what was I to do? Wallow? What would that bring me? Nothing but gut-wrenching misery. So I put a bright smile on my face and tried to move forth—forget you."

"And you succeeded, Lily." Garek couldn't keep the edge out of his voice. "You moved into society easily—enjoyed all I could not give you."

She scoffed a laugh, her head shaking as she leaned back in the booth, her arms crossing over her belly. "Did I?"

"Enough to get foxed nightly, laugh loudly, gain a new fiancé. Rather well done. I witnessed it myself."

"Yes, you are right, Garek. Always right. Thank you for watching me without ever once showing yourself to me." Her eyes went to the ceiling, her head shaking. "Yes, I did drink too much, laugh too loud, flirt too much."

She lifted her fingers, rubbing her forehead before her eyes dropped to him. Her voice, always so hypnotically smooth, went rough, words shaking. "I pretended quite well, didn't I? Pretended I was whole. I thought it was what I could become— what everyone saw—a darling of society, a pretty woman to set upon an arm. Such high—hollow aspirations. I could actually become that woman if I tried hard enough. And kept trying. Kept smiling. What everyone wanted to see. What Brianna wanted to see. What the Duke and Wynne wanted to see. Do you think that was easy?"

Garek shrugged, his look boring into her. "It appeared to be."

"Especially with sherry. Or Madeira. Or punch. Or whatever was handy." She reached across the table for his brandy, her eyebrow cocking at him when he didn't stop her. She set the glass to her lips, taking a long sip.

Not forfeiting the glass, she kept her hands cupped around it, spinning it on the wood of the table. Her eyes stayed down, watching the amber liquid swirl slowly. "Maybe I am different. Maybe I did become that woman. How would I even know? But in all those ballrooms, all those parties, all those dinners, I never found happiness like Brianna said I would. Peace—she promised me peace, but I never found it. And the men...I never loved any of them—and they certainly did not love me." Her blue eyes lifted to his face. "Not like you did once. No one has ever looked at me like you did, Garek."

"How did I look at you, Lily?" Garek asked, his voice low.

Her eyelashes fell closed as her head sank back, swinging back and forth. It took a long moment for her to drop her chin and open her eyes to him. Sadness flooded the blue depths. "You looked at me like I was whole, complete, real...cherished."

His eyebrow arched.

"Like I was something to be cherished." Her voice dropped, weary and soft. "Like the one thing you wanted in life was to make me happy. Every word I said was important to you. Every glance, every touch—like you were fighting yourself to not pick me up and bring me to bed. Cherished."

"And then I disappeared."

"When you left, Garek, I was hollow—nothing. And Brianna was still a ghost—she still has never told me what happened to her, to our father. I had lost them, and then you. So when the invitation came to stay with the Duke and Duchess of Letson, I thought it would snap Brianna out of her grief, help her move on."

"It would seem your sister moved on splendidly." Garek reached forward, grabbing the brandy from Lily's hands to take a hefty swallow.

Dammit, he was waning.

He still wanted to hate Lily. Hate her for asking him to leave—which she never did, if he could believe her. Hate her for laughing at him on that London street. Hate her for making him love her in the first place. Hate her because it had been the only thing he had lived for these past months.

But all of that was waning.

Watching her, her softness, the heartache wrenching her voice—the hatred that had kept him moving forward was dissolving, even though he wasn't ready to let it go.

Lily nodded, a soft smile on her lips. "Bree did move on. She found peace." The smile faded. "But I...I have stumbled through the last year of my life—questioning everything—my mistakes left and right. And always in the back of my mind, I was trying to forget that you left me—that I was not worth staying for—not worth more than the money."

Her palm came up, shoving away the wetness in the corners of her eyes. "So I tried for normal. What everyone around me told me I should want—normal. And I decided to settle. I decided to accept Lord Newdale's proposal. I could not have you, but at least I could have what everyone said I should want—a husband, children—at least my life would be normal—and then maybe I would feel it as well."

"And did you?"

"Yes. No." She shrugged. "Maybe. I was striving for normal—but I do not know what it is. I have never had it, not truly, so I do not know if I achieved it."

Her head tilted as she looked at him, her voice down to a whisper. "Only with you. I think with you, Garek, I had it. Maybe."

"But you did not believe in me, Lily. You turned your back on me. Laughed at me. Betrayed all of the love I had for you."

"And now you hate me for all that happened to you." He expected a fight, but she merely nodded, her words defeated. "But I never did anything to you, Garek. Whatever you may believe, I never did anything to you. Except for love you. That…that I did do."

Garek stared at her, silent.

Stared at the pain she had lived with for the past year and a half. Fighting the realization that was slowly sinking into his gut.

He had caused this. He had left her.

The mere thought so thoroughly shook him that he had to look away from Lily.

Staring at the barmaid cleaning glasses, he cleared his throat. He couldn't deal with Lily. Not yet. Not with his mind whirling. "You need to go up to the room, Lily. I cannot trust you down here."

"Trust me? Trust me for what?"

Without a glance her way, he stood. "Trust you not to continue to imbibe. To do something unbecoming."

He offered his hand to her, but she slapped it away, getting to her feet and trudging past him.

Following her in silence up to the room, Garek opened the door for her, then stopped in the doorway.

In the middle of the room, she turned back to him, her voice aching. "You say I am not the same person I once was—but what about you, Garek?"

He steeled himself enough to meet her eyes. "What about me, Lily?"

"Your compassion, Garek? You lost all of it. It was what I loved most about you, and it is gone."

His head bowed for a long moment, and then he looked up, meeting her blue eyes. "My compassion never helped me, Lily. My compassion never got me you."

He stepped backward, softly closing the door to her.

{ CHAPTER 16 }

Lily stared at the closed door. Stared at it, stunned into stillness for minutes.

How had the man she once knew, once loved, disappeared so completely? So callously?

He was gone. Physically in front of her, but gone. Just like before. Gone, and he did not even have the decency to tell her why.

But then, had she even asked?

He was here. Here and she could ask. Ask what had happened to him. What changed him. If nothing else, she would have answers from him. Not like last time.

She went to the door, turning the round knob. It slipped in her hand.

She tried again. It didn't budge. Jammed?

She pushed on the door. Solidly closed. Wiggling the knob, fury started to build in her belly.

Garek had just locked her in this room.

Locked her in. Holding her captive.

He wanted revenge—but to lock her in a room?

Unimaginable.

Lily spun from the door, growling. This was beyond reason. Beyond sanity.

Her eyes landed on the window. Sparse rain still pattered on the glass, but darkness had not yet fallen.

She was still foxed, but she had learned to navigate through much of life in this way.

Moving over to the window, she looked down. The roof of the dining room area below jutted out underneath her window. Lily unlatched the lock on the window, lifting the sash. It creaked, straining against plump, wet wood, but it moved.

Perfect.

Garek had forgotten one very important fact about her. In all that she may have changed, there was one thing she had not lost.

She was a fighter.

And she would not be locked into a room, ruined, without a battle.

~ ~ ~

Garek rolled his index finger along the rim of the brandy glass, staring into nothingness.

He knew now, in his gut, that Lily had not been lying. She never had anything to do with him leaving Annadale. Never had anything to do with the money.

And now he had to come to brutal terms with what that meant. What he had done in pursuit of a false goal. What he had just done to Lily.

He caught the barmaid's eye and motioned to her, lifting his glass. He was going to need several more of these.

The front door of the tavern opened, a rush of mist blowing in from the dark night.

"Colleen. Rope. Rope. I need a rope." A man, soaked, ran into the room, yelling.

The barmaid pointed in the direction of the stable. "Out back, Tom. Wot's the fuss?"

The man ran through the common area, droplets flying and landing on Garek's forehead as he sped past, headed for the back door. "A girl in the river."

Garek jumped to his feet, his heart stopping.

No. She wouldn't.

He glanced upward, wishing he could see through wood and plaster. Wishing he could see Lily safely in bed.

But he knew instantly it was her.

Not bothering to go upstairs to verify Lily was missing, Garek ran out the front door of the tavern in full speed toward the river.

His boots slipping along the muddy road, slowing him, he made it to the crowd at the edge of the swollen river within minutes.

Pushing his way through several men holding up lanterns, he searched the swirling waters in the darkness.

"Where? Where?" he managed to choke out between heaving breaths.

One of the men pointed, holding his lantern up. "There. She's 'olding onto that branch. Albert told 'er she ain't gonna reach the bridge, but she waded in anyways 'fore 'e could stop 'er. Said she could make it. Current got 'er right quick."

Garek desperately searched the area the man pointed to. A line of trees that yesterday had lined the riverbank were now swallowed by the rushing current. Limbs and branches scattered into the river, dragged down by the waters.

"Where?" Garek demanded.

"'Tween the second and third tree." The man jabbed his finger at the water. "Oye, she gone under again. She's 'olding onto that tree branch, water rushing her. We can't get rope to where she can snatch it." The man leaned forward, squinting. "There—she be up again."

His eyes searching the branches, Garek finally spotted a hand. Then the other. Then her face, just clearing the watery foam.

Lily.

The sound of the rushing water drowning out all noise, Garek could see her gasping, struggling. Her top hand slipped on the branch, jamming into her lower hand.

"Where's the rope, man?"

"Here." The man pointed to the end of the row of gawkers. "But we tried. We can't get it to her."

Garek bolted to it, stripping off his jacket and boots, and then flipped through the heap of rope until he found the ends. He shoved the one tattered end into the nearest man's hand. "You all will hold this?"

"Sure, but it be your funeral, lad. That current will snatch you. It is nasty strong."

"I am stronger."

Wrapping the rope along his arm, Garek moved into the water, almost immediately dropping as the land gave way below his feet. In an instant, water rushed up to his ribcage. Only by the grace of fate did his left foot find a boulder where he could wedge himself against the heavy current. It gave him a precious second to find the ground with his right foot, regaining his balance.

Righted, he barreled forward, every step requiring him to regain his balance, his lean against the floodwaters. Halfway to her, Lily disappeared below the surface of the water again, her hands slipping further down the branch.

"Fight it, Lily. Fight it," he screamed above the waters, knowing she couldn't hear him, but yelling anyway. "Up. Get to air. Get to the damn air, Lily. Fight it."

Her forehead broke free, her head twisting as she tried to get her mouth to air.

Her hands slipped below the surface of the water, the branch straining.

"Dammit, Lily. Fight."

Her head dropped below the water. Gone. All of her gone.

Water up to his chest, Garek plowed through the last few steps to where Lily was, caution be damned. His hand diving, he searched, trying to discern what he was touching through the debris.

Then under his thumb—skin. Her wrist. He wrapped it in a vise, yanking her from the branch, yanking her to him.

Her head broke through the water, and Garek dragged her to his body, threading his arm around her chest. Tight, too tight, but he wasn't about to chance her slipping from his grasp.

He turned, gripping the rope, and the men on the shore started hauling the rope, helping him move back through the raging current.

Three last desperate steps up the hidden slope at the edge of the river, and Garek's feet found solid land.

Limp. She was too limp.

Shaking the twisted rope free from his wrist, he spun Lily in his arms, supporting all her weight. Her eyes were closed, her head bobbing from the movement.

Garek laid her onto the ground, flipping her over and slapping her back. She heaved instantly, water spewing, hacking from her lungs.

His arm wrapping under her belly, he lifted her, propping her up from the ground on her hands. His thumping on her back eased into a rub as she expelled the last of the river water from her lungs and belly, her body shaking.

"Is it out?" Garek asked, close to her ear so she could hear him over the coughs.

She nodded, trying to lift her hand to her mouth. Unsuccessful, she turned her head to wipe her mouth on her shoulder, but it made her lose her balance, her body collapsing.

In one swift motion, Garek flipped her body, picking her up. He started toward the inn, the gathered men bustling with their lanterns in front of him.

Her sopping dress added at least half her weight. But not her boots—they were long gone, her bare toes limply bumping into his thigh with every step.

Two-thirds of the way back to the inn, Garek had reined in his anger enough to speak without swearing, and he looked down at Lily. Her eyes were open in a blank stare.

"Of all the inane things to do, Lily."

Her eyes found his face, her voice beaten. "Why? Why save me? You hate me, Garek."

The words sliced through his heart.

He had created this.

Him, and him alone.

He inhaled heavily, then exhaled a sigh, her body riding his chest. "I do not hate you, Lily. I do not."

She looked at him for a moment, no emotion crossing her face, no response. Her eyes slipped down, returning to the far-off, vacant stare.

Garek bit his tongue against all that he wanted—needed—to rail at her for the sheer stupidity of trying to cross a flooded river. His heart still wildly out-of-control, he set his eyes forward.

Her body spent, Lily drifted to sleep before they reached the inn. Even once in their room, she could not be roused. So Garek stripped her out of her sopping clothes, wrapping her under several blankets on the bed.

Jabbing at the fire, Garek heaved breath after breath. He hung the iron poker alongside the fireplace and turned to Lily, watching her sleeping form. This would have been the moment. The perfect chance to walk away. Desert her, just as he had planned.

But plans had an amazing capacity to change.

He didn't even have to war with himself. That war was over.

He stepped across the room to her, the knuckles of his fingers running gently along her forehead.

With a deep breath, he walked out the door.

~ ~ ~

Lily sat up in the bed, looking around the room.

Silence. For the first time in hours. Silence. No rain constantly beating down upon the roof. The fire still gave off light, and she could see her riding habit, chemise, and stays hung neatly over the backs of two chairs positioned to dry them by the fire.

She peeked under the blankets she had clutched to her chest. Yes, naked.

The last thing she recalled was Garek carrying her. Telling her he did not hate her.

She shook her head.

She was not about to think on that yet. She needed food. Food to stop her hands from shaking. To quell the pit in her stomach.

Lily swung her legs from the bed, wrapping the blanket around her as she went over to her clothes. Still wet. Even her chemise was too damp to put on.

Her jaw shifted sideways as she looked around the room. It was late enough that the common area would be empty— hopefully. And as unseemly as it was, no one would blame her for popping in there with makeshift clothes on.

She went over to Garek's bag, finding one of his white linen shirts on the top. Slipping it over her head, she found it dropped almost to her knees. She cuffed the sleeves and wrapped one of the blankets around her waist in a make-shift skirt.

Hanging the other blanket around her shoulders, she figured she had concealed all she needed to and went to the door. Her breath held as she turned the knob.

It easily opened.

Her bare feet padding along the planks of the wooden floor, she made her way down the stairs.

Thank the heavens, the common area was empty, the last flames of a dying fire flickering in the enormous stone hearth along the far wall. Two lanterns by the front doorway remained lit, casting just enough light for Lily to move about without bumping into chairs.

She went to the bar, stepping behind the long counter to search for something to eat. Her rummaging rewarded quickly, she found a platter of breads covered by a flour-dusted cloth.

Pulling one loaf from the platter, she bit into the crusty end as she walked from behind the bar, needing to sit before her legs collapsed on her.

She aimed for the nearest chair, but the slight movement of a shadow in the rear of the room caught her eye. Then a squeak of wood echoed from one of the five booths.

Lily stopped in place, indecisive about what to do. Sit and pretend whoever was in here, wasn't in here? Or grab another loaf and scamper back up to her room?

A quick look downward at her attire, and she opted for the demure route. She quickly snatched another loaf from behind the bar and began walking back toward the stairs. When she passed the booth she had heard the squeak come from, she couldn't resist one quick glance at the occupant.

Garek.

Leaning forward, hunched over a half-filled glass, he stared at the table. A large carafe of brandy sat nearly empty next to his left hand.

Her feet stopped.

"Are you drunk?" She spat the words out. For how he had chastised her every time a wee bit too much alcohol touched her lips—now he sat there, clearly sauced.

His head was slow to turn and look up at her.

"You are."

She shook her head, her right hand tightening around the loaf, crunching the bread. She turned, but before she made one step, his voice, gravelly, stopped her.

"Revenge is not easy, Lily."

Her look shot to him.

His fingers ran through his dark hair, rumpling further the mess of it. He met her glare. "I do not hide from it—I came back to ruin you, Lily. Ruin your life, just as you had done to mine. I saw a chance opportunity, and I took it. I thought to ruin you, and be done."

"Congratulations, Garek. You have marvelously succeeded."

"I cannot do it."

She charged the table. "Blast it, Garek. You have already done so."

"I cannot let you go, Lily."

The bread slammed down onto the table as she leaned in at him. "You have had your vengeance, so why? Why keep me? Why even talk to me? Throw me out. Be done with me. You have hurt me just as you were hurt. Is it not enough for you? Must you continue to torment me?"

His head shook. "I thought I could do all of this. Do this and be done. Start anew. One last thing to take care of."

"Then be done and let me go, Garek. Let me walk away— hell—let me drown. Just—"

"No." His fist smashed onto the table, making Lily jump. "I sure as hell am not going to let you drown, Lily. Do not even utter those words."

He drew a breath, his fingers rubbing his forehead, his hand covering his eyes. "I do not know what the devil I am doing, Lily—not anymore. I came here for you—to ruin you—to take you away—to love you."

His hand dropped from his face, his hazel eyes moving up to meet her look. "This was for revenge. But I was wrong. Very wrong—about everything. Even with that—from the very start— if I am utterly and harshly honest with myself—I came here for you, Lily. The revenge was just an excuse. A way back to you. It has always been you, Lils."

Her chest tightened, her stomach balling into a hard rock. This was not fair. Not now.

She leaned closer to him over the table. "You are drunk. Do you even hear yourself? You hate me, Garek."

His palm slammed onto the table again, sending the glass rattling. "Dammit, Lily. I still love you. And I have been lying to myself about that very fact every single step I have taken since I left Annadale."

Her head shook. "No. You are trifling with me. This is a trick. You are trying to make me crazy so I do not know what to believe. So I do something else stupid."

She pushed up from the table, grabbing what was left of the two loaves of crumpled bread.

"Wait, Lily. Please."

The words, raw and desperate, stopped her from walking away.

Garek's hand dove under the front of his dark jacket, his finger digging into a pocket.

Lily waited for moment, watching. Then her anger won out over curiosity, and she took a step away.

"This."

She looked back to him.

His hand came up, clutching something small. Fingers hovering over the table, he dropped it.

A short ribbon, the ends frayed, fluttered to the table. Through the dirt streaked along it, she could tell it had been a sparkling peach color at one time.

"A ribbon?"

He looked at her, his eyes solemn. "Yours. It was the one tying your hair when we first met."

"How do you have it?"

"After Sneedly kicked you out of Weadly Hall and I went back for your possessions. I brought you your tin of ribbons. But this one…this one I kept—slipped it into my pocket. I do not even know why I did it, but I did."

His fingers clutched the end of it, gently rubbing the frayed threads. "It has always been on my body. Even through prison— the hell of it—I kept it hidden, safe. Every day. Always in my pocket, on my body—every day, Lils."

His eyes rose to meet hers. "At first it was for hope. And then I thought it was to remind me of my hate. But I was wrong. I took it in love. A little piece of you. And that is what it is. Love that would not let me go. Love that I cannot let go."

Lily's eyes closed as she shook her head, her face tilting to the dark wood beams spanning the ceiling. "You are drunk, Garek, and you produce a ribbon and I am supposed to forget you came here to destroy me? Believe that you no longer want to do so? Ignore that you condemned me—hated me—for something I never did?"

Her eyes opened, her look falling to him. "I do not know what to believe, Garek. And you cannot ask me to trust anything you are saying. Not tonight. Not right now."

Her bare foot found a step backward as she fumbled the bread in her fingers. Tightening the blanket around her shoulders, she made her way to the stairs.

She was suddenly very cold.

Bitterly cold.

{ CHAPTER 17 }

Hooves clomping once more over the wooden bridge, Lily's hands tightened on the reins as she averted her eyes, setting them on the far-off horizon aflame in the early morning light. She wasn't about to glance down at the river, look at the trees, the spot where she had almost drowned.

A shiver scuttled down her spine. She had been so very close. Slipping, darkness swallowing her. And then Garek. Lifting her. His arm clamped around her. Saving her.

He had always been so very good at that. Saving her.

So it only made sense that he was also so very good at the opposite—destroying her.

The horses' hooves sank into the muck on the far side of the bridge and Lily exhaled her held breath. She was finally away from the Golden Pheasant Inn. Free from the suffocation.

Garek had collected her in the morning, producing replacement boots and telling her the bridge was passable, and they could leave. But leave to where, he did not say.

Lily looked ahead on the road. Without a word from Garek, she knew she could turn south at the upcoming split in the road, and he would not stop her. Several hours of riding, and she would be back at Notlund.

But back to what? What was there for her? Pitying looks, unyielding gossip from the wedding guests still there. Horrified faces watching her crawl back into the castle, a bamboozled woman, now ruined beyond repair.

In front of her, Garek moved his horse off to the side of the road, waiting for her mare to fall in line with his. They rode in silence for a length of time, only the squawking of overly robust birds echoing along the road. Garek occasionally looked at her, while Lily tried to ignore his presence.

"Forgive me." His sudden words, soft and earnest, broke the silence.

Anger instantly swelled her throat. "You are asking for a miracle, Garek."

The horses took several steps before he answered, his voice calm, controlled. A ghost of the past, much like he had always been at Weadly Hall. "I am not demanding a miracle, Lily. I was wrong, so very wrong, and I am sorry. I am only asking for the possibility—give me that—the possibility that you can find a way to forgive me. Find a way back to me."

"Or I could find my way back to Notlund."

"You are already ruined, Lily."

She looked away from him, her eyes on the branches of the passing trees, her head shaking. "You do not need to remind me what has become of me."

"There is nothing for you there, at least not now." He cleared his throat. "Can I suggest a different option?"

Eyebrows arched, her look swung back to him.

"I will deliver you to Coldstream. Your sister will be there."

"Brianna will be there? Why?"

"I wanted her out of the way—not able to save you. So while she was talking to you at Notlund, I arranged with her husband for them to be part of the elopement—to attend the wedding in Scotland." His head cocked with a wry grin. "I posed it as a peace offering of sorts to your sister. They were to leave the same night after the business with Lord Newdale was concluded, though I imagine the rain has either delayed them, or altered their route."

"How could delivering me to Coldstream possibly help me?"

"I will accept it if you cannot forgive me, Lily, and I will do whatever it takes to clear scandal from your name. Including standing by the story that you left Notlund with your sister— not me. That the elopement was just a rumor. That you were overwhelmed with worry, collapsed because of nerves, and left to escape the marriage to Lord Newdale. Brianna left Notlund at the same time, and is travelling to Scotland, so it is entirely plausible."

Lily's jaw shifted, considering his words. The possibility of avoiding ruin was tempting. Especially considering the scandal she would face arriving back at Notlund. "But Brianna knows exactly who I am with—and she may have already circulated the story about the elopement, about my leaving with you."

"Yes. But she will also do absolutely anything in this world for you. She will recant her story, admitting you wanted to elope, but she convinced you to leave with her instead. You disappeared to hide, because you were so distraught at having to break the engagement with Lord Newdale."

His voice dropped as he stared at her, the blue in his hazel eyes shining in the sunlight. "But you were never with me, Lily. That will never be known. You will have to live quietly outside of London for some time, and you will be pitied for your collapse, but after a year of quiet, you will still be marriageable. Maybe not to highest echelons of society. But you will be marriageable. I will see to that. I will use everything in my power to see to it. You can still have your normal, Lily."

"This is all—such a very long stretch." Her head shook. "You cannot make this happen, Garek."

He sighed, his face tilting to the sky. It took a moment for him to drag his eyes down to her. "I can, Lily. I am a blasted marquess."

Lily yanked up on her horse's reins, coming to a standstill. "You are what?"

It was a moment before Garek could stop his horse and turn it back to her. His hand slapped onto his thigh, thumb tapping on his buckskin breeches. "I am a marquess, Lily. The Marquess of Wotherfeld. One day I was in Newgate. The next I was being dragged to my feet, freed, and given a title that I was six times removed from. A freakish twist of fortune. I did not even know I was in line for it."

Her mouth open and she drew in a quick breath, expelling it as her eyebrows collapsed together. "And you did not think to tell me this, Garek?"

"It was not necessary to what I had planned."

"Of course not." Her hand flew up, waving in the air. "Of course there was no need to tell me."

She rubbed her forehead, the soft kidskin gloves dragging across her skin. "What…" She shook her head. "I do not even know what to say to you, Garek. To say to this."

He nudged his horse a few steps so he was within reaching distance to her. "I have the means—whatever you decide—to make sure this does not ruin your life, Lily. But you need to let me. Let me bring you to Coldstream. Let me fix this."

Her eyes went to shrewd slits. "And the price?"

"There is no price. I demand nothing." He reached out, his gloved hand landing lightly on her knee. Lily flinched at the touch, but did not pull away. "But in the time that we have left together, I ask, humbly, that you entertain the possibility of forgiveness. I offer no excuses for my actions, just know that I now recognize quite clearly what I have become. And what I will be no more."

"Which is?"

"A man that lost his way." His hand squeezed her knee. "I have found it again, Lily, and I will be damned if I am going to let it go without a fight. Let you go without proving that I can once more be the man you always thought I was."

Lily stared at him. At the hard set of his jaw. At the determined crinkle edging his hazel eyes. At the lips that spoke words of forgiveness, of redemption. Lips, voice that she used to love.

Her eyes fell closed with a heavy exhale. There was nothing for her at Notlund. Only forward. Forward with Garek. At least for the next few days.

She nodded, praying this was not another trap, not another mistake.

Fate couldn't be that cruel, could it?

~ ~ ~

The screams woke her up.

The window was cracked to the night air in the room of the inn. Cracked to the screams that tore along the main road through the small village.

Lily sat up in bed, her bleary eyes searching the room, trying to orientate herself. Trying to figure out if the screams were real or part of the dreams she still had about Brianna being attacked.

She glanced about the foreign surroundings in the light afforded from a lit lantern just outside the window.

Her mind clicked. She was in the next coaching inn, another day's travel from Coldstream. As they had at the Golden Pheasant Inn, they were pretending to be married so as to not arouse suspicion.

Garek—where was he? She leaned over the side of the bed to look at the floor. Fully clothed—as he had been when she shut her eyes—Garek lounged long on a blanket covering the floor, his left hand propped underneath his head as a pillow.

A scream, high-pitched and tortured, floated in through the window.

Lily bent over the edge of the bed, poking Garek's shoulder. His eyes popped open.

Another scream ripped through the night.

He sat up, rubbing his eyes. "What in hades…"

Lily pointed to the window. "From out there. How did that not wake you?"

He shrugged. "I learned to sleep through much worse…"

A staccato shriek, three times over, echoed in.

Lily finished his thought. "In prison?"

"Yes. And the war." He stood, his movements suddenly swift as he went to his boots and yanked them on. "That's a scream of pain, Lily. A woman. I have to follow it, help if I can."

He moved to his bag, digging deep for the wallet that held his surgical tools.

Lily jumped out of bed, quickly sliding on the skirt and jacket of her riding habit over her chemise.

Garek glanced up at her. "You are not coming with me, Lily."

"I am." She went to her boots, dragging them on, her fingers nimble on the laces.

"No. We do not know what is out there—what happened. I do not know if it is safe for you."

Bent over, tightening her left boot, Lily craned her neck to look up at him. "Whatever has been done, it is done, Garek, or there would not still be screams. There is now someone obviously in need of help. You know I can help. Extra hands, just as I did with Brianna."

She stood, hands on her hips as she stared at him.

The next screech filled the air, and Garek nodded, going to the door.

They were down to the street, following the intermediate screams along the buildings lining the road. Some buildings had lanterns lighting the night, most did not. They stopped as a wretchedly bent old woman stumbled out the door of the bakery and into the street right before them. A long apron, streaked with blood, covered the front of her. Her grey head down, she bustled past Garek and Lily.

A scream came down from the rooms above the bakery. Garek snatched the woman's arm.

"Good lady, what has happened?" Garek pointed up at the building.

"The babe ain't right in her." Her gravelly old voice held little compassion. "Ain't nothing to be done fer her."

Garek shook her arm. "You are the midwife and you just left her, woman?"

"Mind yer business. I been here fer two days and nights." She jerked her arm free. "Ain't nothing more I cin do."

She pushed herself past Garek and Lily, moving down the road.

Garek opened the door to the shop, looking around. Finding stairs off to the side, he moved toward them, looking upward to the light on the next level. "Hello?"

A screech came down as reply.

Garek ran up the stairs with Lily at his heels.

Low angled ceilings made Garek duck in front of her as he moved to the doorway next to the stairs. The door was open, and Lily bumped into Garek's shoulder, looking past him. Her stomach curdled at the sight.

A woman thrashed on the bed, doused with sweat, delirious, the bottom half of the bed soaked in blood. A man stood next to her, his head bowed and shoulders shaking. He pulled the woman's arm straight, her hand captured in his grip, hugging it to his chest.

"Sir, I am a physician. Garek Harrison." Garek stopped just outside the entrance to the room. "We passed the midwife on the street. May I be of assistance?"

The man's head turned to the doorway, his eyes hollow, beaten. His look dropped from Garek to Lily. Slowly, raw shock slowing his movements, his eyes went back to Garek. He nodded.

"My wife…" The man broke, hiding behind a hand as a sob overtook him. He sucked in a breath, looking at his wife. "She said there be nothin' to do. Three days it's been." His voice cracked. "The midwife gave her up for death. The babe is already gone."

Garek handed Lily his surgical wallet and stepped into the room. He motioned to the woman's swollen belly, the bloody sheets covering her. "May I?"

The man nodded.

"Your name?" Garek asked.

"Fallow. Jonathan Fallow. Me wife is Brittalynne."

Garek pushed aside the red-sopped sheets and set his hand on the woman's stomach. Her body went into spasms under him, and he moved his hand along her belly.

A gasp, and he looked up to the man, his voice a whisper. "A kick. The babe is still alive."

The man sprang next to Garek, leaning over the mound of his wife's belly. "No—no—no—no—she said—no."

Garek grabbed Mr. Fallow's hand, placing it on the lower side of his wife's protruding belly. "Here. Feel it here. There. It is still alive. But it will not come out this way."

"The midwife said—" Mr. Fallow shook his head, one arm still clamping his wife's hand to his chest. "She couldn't turn it. She said it was dead."

Garek released Mr. Fallow's hand. "I may still be able to get the babe out. But your wife, Brittalynne…she will not survive it."

Mr. Fallow looked down to his wife's face, her head rolling in agony back and forth on the bed. "Will she survive at all?"

Garek shook his head, his voice solemn. "No. This will speed it."

Mr. Fallow watched his wife for a long moment. Fevered, tortured moans rolled from her chest, pain contorting her face.

Long moments passed, time frozen, and then his head dropped, his mouth going to her hand. "Do it. She is in nothing but pain, now."

Garek nodded, pushing all of the bloody sheets away from the woman's belly.

Lily had hovered in the doorway, not sure if she should enter. But at Fallow's last words, she stepped into the room, backing into the closest corner, only to bump into something squishy. She spun to find a small girl, maybe five or six years old, staring up at her with wide, horrified eyes.

She stepped away from the girl.

"Lily, I need help. Unbind my instruments."

Lily turned back to Garek, the mess of blood and the ravaged body of the woman up close nearly stopping her. She swallowed hard, grabbing a wooden chair from the wall and dragging it next to Garek. Unlatching the wallet, she set his tools on the seat, splaying them out as quickly as possible.

Both hands on the woman's protruding belly, Garek pressed through her skin, every jab causing a scream. It didn't slow Garek, concentration consuming his face. "The babe is here. Lily, hand me the scalpel and gather cloth, blankets—clean—quickly."

Lily handed him the scalpel as she searched the room, seeing nothing but blood-soaked sheets. She spun and ran out the door, finding another bedroom a few steps away. A small bed sat under an angled roof. Lily stripped the sheet from the bed, speeding back to Garek.

Her feet skidded to a stop.

Garek was cutting through the woman's skin, into her belly. Pulling the cut wide. She looked up to the woman's face. Delirious, Brittalynne didn't even seem to understand she was being cut.

Lily's eyes went back to Garek's hands, and she saw it. A blood-covered foot, tiny, flailing into the opening.

Garek's fingers—so large, so gentle—grabbed the foot, pulling the babe from the woman.

Gore and blood and babe and cord blended in a wiggling mass, Garek cradling the whole of it in his hands with reverence.

"Lily. The cloth."

Spurred into movement, Lily jumped forward, making a sling with the cloth. Garek set the babe into it.

"Wipe its eyes, its mouth."

Garek's fingers moved to cut the cord and tie it the best he could while working around Lily's hands both cradling and trying to clear the muck from its face.

The cord tied off, Garek looked at Lily as he wiped his hands on a trailing fold of the cloth. "It breathes?"

Lily looked down at the face of the babe—she had assumed it was, but maybe it had been her jostling the babe instead of the babe moving on its own.

Garek moved to the babe's head, his fingers running over its mouth. He put his ear next to its nose. Breath held, Lily watched Garek's face, waiting for something—anything—to flicker across his features.

A slight smile.

Lily exhaled as Garek stood, looking over his shoulder to Mr. Fallow. "It is a girl, and it is alive."

A nod, and Mr. Fallow crumpled around his wife's arm, his shoulders trembling. His wife had stilled, only shallow breathing, gurgles, coming from her lips.

Garek set his face in front of Lily's eyes, blocking her view of the woman. "Take the babe and clean it, wrap it to warmth. Wait outside."

Frozen, her breath suddenly not reaching her lungs, Lily could not move. Could not understand the death that was about to happen before her. The cruelty. A mother dying.

Garek's hands went to her shoulders, squeezing as he set his lips on her forehead. "You did well, Lils." He pulled away, bending so his eyes were only a breath from hers, his voice soft. "Now you need to go downstairs and take care of the babe."

It edged her out of her stunned trance. "Yes." Lily could only force the one word through her choked throat.

Clutching the babe to her chest, Lily backed out of the room, going down the stairs. She walked about the rooms on the ground level, going from the front area, where the baked goods were made and sold, to the open back room.

Dried to crispness on a rope by the hearth, several simple wool dresses were hung. Lily set the babe on the floor, found a flint box and quickly lit a tallow candle and the peat log in the fireplace. She took one of the dresses and found a bucket in the corner that held clean water.

The babe, tiny with flailing arms, took the quick washing Lily gave it with several soft whimpers, but not the slightest cry. The babe cleaned as well as Lily could manage in the limited light, she tore the skirt free from the dress and wrapped the babe snuggly in layers of warmth.

No further screams came from above, which told Lily exactly what transpired up there. Her heart breaking for Mr. Fallow, for the little girl in the corner, for the babe in her arms, Lily swallowed back tears and went out the rear door into the night air.

She paced outside for an hour, the babe snuggled against her chest, tiny puffs of the babe's breath constant on Lily's neck. The night air still held a whiff of the heat from earlier in the day, but the land was calm—too calm, void of respect for what she had just witnessed.

Her eyes to the stars above, Lily stared at the vastness of the sky, cursing over and over the brutality of what had happened to this family. To the mother.

The door opened behind her, soft sobs entering the night.

Lily turned to see the little girl from the room stomping out onto the well-worn grass Lily had been pacing on.

"Aah, sweet one," Lily exhaled, juggling the babe into one arm and wrapping her other arm tight around the little girl.

The girl didn't resist, her tears soaking through Lily's skirt to the skin at her waist. It took long minutes before the girl drew back, pulling away from Lily's arm. She turned from Lily, furiously wiping her eyes before crossing her arms over her chest and kicking the dirt.

"Papa made me leave."

Lily stepped in front of her, gently brushing the brown hair along the girl's forehead to the side. "What is your name, sweet one?"

"Julia."

Lily tilted the babe down from her chest, holding her out. "Do you want to hold your little sister, Julia?"

"No." The girl flung her hand through the air, almost swiping the baby. "No, no, no. I hate her. I hate her. I hate her."

Julia ran around Lily and the babe, growling as she disappeared into the line of trees behind the building.

Mouth agape, Lily watched her run, the quarter moon not shedding enough light to see where the girl disappeared to amongst the trees.

With a glance over her shoulder at the upper level of the home, Lily tucked the babe against her chest, following the girl into the trees.

Fifty steps into the line of woods, the trees cleared to a stream. Lily found Julia immediately, standing in tall grasses next to the bank of the water, her hand wrapping along the seeded tops of the blades of grass, and yanking them, one by one. The girl wasn't crying, just angrily ripping apart the grasses.

After a few minutes of watching her from the trees, Lily took a deep breath, snuggling the babe under her chin. She walked over to little Julia, stopping beside her and facing the stream.

Lily looked down at the top of her head. "You will miss your mama terribly, I can see that. I am so sad for you, Julia."

"It ain't fair."

"No, it is not. You are very right." Lily gathered all of the gentleness she possessed, infusing it into her voice. "This is terribly unfair. For you. For your father."

"I need her. Papa needs her."

Lily set her arm along Julia's shoulders, pulling her to her hip. "Your little sister needs her too, but will never even know her."

The girl pulled at Lily's hand for the merest second, then relaxed, leaning back into Lily, silent.

"You need to know, Julia, how very important you will be for your little sister."

"Me?"

"Yes. You will be the one that guides her, protects her. Your papa will need you to do that. She will need you to do that."

"But I hate her."

Lily's hold tightened on Julia's shoulder. "I know. I know you do right now, and that is what you must do in this moment. But it will fade. For the most part, it will fade, even though I think you will still hate her at times, because she took your mother." Lily swallowed hard, trying to control her voice. "But you must hide it from your sister. Never let her know."

Julia looked up to Lily, her eyes wide. "Why? How do you know that?"

"My own mother died in childbirth."

"And you have a younger sister?"

Lily shook her head slightly, careful not to rouse the babe under her chin. "No, our mama died having me. I am the younger sister. I did not even know how she died until I was five. My papa told me. But my sister, her name is Brianna—"

"That is pretty."

Lily smiled. "It is. In all of our lives, Brianna has never once—even though she must have thought it a thousand times over—blamed me. Never once said I was the cause of our mama's death."

"But you were."

"I was." Lily's heart clenched. "And I knew it."

Lily looked from the girl's face, her eyes settling on the water. "I have always hated myself for it. Hated myself for killing her. Hated myself for taking her away before I ever knew her." Her head shook. "I asked Brianna once if Mama ever even got to hold me, touch me. Bree did not know the answer. She just gave me a hug. The only thing she could tell me was that our mother was very kind, and could sing, beautifully. Bree says I have her voice. A voice I never heard—a voice I took from this world."

Lily looked down to little Julia. "Do you see how important it is? How important you will be to her? Your sister will never be whole, no matter what she does. She will always have this hollow, rawness in her heart—knowing she took her own mama's life. It is something she will never escape, no matter how she tries."

"That is stupid."

"What?"

"I know I just said it, miss, but I didn't mean it. I was mad. Ain't no way a babe can kill an adult."

Julia looked over her shoulder into the woods, then back up to Lily. "No disrespect to you, miss. Papa don't like me arguing with adults. But my little sister ain't doin' no harm. Look at her. She done nothing wrong. She almost died too."

Lily stared at Julia for an aching moment. Slowly, she shifted the babe downward, her eyes dropping to the fuzz on the babe's head, then to the closed eyes, little slits wrinkling her face. Tiny nose. Sweet heart-shaped mouth. Lily's tears started to stream, falling onto the blanket, soaking it.

"Yes." Lily's voice cracked. "I suppose you are right."

Julia's small hand wedged between Lily and the babe. "I think I need to take my sister from you, miss. Don't want her to get cold, what with your wet tears."

Lily smiled through her tears, loath to relinquish the babe. But she let little Julia take the babe, gently, from her arms.

"Best get back to the house, miss. Papa will be worried if we are not there—his girls."

Lily nodded, her hand wrapping along the crown of Julia's head, stroking her brown hair. "Yes. Let us return."

They started walking back through the woods.

"You are going to be the very best big sister, Julia. I can already see it."

Julia looked over her shoulder up to Lily. "I plan to, miss. I plan to."

{ CHAPTER 18 }

"You have not said five words since we left the Fallow family." Garek's deep voice slipped through the air, entering Lily's thoughts.

His footsteps crunched along the rocks lining the river they had travelled parallel to for most of the day. The crunching stopped as Garek came to a stand next to her.

Lily looked over the water to a wide green field dotted with bleating sheep. The sun had dipped to the tips of far-off trees. She propped her heel up along the large boulder she sat on, wedging her toes into the pebbles. "Will we reach Coldstream by nightfall?"

"No. I had hoped to. But no. One more night."

Lily nodded, not looking up at Garek even though she could feel him staring down at her. "I did not like leaving them."

"No. But there was little more we could do for them. I arranged with the wet nurse for her services for the next six months. And their neighbor said she would care for the household and cook until I can send a proper nursemaid when I arrive back at Wotherfeld. They will be able to use her for as long as they need."

Lily glanced up at him. The sunlight was coaxing out the blue in his eyes. "It is generous of you."

He shrugged, looking across the river to the field. "I can think of nothing better to do with the Wotherfeld fortune. It should do some good in this world."

Garek sighed, rubbing several days' worth of dark stubble along his jaw. "Are you tired?"

Lily shook her head.

"I am sorry you had to witness that, Lily. I did not intend—"

"No. It is fine. If you recall, I am sturdier than my gentle-bred backbone would have one believe."

"I do recall." A slow smile lifted his right cheek.

"In all of that bad, it was good for me to be there. To witness it. It reminded me of you—the you from a different time."

His mouth pulled back into a hard line. "I am still the same person, Lily."

She stared up at him, watching his face, searching for the man, the soul she had adored. "I am beginning to see that. Last night I recognized you. You have changed, but you are still capable of such good. Compassion. What you can do with your hands. How you can save another. How you can save a babe that was defenseless against death."

"It was right, Lily. It felt right. Even in the cruelty of death, it felt right." His hand scratched the back of his hair, his head shaking. "Not leaving that family to suffer the death alone. Not giving up on the babe."

"That was the man I loved." A gentle smile came to her lips, hesitant. "I am glad you have not lost it."

Garek nodded, walking around her feet to reach the side of the boulder where there was space for him. He sat, propping his hands on his knees, his eyes on the rolling water. "I did lose it, Lily. You are not wrong about that. I lost that—who I was—for some time. But I am trying to find it again."

Lily stared at his profile, watching the strength of his jawline, the crinkle at the corner of his hazel eyes. He was searching. Just as much as her, if not more. Searching for a life worth living.

She took a deep breath, slowly exhaling it. "Seeing all of that—seeing a family torn apart. Life gone. It reminded me that I am nothing—that my problems, my anger, my fear—it is nothing compared to what just happened to the Fallows. My world had become so small in London—dress, dance, eat—the same people, again and again. Abundance in even the smallest corner. I had lost sight of just how cruel the world can be."

"Yet beautiful—that babe breathing—beautiful," he said, his eyes far-off.

Her lips curled into the softest smile at him. Of course he would see beauty in that. In the smallest thing. A breath. That was the man she had known. "Do you know I used to be so certain, Garek?"

He looked to her. "Certain of what?"

"Long ago, with you—I was certain of everything. That you would save Brianna. That you loved me. That you would... that you would never hurt me."

"And now?"

"I am certain of nothing. Absolutely nothing. Not since you left me."

Garek's hazel eyes pinned her. "And do you need certainty to move onward?"

She shrugged. "I have lived with this, without certainty before—after you left, I did not know how to move forward. So I hoped if I cared about something—anything—then I could find feeling again. Find certainty. Find a way forward. And the easiest things to care about were dresses, and parties, and people I did not care for, and fine gentlemen telling me I was delightful. All the very wrong things to care upon, but I did not stop. I just wanted to feel something again. Anything."

"So did you?"

"No. No feeling. Just emptiness." Her cheek lifted in an aching half smile. "I never forgot you, Garek. Never. No matter what you saw in London."

Lily leaned forward, plucking a stem of ragwort that grew from a mossy crack in the rock beside her knee. She rolled it in her fingers, staring at the yellow petals. "But I did forget just how important people—the very few that are truly loved—are the only thing that should matter. Those moments of happiness with them. Happiness, so that when the bad comes, there is something to hold onto. Even if it is only a memory. Little Julia will have that—memories of her mother—only a few, but at least she will have those."

She plucked at the yellow petals of the ragwort, the silky powder of the flower rubbing onto her bare fingers. Her voice went quiet. "Do you remember, Garek, when I was talking about striving for normal?"

"Yes."

She gathered breath deep into her chest. If she was going to say this, admit to this truth that had sat upon her for her entire life, then she could not hide.

She looked up from the flower, meeting Garek's eyes. "I realized when I was talking with little Julia that I have never been normal. I will always be a babe that killed her mother."

"Lils. No." His palm instantly slipped onto her cheek.

"It is true, Garek. I have known it my whole life. How is being a babe that killed her mother normal? I will always live with that darkness—that sadness for what never was. There was never a mother for me. And I took her from Brianna—she only had her for a little while, a few years." Tears started to slide down her cheeks. "But it was too short. Too short for Bree—I took her mama away from her. I killed my own mother. How could I ever be normal knowing that?"

Garek's other hand clamped onto her face, holding her from turning from him. "You cannot bear the blame for that, Lily. You cannot. It was never your fault. You were only an innocent babe, fighting to live."

She chuckled through a sob gripping her chest. "I know. Little Julia told me that very same thing. Even a five-year-old knows it. I know it."

Her head shook slightly in his grip, swallowing a sob threatening to overtake her body. "But that does not make me believe it. Not in my heart. I do not think I can ever rid myself of it. My mother left me. She did not fight for me. She left and abandoned me with this…this burden, this pain in my heart that I cannot escape, no matter what I do."

"Lils...hell..." Garek's voice raw, he pulled her onto his chest, holding her as silent sobs racked her body. His hand clutched the back of her neck as his lips settled onto the crown of her head. "I would give anything to take this pain from you, Lils."

He gripped her in silence for long minutes, until the sun began to disappear beyond the far-off trees.

Tears spent, her breath solid in her lungs once more, her fingers crawled up onto his chest, touching the cloth of his jacket that was now sopped by her tears.

She leaned backward, and Garek slightly loosened his hold on her, but kept his arms around her body, his hands wrapped behind her waist.

Clearing his throat, his head tilted to the horses by the bank of the river. "I do not want to leave this moment, Lils, but we need to make way to the next inn before nightfall."

Lily nodded, silent, numb.

~ ~ ~

The last glow of the evening sky waned, thick darkness setting in just as their horses came to a stop before the stable at the Wallton Inn.

Garek had first checked on availability and purchased them a room for the night while Lily waited outside on her horse, staring at the darkening orange-streaked sky.

After leading both of their horses to the stable, Garek came to her side to help her dismount, waiting patiently as she loosened the reins she had wrapped tightly about her palms during the silent ride.

Feet on the hay-strewn dirt, Lily stripped off her gloves and flexed blood back into her hands. Garek grabbed the reins of both horses, leading them into the long barn. Lily followed a few steps, stopping just outside the opening as a stable boy ran up to Garek, taking the horses.

Garek slipped him a coin, and the boy's eyes went wide. The boy turned with a near skip, leading the horses to empty stalls.

Turning back to her, Garek peeled off his gloves as he walked out of the deep shadows of the barn and into the yellow light of the lanterns hanging aside the main opening of the stables.

He paused next to her, holding his hand out toward the inn door, and started walking.

Lily didn't follow, her feet solidly stuck.

A few steps by himself, and Garek spun back to her. "Are you not ready to go in, Lily?"

Words lodged in her mouth, her tongue suddenly foreign to her. She shook her head.

Instant concern lined Garek's brow as he moved back to her.

Lily glanced about. They were fully alone outside the inn, save for the stable boy deep in the barn.

Garek's fingers went to her upper arm in a gentle stroke. "What is it, Lils?"

Lily looked up, finding his hazel eyes as her tongue uncurled. "You did not fight for me, Garek."

"What?"

"Of everything, it is the one thing I cannot come to terms with. What has happened since we left Notlund I can reconcile in my mind. But back in Annadale. You left. You took the money from Brianna and left. The money was more important. More important than me. You could have stayed. Fought Brianna. Not believed that I would have condemned you. Come for me. Talked to me."

His hands came up, palms open to her. "Lily—"

"No." She cut him off, but her words were soft, raw. "You took the money, Garek. You took it and left. You did not stay and fight for me. Fight for our love."

His head dropped, shaking as he raked his fingers through his hair. "What the hell do you think I have been doing for the past eighteen months, Lily?" His eyes came up to her, a hard glint in them. "I have been fighting. Fighting every damn step of the way. Fighting to get out of prison. To make a life. Make a life where you would want me again. A life that would make you love me again. And all that time, fighting my own damn self, my own hatred. Even with the hatred, I was fighting for you."

"But not in the instant it mattered most—not in the moment you took that money and walked away from me. We could have avoided all of this. But I was not more important than that money."

Garek grabbed her arm, ushering her to the side of the stable and trapping her against the wood slats of the barn wall. He leaned in, his voice vehement. "Do not speak idiocy, Lily. You were always more important than the money."

"Then why did you do it?" She stared up at him, her chest rising high as the ire in her belly rose. "Brianna told me that it was the money you were after, but I could never believe it. But maybe it was true—true all along. You were always after the money. Maybe even now you think to entitle yourself to my dowry."

His hand slammed against the wooden slat beside her head. Moving his face close to her, his voice tinged with bitterness. "I don't need your damn dowry, Lily."

He heaved a breath and then pushed off from the wall, giving her space. "I was ashamed, Lily. Ashamed."

His head tilted back with a heavy sigh, his face to the dark sky. "I had no money. No prospect to give you a life."

Garek's eyes dropped to her. "What was I supposed to stay and fight for, Lily? Stay and fight to put you into poverty? Stay and fight, only to have to watch your face when they dragged me off to prison?"

She rocked back on her heels, leaning against the wall of the stable as her arms wrapped her belly. "Stay and fight for me, Garek. I had my dowry. We could have left together— disappeared."

He turned fully from her, his head hung as his words slipped low into the darkness. "I took the money because it meant I could correct my failure of a life—it could save the one man that I owed my life to."

Staring at the back of Garek's dark hair, it took long seconds for the words to settle into Lily's mind. "Your uncle? How? Why did you not tell me?"

"I had a life before you, Lily. Responsibilities to that life, what I had done, what I had not done. And that day…that day with Brianna, she forced an impossible choice upon me. And I was ashamed. My uncle was in prison—debtors' prison."

He looked over his shoulder to her but kept his distance. "He was in there because of me. Because of all the debt he incurred in order to keep me at Dr. Halowell's practice. I never knew what he did until they came for him. Never knew my time there was so costly. He always told me everything was well managed. And I believed him. Did not think to ask. When they finally came for him, the debts were far too insurmountable."

"Garek, why did you not tell me?"

"I was too ashamed to tell you. I did not take care of my own life—my own responsibilities, and he suffered for it—I could not afford to get him out—especially when he needed it most. A complete failure."

Lily's eyes narrowed at him. "What does that mean, Garek, 'when he needed it most'?"

"He was dying, Lily. Dying in that filthy prison and that money from your sister was the only way I could get him out. I found out the day I left Annadale, right before Brianna visited me, that he was not long for this earth. That he was dying in the stench of that place. And then your sister walked in and offered me the money. Offered me the exact thing I needed to save him."

Garek shrugged, his hands tightening into fists. "So yes. Yes, I damn well took it. I had already lost you. Brianna convinced me of that. So I took the money to get him out. I tried to save the one thing that still meant anything to me."

Lily's arms dropped to her sides and she took one step away from the wall toward him. "And did you save him?"

"Yes. I saved him from prison." Garek exhaled, heavy. "But I was too late. Death was already consuming him. He died two months after I got him out. But I was in prison, not there with him at the end. Right after I handed over the money to clear his debts, I was tossed into Newgate for robbing graves."

"Did you get to see him? Speak to him?"

"No. I did not get to talk to him. Apologize. Thank him. Ask for forgiveness. None of that." His head bowed. "He would be so disappointed in me."

She took another small step toward him, her voice soft. "Why?"

His head shook. "What I have become—I am not the man he raised me to be—expected me to be. He was hard, complicated, but he believed in the good—in the honor in everyone."

Garek turned to Lily, his eyes solemn. "In prison, when I started to lose faith—to blame you—when my hope, my love started to turn to hatred. He would have told me I was stupid. To rein in my anger and believe in you. Instead, when I learned he had died, I knew in that moment what I had done—chosen a fickle woman over my uncle."

A small gasp escaped from her lips. "You delayed going back to London because of me? Because I needed you?"

"It was my choice, Lily. I chose to stay at Weadly Hall, to stay with you and delay my responsibilities. I thought I had time...I convinced myself I had time. "

"But why did you go back to London when you knew you would be arrested? The debts could have been erased from afar."

"It was time. I did not have you, and while I knew I could have sent the money and disappeared, I was not about to run from something I knew I had not done. It was time to face my failures. All of them. Face what my uncle suffered because of me."

His eyes dropped to the ground between them. "And then when I got out of Newgate—that day on the street I saw you hanging out of the carriage. That was the moment when I embraced my hatred. Idiocy that it was."

Lily's hands clasped around her gloves, wringing them. "I still do not remember that, Garek. But I would have never, in my right mind—"

"I do not need you to remember, Lily." His head did not lift, but his eyes came up to her. "Everything I thought of you during that time was based on a lie—you were never the fickle one. And I never should have believed you were."

She took a deep breath, steadying herself. "No. You should not have."

A sad smile, and he nodded. "I did not tell you before—I was walking out of the cemetery that day in London, right before your carriage rolled by. It was the first time I had visited his grave. The first time I could talk to him. And he was in the ground."

"Garek—"

"I just need you to understand, Lils, how everything twisted bad in that moment on the street. When it should have twisted good—twisted into forgiveness. If my uncle had survived, he would have reminded me in that moment that everyone struggles with demons—that some are shown to the world, some are not. He would have been so disappointed. He would not have hidden that from me. He never did. He always expected me to be more."

"I know he meant the world to you, Garek." Lily wanted to rush forward, touch him, share the burden of his pain.

But she couldn't.

Not when she didn't understand. All of it—everything— could have been avoided if he had just told her long ago about his uncle.

With her dowry, she would have had the means, with or without Brianna's support, to get his uncle out of prison. She could have paid the debt and they could have left the country before he was arrested.

If only he had told her.

Her eyes dropped for a long second as she took a deep breath. If only.

She looked to him. "You were ashamed, Garek? Ashamed to tell me?" Her voice softly shaking, Lily took one more step toward him, her hands dropping into the skirts at her sides. "There is no shame in any of this—not between us. That is what you said. Exactly. I have held onto those words for so very long."

She exhaled, her eyes closing. "But I was the only one that truly believed them, wasn't I?"

"I was not a man, Lily. Not a man that deserved you."

"No. You were." Her eyes flew open. "You were the man I deserved—there was never another higher, never another I could love more. And I was yours. All of me." A single tear slipped down her cheek, and she slapped it away.

She would not cry. Not now. Not again over this very thing she had already spent an ocean's worth of tears for.

Her jaw thrust forward, her words quivering. "It does not matter if you were ashamed, Garek—you were too damn proud. You could have told me a year and a half ago, and I could have helped. Or you could have come to me in London and told me why you left, and I would have forgiven you in an instant. For what was your choice but an honorable one—to save him? Did you think I would not understand that? That I am too simple— too jaded—too selfish?"

"Lily, no, none of those things."

"Yet still, you did not trust me enough to tell me. Your pride, how you thought I would react—it does not matter. Instead of telling me, trusting me, you become a man bent on vengeance. On making me hurt." She took a long step backward, distancing herself from his space. "But you did not even know me enough to understand…"

"Understand what, Lily?"

Another tear slipped and she swatted it away. "That you could never harm me more than when you abandoned me."

"What are you saying, Lily?" He asked the words softly, cautious.

"Me?" She looked up to the dark outlines of the treetops, rubbing her forehead. "I do not know. I do not know what I am saying. What I am doing. When you appeared at Notlund—there was no question in my mind—it was you I chose. Regardless of how mad I was, how hurt, how I did not want to want you. But I did. It has always been you. But then…"

"I ruined it."

Her eyes dropped to him as her fingers moved up, digging into her hairline. "I want you, Garek. I want to forgive everything, but I do not know that I can ever trust you. Is that what you want to hear? That I will never trust you?" Her fingers dropped from her head, her voice defeated. "At least it is honest. At least I am telling you instead of leaving you without a word."

"I will fight, Lily." He took a long step to her, closing the space between them. "I will fight if there is something here to fight for. I will fight to the end. Just tell me there is something, Lily."

Lips cracking open, she drew in a deep breath. Her eyes closed as she let out a long exhale. It took an aching moment for her to open her eyes to him. "I do not know…"

"Lils—"

"I am tired…so tired." She shook her head, her eyes closing against the welling tears. "Save your fight, Garek."

She turned from him, her head sinking, and started to the front door of the inn.

{ CHAPTER 19 }

Three steps, and the sudden arm across Lily's chest stopped her, her feet almost flying out from under her.

Garek spun her around, his large hands gripping her shoulders.

"I do not accept that, Lily. And I sure as hell will not save my fight." He leaned in, his voice fierce. "This is when I fight for you. Here. This spot. On this land. This moment."

"Garek—"

"No. It is now, Lily. You have lost your will and I am the reason for that. I accept it. And if you are not going to fight for us, I accept that as well. It is my responsibility to bear."

A small step, and the front of his hard body brushed hers. He leaned down, his mouth hovering above her lips, his hazel eyes burning like she had never seen them. "But make no mistake, Lils, if you will not fight, I will fight for both of us."

Her breath lodged in her throat as his mouth moved even closer to hers.

"And you need to not only hear it, Lils, you need to feel it."

His lips met hers before her breath caught, taking control of her mouth, of her senses. His grasp on her shoulders tightened, not letting her move from him. Not that she could.

He edged up slightly, breaking the kiss even as his lips brushed hers with every word. "You cannot trust me?"

He held in place, waiting for a response, his breath mingling with hers.

She exhaled, her lips sweeping his as she gave the slightest shake of her head. "I do not know, Garek. You had all of my trust once, but now…it is gone and I do not know how to revive it."

He nodded, his hands moving up from her shoulders to capture her face. Warm palms on her cheeks, his fingers curled into her hair. "I cannot conjure trust for you to feel, Lily, but I can vow to spend every minute from here, till death, proving to you that you can."

He shifted closer to her, lining himself so she had to feel his body on hers from his chest to his thighs.

Lily half gasped at the touch, fire instant in her core.

Moving from her face, Garek's left hand dropped, trailing along her shoulder, down her side, until he slipped it around her waist, pressing her body into his. His mouth left her lips, and the stubble along his jaw slid along her cheek, roughing her skin.

His warm breath tickled her right ear with his gravelly whisper. "Feel me, Lily. Feel how much my body craves you. Every minute since I left you. Every minute in prison. Every minute since then. Even when I hated you, my body ached for yours. I could not even stomach the thought of touching another."

Her eyes slid shut, resistance waning. "Yes. But our bodies have never disappointed us, Garek."

"You are afraid I will disappear again, leave you?"

She held still—silent—her mind railing against the very thought. If she never let him into her heart, her soul again, then he could not hurt her again. It was the safe—the sane thing to do. Resist.

"Admit to it, Lils. You are afraid." His fingers trailed up her spine and back down, teasing the bumps along her back, sending her skin to tingle. "I am not going anywhere until we resolve this, Lily. Not a step. And neither are you." He pulled back, searching her face. "Are you afraid, Lily?"

"Yes—yes, I am." Her shoulders leaned back as her hips pressed into him—her own body unable to either accept or deny him. "I cannot suffer the loss of you again, Garek."

"You have to let it go, Lils. You cannot worry on what the next day brings."

He met her eyes as his hand that was still on her face moved inward, his thumb tracing her lower lip. "Know this now—I will never leave you again of my own free will. Never leave your presence without a word, without telling you I love you. But I cannot make you believe my words, Lils—you are the one that has to take the chance—has to trust in the possibility of me again. Trust that giving over to the moment, the lifetime with me, the memories to be made, will all be worth taking this chance."

Her hand came up, gripping his elbow, holding it to steady herself. "Garek..."

Lily's voice left her as she looked into his eyes, searching for the honesty in his soul. If he was lying again, lying about wanting her—she knew it would destroy the last of her hope, any remaining ability she had to ever love another again.

"Do you feel safe, Lils?"

"I do not want to surrender to it, Garek." Her words came out in the merest whisper.

"You are on the wrong side of the war, Lils. Stop fighting it. Choose to fight for us. Us." His voice dropped, raw. "In my arms, Lils, do you feel safe?"

"Do you know what you can do to me, Garek—how you can destroy everything I am?"

"I do." Not a second passed before his reply. "And I refuse to shy from that responsibility, Lily. I am strong enough—in who I am, in what I am capable of—to never disappoint you again. And you are strong enough to love me again. To trust me wholly and completely."

His left hand came up, cradling her face, insistent. "Do you feel safe, Lils?"

It welled from deep within, the sudden and complete disregard of caution, the crushing need just to be his. To be his no matter the consequences, no matter the future.

She was strong enough.

Opening her mouth, the one word took her breath with it. "Yes."

He smiled, the gravity of her answer sending a ripple through his body. A ripple she could feel in his chest, down his torso, along his arms.

He closed his eyes for a moment, breathing. Just breathing.

When his eyes opened, raw heat, guttural, had consumed his look.

"Tell me that is a yes to everything, Lils." His grip along her jawline tightened. "Tell me that. Because if you need time, I will give you all—"

"I need no time, Garek. It is a yes—to everything. Everything in this moment."

His eyes went to the dark sky above as he shook his head. Whatever he was about to say, he didn't want to say it. "We can wait until Coldstream, Lily. Until you are properly my wife."

Lily almost laughed at the resistance she could feel straining through his body, through his fingers on her face. "Would you like to wait?"

His look dropped down to her. "No. Hell, no. I want to rip your clothes to shreds. I want to have you on a proper bed. I want to have you on a proper wall. A proper floor. A proper chair. A proper windowsill."

She laughed. "Then why are we still standing here? Did you not get a bed up above?" Lily pointed over her shoulder to the upper floors of the coaching inn.

"Minx." Garek chuckled as his arms flew around her, lifting her just as his feet started moving toward the side door. The low rumble still vibrated in his chest as his lips came down on hers, ravaging her mouth, tasting her, his tongue exploring the depths. Her legs came up, wrapping around him, not caring in the slightest she would look the harlot were anyone to see them.

Before Lily could take a breath from the kiss, Garek was walking up narrow stairs, her backside bumping against the rough wood of the wall. She curled into him, making herself small against his mass, her fingers curling into his hair, pressing his head down to make sure he didn't even ponder pulling from her lips.

His footsteps fast and heavy down the hall, Garek opened the door without breaking the kiss, only to be rewarded with a high-pitched scream.

He yanked his face from Lily, looking over her head. "My apologies," he said, grasping the door and quickly shutting it.

Lily hid her head on his chest.

"The man said right, not left." Garek went to the opposite side of the hallway, still carrying Lily. A quick knock went unanswered, and he kicked open the door. "No time for mortification, Lils. This room is empty. As is the bed."

The door closed and Lily pulled her face free from his chest, finding his neck with her lips, tasting the saltiness of his skin. The dark stubble roughed her skin raw, but she took no mind, working her way up along Garek's jawline.

A growl rumbled from his lips, and he dropped one of his hands from her back. "Stand, Lils."

Her legs slid down from his body without question, her boots finding wobbly balance on the wood planks of the floor.

"I know I said I wanted to rip your clothes to shreds, Lils, but I am not about to let the opportunity to disrobe you properly pass me by."

His hands moved to the front line of her riding jacket, flipping the gold buttons free from their restraints. "To see your body bared inch by inch, to watch your skin react to my touch."

Lily stilled, staring at the low fire in the small hearth as he walked around her, stripping her plum-colored jacket off her shoulders and down her arms.

From behind, his fingers slid along her neck, moving downward to slip beneath the front of her white linen shirt. Five thin ribbons held it closed, and each one of them his fingers gently tugged at, freeing her skin to the air. He gathered the fabric, pulling it up and over her head.

He stayed behind her, his lips, his teeth running along the lines of her neck. Lily's head dropped to the side, her eyes closing as she let him have full rein on her body.

His mouth did not leave her skin, yet she could feel him moving behind her, hear his clothes fluttering to the ground. Heard his boots clunk onto the wood.

When his hands slipped around her ribcage, moving up between her breasts to unlace her short stays, she looked down to find his arms were now bare, the smattering of short black hair darkening his arm.

Her breath drew in, shaking, at the sight.

Garek bared to her.

His hands baring her to him.

Short stays loosened, he wrapped the straps of her chemise around his forefingers, sliding the fabric down her arms.

In a blink, the last of her clothing, save for her boots and stockings, were a puddle on the floor.

Slowly, inch by inch, Garek pressed the full height of his body into her bare backside, from his legs to his chest that curved around the back of her head. Skin meeting skin, his hardness, the pulsating length of him, pressed insistently into the small of her back.

Her head turned as she looked up to him, and his fingers dug into her hair, setting free the captured strands from the singular braid trailing down her back.

"You are naked."

He chuckled. "I am."

"It is different." She swayed her hips, feeling his skin rub back and forth against hers. "And wondrous."

"And maddening." His hands went down, wrapping around her hips, stilling the motion. "You continue to do that, and I will learn nothing about your body, Lils."

"What do you want to learn about my body?"

"Everything." He smiled, rounding her as one hand trailed across her lower back, and then his fingers slipped down past her backside and between her legs.

She gasped, nearly losing her balance. At the touch, or at the sight of Garek naked in front of her—she wasn't positive which.

She grabbed his upper arm for balance, her eyes travelling down his chest, the muscles lining his stomach, the dark hair starting below his navel. His shaft. Long and beautiful and straining upward, touching his abdomen.

Heaven forgive her, she wanted him in her.

He smiled as he stopped in front of her, dragging his arm behind her upward, his fingers invading her folds.

Lily curled forward, her nails digging into his arm.

"You know it is my nature to study. To see what happens—cause and effect. And I want to learn what pleasures you the most, Lils. What makes you gasp. What makes you beg."

"Is it too early to beg?"

Garek laughed, dropping to his knees in front of her.

"These I know about." He set his mouth right in front of her breasts, taking one nipple between his teeth, sucking to tautness, and then the other. His head angled back, a smile on his lips at her reaction. "These I know make you strain."

His lips went onto her chest, between her breasts, and then started to slip downward along her skin. "But I am curious about further down. And I still have to take your boots off."

His mouth continued the onslaught downward along her body, past her ribcage, over her belly, every spot sending prickles onto her skin. Sending her fingers to bury deep into his dark hair.

His hands wrapped around her thighs, his palms sliding upward until he held her backside sturdy, his fingers wrapping into her inner thighs.

And then he went lower.

First with the flick of his tongue.

Then his lips, parting her folds, his tongue delving deep, exploring.

Her gasp spun into a moan, her body buckling at the rush to her nerves. She lost ability to stand, and she could hear Garek chuckle as his hands took the brunt of her weight. He didn't let her dip in the slightest.

His tongue only became more insistent. Circling. Challenging. Yanking every nerve to a frayed end.

"Garek. Don't...don't..."

"Don't what, Lils?"

"Don't stop." Her voice went into a scream. "Please, Garek, please. Hell. Please."

He went faster, harder.

She curled, gasping for breath as she came, her body lost to her and breaking into a thousand pieces. Spasm after spasm burned through her core, the fire dissipating through her limbs.

She knew she wasn't standing on her own, just that she was still upright, yet it still surprised her when Garek moved upward, his shaft sliding deep into her as he stood.

Picking her up, he wrapped her legs around his waist, already thrusting upwards as his hands went under her backside, holding her against his onslaught.

Her fingers slipping on the sheen across his back, she realized he was right in front of the edge of the mantle, and she reached out, gripping the end of the plank of wood, leveraging herself against his movement.

"I want you to come again, Lils." Garek's voice strained into her ear, rough, fighting the carnal need that threatened to overtake him.

"I cannot." Her voice went ragged, limp with the waves that still crashed through her body.

Garek slid into her from below, again and again, sending new waves coursing through her core.

New waves that were already building.

"I don't think I can."

"You can." The words growled into her ear, commanding her.

Demanding she let the new waves build, replace the throbs of her last explosion. Building deeper, more forceful than before.

"Come, Lils. Come."

Unable to endure any longer, she screamed, her body clenching around him, holding him buried far within her as her muscles spasmed, drawing the very same from him.

His body contracted, trembles ricocheting along every one of his muscles that held her upright, held him upright. An elongated grunt, guttural, shook his chest, vibrating against hers.

Three steps with his clamp around her unyielding, and they fell onto the bed, Lily on top.

Her chin draped over his shoulder, she turned her lips to his ear. "My boots didn't come off."

He chuckled, breathless. "No."

"And we did not make it to the bed."

"We are here now." His arms tightened around her, and Lily could feel his skin still twitching from the spasms rolling through his body. "And we have all night, my love."

Lily snuggled downward, setting herself so she could rest her head in the crook of his chest. Hear his heartbeat.

For an hour, for a lifetime, they stayed motionless waiting for breath to become normal, hearts to steady.

"Garek."

"Hmmm?"

Happy he wasn't asleep, Lily shifted her head on his chest so she could see his face. "There is something I have to confess."

His head came up slightly, voice alarmed. "What?"

She chuckled. "Nothing that warrants panic." Her fingers went to his chin, pushing his head downward back to relaxation. "I wanted to tell you before, but I was afraid."

"Tell me what?"

She looked down, watching her fingers trail circles on his chest. "Holding the Fallow babe—I have never held a child that young before."

"And?"

"It felt perfectly normal. I felt normal. For those few minutes, I felt at peace holding that babe." Her hand flattened on his chest, her palm pressing against the beating of his heart. "Just as I am right now in your arms."

"To love and to be loved?"

She looked up to his hazel eyes, the green flecks that always shone brightest indoors alive and dancing. "Can it really be as simple as that?"

"It just may be, Lils." He kissed her forehead.

She nodded, her head nuzzling under his chin. "We have taken a long time to get here."

He chuckled, the warmth of the sound in his chest echoing under her ear. His hand wrapped along her bare back, tightening her body to his.

"Too damn long, Lils. Too damn long."

{ CHAPTER 20 }

Lily bit the leather tip of the forefinger of her gloves, trying to spy through the glass window at the front of the three-story inn. They had crossed the Scotland border and arrived in Coldstream by the time the sun had reached its peak, and Garek had wanted to rent them a room at the coaching inn before doing anything else—a bed ready for them immediately after they married.

She smirked at her reflection in the sunlit glass.

After Garek waking her up twice more throughout the night, she would have guessed that he would have been sated enough to last through the proper daylight hours. Especially after she had done her own exploring of his body this morning.

She looked at her lips in the glass. Still slightly swollen, bruised. The smile returned. If he wanted to lock them in a room for the afternoon, she was not going to complain. Not in the slightest.

Lily turned from the glass, her eyes sweeping along the main road of the village to watch the midday bustle. At the corner opposite her, a coal porter passed in front of the cheap-jack shining a carving knife from his box of wares. Three buildings away, the chandler chatted with a woman preceding him from his shop as he set a block of cheese on the stand outside the door. The woman's daughter tugged at her mama's skirt, pointing at the pies in front of the pie man. A horse and cart went by. Lily followed it, her eyes scanning the buildings along the street, pausing for a moment on the tall church down the way. A smile edged along her mouth as she started to search the faces in the road, looking for Brianna.

"Good news." The door swung shut behind Garek as he walked from the inn, stopping in front of Lily. "First, is that the clergyman can marry us at any time. The innkeeper sent someone to gather him. They have a wedding room inside or we can do it at the church. Second, is that Brianna and her earl are already here. They rented a suite of rooms days ago."

"So they are inside?"

"No. They left a few hours ago for a ride. They did tell the innkeeper they would be back in early afternoon."

"So any moment?"

"Hopefully." He captured her face, kissing her quickly. Much too short. A smile spread across his face as he pulled away. "I must admit I do like that you are entirely anxious to marry me. And I am the same—I want you to be mine—officially—so I can get you into the room I rented without any wayward glances. We can go over to the blacksmith shop to hurry it along. There is an anvil priest there. But I know you wanted Brianna to be present."

"I do want to wait for her." Lily went to her toes, giving his lower lip a slight nip. "Even if it is not soon enough for me."

Garek chuckled, turning and tucking her hand into the crook of his elbow as he walked to the inn door. "Do you want to freshen up in your sister's rooms—maybe see if she brought any dresses other than riding habits with? That way, we will be ready the moment they appear."

"That sounds perfect."

A half hour later, Lily stepped out onto the small balcony from Brianna and Sebastian's third-floor sitting room.

She watched the street below for her sister, her palm smoothing the front of the yellow dress she had found. Foot tapping, she leaned over the wrought iron railing, her eyes trailing the road.

Far off along rolling green hills, she could see two riders. Brianna and Sebastian? She squinted. Impossible to tell. Although the riders were fast on their horses, and that probably meant it was her sister and brother-in-law.

Her stomach fluttered. She was almost married to Garek. Minutes away. Finally.

"The yellow suits you much better than the black."

The words floated from the room out onto the balcony, and Lily turned to face the sitting room, not sure she heard them correctly. Not sure that she heard the voice correctly.

A voice from long in the past.

Before her eyes landed on the figure in the room, Lily recognized the voice. Recognized it, but could not believe it.

Her jaw dropped, her fingers clutching the frame of the balcony doorway. "Mr. Sneedly?"

He stepped into the room, away from the closed door. "I almost did not recognize you, Lily. Not in the yellow. But I have been watching. Waiting. And then you appeared on the balcony."

Shivers spiked along her spine. What the hell was Mr. Sneedly doing in Coldstream—in Brianna's room?

Lily's eyes darted to the closed door. Sneedly was between her and escape. She forced her voice light, hiding her rising panic. "Mr. Sneedly, it is delightful to see you again after all this time, but whatever are you doing here in Coldstream? In Lord and Lady Luhaunt's room?"

"Do not play the fool with pleasantries, Lily. You are not happy to see me. But you will be, eventually." He took two steps toward her. "They would not let me see you at Notlund, and I know you left the castle to elope. So I followed your sister here. You and that bitch thought you could just destroy my life and be done? Never have to think on me again? You and your sister. You a whore. Your sister a vengeful wench."

Lily shuffled her feet into the room, sliding herself to the right along the wall. She only had to clear the large wardrobe, and then she could skirt past him and get to the door. "Come, now, Mr. Sneedly, my sister is very dear to me, and I cannot have you speaking so ill of her. Whatever you may think has happened—"

"Know that has happened." He took a step to his left. "Then I will just speak ill of you, Lily."

Now he blocked her line to the door, but she could still get past him if she was fast.

"What are you here for, Mr. Sneedly?"

"Even as a whore, Lily, I will still take you." His hands stretched, the fingertips of his black leather gloves collapsing together. "You will be payment enough for what I have suffered since your sister ruined my life—you and your dowry."

Lily ran, spinning sideways to make herself skinny as she edged past him.

One more step.

But then his hand jammed into her shoulder and she flew backward.

She hit a small rectangular table, upending it and sending the chairs clattering to the floor. Landing with her limbs tangled in the legs of the table, she tried to free herself and get her feet back on the ground.

Mr. Sneedly moved toward her, stopping only a step away, lording over her.

She could fight him. She could still fight and get away. To her feet first, though.

It wasn't until she had managed to her knees, her hands crawling up the wall for balance, that she looked to Mr. Sneedly.

Her movements froze.

A pistol.

Aimed at her.

A gleaming silver, long-barreled pistol with the hammer cocked.

"Sneedly...no..."

"You will come with me quietly, Lily. You will walk out of this place, and we will move to the blacksmith's shop. You will marry me without hesitation, and then we will leave this place."

Her eyes flew wide, her heart pounding. Lunacy. Mr. Sneedly was speaking complete lunacy. She opened her mouth to tell him that very fact, but then her eyes flickered down to the gun.

Battling all instinct, her voice went silent.

Now was not the moment to fight.

"Lily." The door swung open. "Lily, I heard a crash from below."

Garek stepped into the room, his foot stopping in midair. His instant growl filled the room. "Sneedly."

Mr. Sneedly jumped backward into the middle of the room, distancing himself from Lily as he swung the pistol toward Garek. "Stop, Harrison."

Garek hesitated for one short second, glancing to Lily. Murder in his eyes, he started to charge Sneedly.

The barrel of the pistol flew back at Lily. "I said stop, Harrison."

Garek froze, his hands slowly rising, reasoning. "Put the pistol down, Sneedly."

"No. No, I do not think it would be in my best interest right now to drop this pistol." Mr. Sneedly ran his free hand across the front of his hair, smoothing the dark greasy strands from his forehead. "Nor to aim it anywhere other than at your slut."

Garek took another step.

"One more step and she is dead, Harrison."

"I am the one that is going to kill you, Sneedly," Garek said, murder lacing every word. "So you had best point that gun at me."

"Garek. No." Lily shuffled forward from the wall, moving around the upended table and chairs. "Mr. Sneedly, it is me you want. I am the one that you hate. The one you want to punish. I am the one that refused you. Did not want you because you resemble nothing near a man. A quivering coward, Sneedly, that is what you are." She moved another step forward.

"Shut your mouth, Lily." Out of the corner of her eye, Lily saw Garek's entire body clench, coiling, his hands curling into fists.

"Yes, shut your mouth, whore, unless you would like to hasten your own demise." Mr. Sneedly sneered the words out the corner of his mouth, but his eyes stayed focused on Garek.

"You pull that trigger and it will be the last thing you do on this earth, Sneedly."

Mr. Sneedly shrugged. "My life is not worth much at this juncture. So that threat has very little weight to it, Harrison."

Lily edged another step forward, trying to force Mr. Sneedly to look at her and not Garek. "Garek, you need to leave the room. It is me Mr. Sneedly wants, so let us finish this without interference. Mr. Sneedly would like to marry me and I am considering it."

"Utter madness, Lily," Garek hissed.

Mr. Sneedly's eyes shifted to Lily.

"Look at me, Sneedly." Garek's voice thundered. "I am the only thing you need to worry about. I am the only thing that is going to crush you."

Mr. Sneedly's eyes flickered between the two of them. "Is this not the sweetest moment? Both of you, attempting to save the other. It would seem that no matter who I kill, both will suffer. It is more than I could have asked for. Other than to have Lily clear to the blacksmith's, of course."

Garek started to move. "Sneedly—"

"Too late, I have already made my choice."

The loudest bang filled her ears, filled her head. And then Lily was falling, flying through the air, Garek on top of her.

Thud.

She hit the floor hard, her head knocking against the wood planks, all of Garek's weight landing, uncurbed, onto her body. Smothering her.

In an instant Garek was off her, up to his feet, charging across the room at Sneedly.

Trapped far from the door, Mr. Sneedly started blubbering, his feet scampering backward, as his hands blocked his face. "No, no, no. I didn't mean to fire." The pistol dropped out of his hands, clanking to the floor. "I did not mean it, Harrison."

Lily sat up, her mouth opening, but no words could form. Her hand landed on her side, hit hard by Garek's weight.

She felt it immediately, the warmth, the stickiness spreading along her fingers. Slow, in a trance, she looked down.

Blood. Bright red. Spreading along her dress. Her wedding dress. Her beautiful, yellow wedding dress. Blood.

Lily ran her hand along her side, searching for the tear in the fabric. Searching for the pain of a bullet.

She looked up the very instant the balcony railing hit the back of Sneedly's thighs, and he tipped, arms spinning. A second before Garek reach the balcony, Sneedly dropped out of view.

Garek slowed, taking another step forward to peer down over the edge of the balcony.

He turned from the railing, shaking his head at her as he moved back into the room. "Dead. He is dead."

Lily's eyelids squeezed shut, relief shaking her shoulders.

Garek's footsteps into the room slowed to a stop. Lily's eyes opened, looking up at him.

His face had gone pale.

Lily looked down at her side, then up to Garek, desperate.

She wasn't shot.

He was.

{ CHAPTER 21 }

Everything in her body stopped. Frozen. Mud swallowing her.

She couldn't get to her feet, couldn't make her legs work, so she scrambled, hands dragging, feet slipping, across the floor.

She wasn't fast enough. Garek dropped to his knees, heavy. He collapsed before she could get a hand under him, an arm to soften the blow. He hit the floor hard, his forehead cracking the wood.

The sound twisted her stomach, ravaged her chest, but it also released her from the sludge holding her captive. To Garek's side in the next breath, her hands ran over his body, over the dark cloth of his jacket and trousers until she found the wetness. The blood.

Ripping his jacket and waistcoat off, she rolled him onto his back, pushing his linen shirt up his torso and over his head.

"Lils—" Clear of the shirt, Garek's hand came up, trying to reach her face.

She snatched his wrist out of the air, setting it on the floor. "Do not move. Do not speak, Garek. The damn bullet hit you."

"Good."

"No. That bullet was to be mine, not yours." Lily grabbed her skirt, wiping away the blood that had smeared all over his belly. Most of the blood cleared, she found the hole tearing into Garek's side, just below his ribcage.

Blood sputtered from the hole, seeping down his skin to pool on the floor.

Her hand slammed onto the floor. "Damn you."

"Me?"

She looked up to his face. "Yes, you. Damn you. Damn you for saving me. It could have missed me. Or if it did hit, you could have saved me. You could have done that. You. But now you think to leave me."

"No. I will not leave you, Lils." His chest rose in a shaky breath, setting a gurgle to his words.

More blood oozed from the wound. Lily balled up her skirt, pressing it against the hole. Wetness soaked through, squeezing between her fingers.

Dammit to hell.

She needed her sister. She needed Sebastian. She pushed Garek's shirt in front of the wound and ran to the balcony, searching the street below, the crowd gathering around Sneedly's body and pointing up at her.

"Lily—Lily."

The scream rose above the crowd, and Lily looked up the slight hill to her left. Their horses in full gallop, Brianna screamed her name.

Brianna and Sebastian pulled up their horses just before tramping into the crowd.

Lily raised her bloody hand. "Surgeon. Get a surgeon," she screamed as loud as she could.

Brianna and Sebastian nodded, and Lily ran back to Garek's side.

They would be up here soon enough.

~ ~ ~

"No. Absolutely not." On his side, Garek gasped a cough, his body curling.

Lily lifted the linen shirt she had bunched against the wound to see blood still seeping. Her free palm went flat on the bed next to Garek's chest as she leaned down to put herself in front of his face. "Garek, he is the only surgeon nearby."

Garek lifted his hand from the bed, pointing past Lily at the skinny boy, sixteen at best, standing against the wall next to the door. "How many bullets have you taken out, boy?"

"None, sir." The gangly boy fiddled with the black satchel he held in both hands. "My father was the main surgeon. He just died two months past. I only watched him."

Garek looked up at Lily. "So, no, he will not touch me."

Lily looked over Garek to Brianna and Sebastian, standing on the opposite side of the bed. Her face drawn in worry, Brianna shook her head, shrugging. No help there.

Lily looked down to Garek. "Garek, we have to get the bullet out. You said yourself we do. He has to save you. Please just let him."

"No, Lils. He won't save me. Leave, boy."

The boy scurried from the room.

Lily growled, standing straight from the bedside and turning to go after him.

Garek grabbed her wrist. "He won't. But you will. You will save me, Lils."

She looked down at her fingers clutching the bloody shirt. "I don't know what to do."

"Look again, Lily, just to make certain." Garek sucked in a wheezing breath, his body clenching. "It did not go out, the bullet?"

Lily lifted the cloth, wiping away the fresh blood from around the wound. Her fingers running over his skin, she checked both the front side of his belly and his back. No bullet hole. "No. No other holes."

"Then you need to get the bullet out of me."

"No. I cannot."

"You can, Lils. I will tell you what to do. I do not want a butcher boy touching me. I would do it myself if I could." He sucked in a breath, wincing against pain. His fingers slipped down from her wrist to her hand, squeezing. "These hands. These hands can do it. I watched you help heal Brianna. You will listen to what I tell you and you will do it. You can. There is no one I trust more, Lils."

Lily stared at the side of his stomach, refolding the fabric of the shirt to a fresh spot and pressing it against the wound. If only the blood would stop. The bullet would be fine. They could leave it in. Stop the blood, and he would be fine. She pressed harder.

Garek recoiled, his body cringing from her.

"It has to come out, Lils. It has to or I am dead."

Her hand went up to his forehead, blood smearing onto his face as she tried to flatten the creases of pain marring his skin. She pushed the hair back from his face. "I will do it. I can."

She stood, steeling herself with a breath.

She could do this. She had to.

A few minutes of frenzied preparation in the room passed, and Lily looked down at Garek's face, swallowing hard against the grey color lining his cheeks. "There is nothing else I need? You are certain?"

"I am. Everything you need is with my tools."

"Lily, we need to do this quickly, before he loses consciousness," Sebastian said, positioning himself at the head of the bed they had dragged away from the wall.

"I will be awake." Garek's eyes did not leave Lily.

"You will not drink any brandy?" Sebastian asked.

"No. I cannot have my mind altered if I have to guide you— if you find something dire in the hole."

Lily nodded. "Sebastian, get that strap in his mouth."

She made a fist, squeezing hard, trying to eradicate the shake in her fingers before she picked up the scalpel. Garek didn't need to watch her cut into him with a shaking hand.

Lily glanced over to Brianna. She stood at Garek's feet, hands around his ankles should they start to flail. Her sister's look was set firmly at her husband, high above Garek. Brianna was not going to let Lily do this alone, yet she also wasn't about to look down and see the wound, the cutting, the blood.

Lily's eyes swung to Sebastian, giving him a nod. She couldn't look at Garek's face. Not with the leather strap in his mouth. Not with what she was about to do.

Garek had run through the many possibilities that Lily may discover in the wound. Organs, blood, flesh, pus—but the goal of it—quite simply, was to get the bullet—and any cloth that had been dragged in with it—out of the wound.

Waiting until Sebastian secured his solid hold down on Garek's shoulders and nodded, Lily picked up the scalpel in her right hand and the forceps in her left. Leaning down, she got close to the wound and used the small forceps to stretch the skin apart.

Garek twitched under her, but she ignored it—ignored him.

She started to dig. Tweezers. Scalpel. Forceps.

Muffled screams, Garek's body strained. But Lily shut all sound from her ears, digging through the mess of Garek's innards.

Clink.

Metal, not flesh. The bullet.

She stretched the wound wide, easing the tweezers around the lead ball.

Dropping the bullet onto the table next to the bed, she dove into the wound one last time, snatching from the depths the black threads she had seen, remnants of Garek's jacket.

Lily grabbed the bottle of brandy, dousing the wound and sending Garek's body into spasms.

She gave him a moment, then picked up the curved needle and thread at the ready and quickly stitched the wound closed.

Using the fresh cloth from the bowl of water on the table, she wiped the blood clean from Garek's skin, relieved to see the flow of blood was already slowing with the closed wound.

Setting thick gauze over the stitches, Lily quickly washed her hands in the water and then lifted her chin, blinking hard against the dry eyes from the daze that had encompassed her.

Her look went to Brianna and then to Sebastian. Identical looks sat on their faces. Both their mouths agape.

Terror shot through her. She had avoided it—looking at Garek—not wanting to see his face in pain because of her. Her gaze dropped to him.

"You are done?" he asked, his voice weak, but his hazel eyes—clear—fully meeting hers.

"Yes?" A new wave of fear gripped her. What had she done wrong? "I found the bullet, the cloth that had torn free and embedded. There was nothing else in there. I looked closely. I did not leave anything, Garek."

He gave a slight nod, the motion appearing to sap his last remnants of energy. "I know. It felt deep. Was it deep?"

"This deep." She held her fingers apart about a forefinger's length. "What? What is going on? What did I forget?" Lily's eyes chased up to Sebastian and Brianna.

Sebastian cleared his throat in a small cough and moved to the foot of the bed to stand next to Brianna. "It is merely that... fast...you were fast. I have never seen a surgeon remove a bullet so quickly. And I was on battlefields."

"How did you..." Brianna shook her head. "I am just—in awe—I had no idea you could do something like that, Lils. You did not give the slightest squirm—Garek was writhing and you just...you did not stop."

Her head whipped to Garek, blood draining from her face. "You were writhing? No. I hurt you? I heard the scream, but it was muffled and—"

"I was already hurt, Lily." A soft smile came to his lips, his voice just above a whisper. "You did good, Lils. I knew you would. You have the hands. The mind."

The blood that had drained from her face returned in a rush, sending her cheeks into pinkness. Cutting into flesh was not exactly a delicate pursuit for a proper lady, and her eyes flickered to the earl. No judgement on her brother-in-law's face. Thank goodness.

She exhaled, looking to Brianna. "Bree, can you please find me another dress?" Her hand swept over the large swathes of bloodstains covering the front of her yellow dress. "This one I seemed to have ruined."

"Of course, Lils." Brianna looked at Garek's face. "And I believe Dr. Harrison needs his rest. I will have them bring fresh water up and set out a dress in the sitting room, and we will move into the rooms you rented."

Sebastian set his hand atop Brianna's shoulder and they made their way out of the room.

Lily watched the door close, then looked at Garek. His eyes were already shut.

She stared at him a long moment, trying to breathe normally once more. A full breath, deep into her lungs—something that hadn't happened since Mr. Sneedly had appeared in the adjacent sitting room.

Garek needed to rest, and she had to change out of the bloody dress—she knew that—but she was having a blasted time trying to move away from the side of the bed. She forced the heel of her borrowed slipper backward.

"Don't leave."

The soft words slipped out into the pounding silence of the room, gripping her heart.

Garek's eyes didn't open, but his fingers twitched, beckoning her.

Lily clutched his hand, moving up along the bed toward his head and leaning over so her face was above his. "I hurt you, Garek—tell me the truth."

He sighed. "You had a scalpel, forceps, tweezers, and your fingers in my innards, Lily. And yes, that hurts. A pain like no other." His hazel eyes cracked open, the green flecks dull. "But you had best not apologize for it. You had to do it. I asked you to because you are the one I trust. You saved me, Lils."

The sweat still thick on his brow, Lily smoothed the dark hair back from his forehead. "You save me, Garek. I save you."

He chuckled, the movement sending him wincing on his side in pain. It took several breaths before he could open his eyes to her. "You have your fight back about you."

A half smile lifted her cheek. "I do." Her fingertips played along his brow, twirling his short dark hair. "And you need to rest. I will change clothes, but I will be right here when you wake up."

Garek's fingers tightened around her hand, his grip suddenly insistent. "I said I would never willingly leave you again, Lily, and I meant it. But you know what can happen after this."

Her head bowed, avoiding him, avoiding what he said.

He squeezed her hand, his voice wheezing to get louder. "You know, Lils. I want to hear the words."

Lily lifted her eyes, meeting his look. "I know."

"Say it."

Her mouth tightened, her head shaking as she stared at him. Her chest seized upon itself, stealing her breath.

"Say it, Lils."

"You may die." The words fell, curdling her tongue.

He nodded, his eyelids closing for a long breath. When he opened them to her, the green flecks in his eyes had sparked to life. "Then let me say this now—in case I cannot tomorrow. You are worth everything, Lily. The time we were apart, the time in prison, all of those days, those hours, were just a sacrifice to suffer in hopes fate would return you to me again."

His fingers twitched against her palm. "These last days with you, Lils—these are the memories. My love you hold onto. This is the love you need to remember, because it has never burned brighter than in these moments. You were always worth fighting for, Lils."

"Do not speak as though you are already dead, Garek. I will not have it."

He continued on, ignoring the anger in her voice. "If I die, Lils, you need to move on with your life. You keep these moments, keep them in your heart—but you cannot become stuck in these moments, you cannot let them drag you to lifelessness."

"Garek, stop. Stop this instant." She wiped clear a tear that had fallen from her face onto his cheek.

Drawing a deep breath, she yanked his hand up to set their entwined fingers onto his chest. "You are making me cry, and I am not yet ready for tears. I am ready to fight. This is my time—my time to fight for the both of us. I am not about to let you die."

"You cannot fight what is done, Lils. An infection that may have already begun. What is fate."

"Wrong. I can fight—I do not give a damn about fate—I can give you the will to stay with me, and don't you dare tell me I cannot."

"Lils—"

"Do not even think upon giving up on yourself." Her fingers burrowed into his chest. "Your heart will keep beating, Garek, because I am demanding it of you."

"It is not that easy, Lily."

"No? Do you remember what you said—about your mother—that you never wanted to watch another person you love die?" She moved closer, her nose almost touching his. "You will be watching me die, Garek if you do not hold on. Do you not see that in my eyes? You are my everything, and if you give up and leave me, I will live, a shell, dead inside, until I can meet you on the other side. Do not make me suffer what you suffered those many years ago. Do not."

He held her eyes for seconds that drifted into lifetimes.

His head moved in a slight nod. "I will hold on. Fight."

She smiled, her lips brushing his. "That is all I ask."

CHAPTER 22

The nudge on her shoulder jolted Lily, sending her sprawling as her elbow slipped off the armrest of the settee Sebastian had dragged into the room.

Brianna caught Lily's shoulder before she slipped to the floor, righting her.

Lily's eyes found Garek immediately in the low light of the fireplace. She stared at the blanket over his bare chest, not blinking until she saw the even rise and fall of his lungs.

She said a little prayer. His breathing wasn't labored. Not yet.

Sinking down next to Lily on the settee, Brianna offered a steaming cup of tea, her voice just above a whisper. "I did not want to wake you, Lils, but you have not eaten or drunk anything since you arrived in town. Plus, it gave me an excuse to come check on you."

"I was not asleep, not truly. I do not cry as long as my eyes are closed, that is all." Lily took the cup, cradling it as she sipped from the edge. Her eyes drifted from Garek to her sister. "What?"

Brianna smiled, finding Lily's knee in her skirts and squeezing it. "It has just been a very long time since I have handed you tea, and you have not asked if there was a dollop of brandy mixed in."

Lily's eyes dropped. "Yes, well…" She looked up to Garek. "I do not want to hide from this. I need a clear head."

"It is nice to witness."

Lily shrugged, taking another long sip of the tea and then leaning to the side table to set the teacup down.

Brianna slipped her arm along Lily's shoulders, pulling her close. "I am proud of you, Lils. What you did today—something I could never dream of doing. Where I would have been running about panicked, you had a clear head about you."

"Sebastian was not horrified to be related to me?"

"Hardly. I think he already has plans to entice you to stay around Notlund so you can tend to the riders when there are mishaps with the horses. How good are you at setting bones?"

Lily chuckled, settling her head on Brianna's shoulder and pulling her bare feet up to tuck them under her skirts on the settee. "It is the middle of the night, Bree. You should be asleep."

"Says the one that is curling up with me." Brianna squeezed Lily's shoulders, keeping her in place. "I cannot sleep. I have been waiting in worry for days for you, so forgive me for just wanting to be near you for a spell. Besides, you know we are bound as sisters—if you are anxious, I am anxious. It is just the way it is."

"I did not intend to worry you. We were delayed in our trip."

Brianna stroked Lily's unbound hair. "What happened on the way here from Notlund? I know Seb and I ride fast, but you and Dr. Harrison had a half day's start on us. I have been rather worried."

"We were stuck on the wrong side of a river when that storm barreled along the land." Lily tilted her head further, easing into the comfort of Brianna's hold as her gaze stayed on Garek. "You did not get stopped by it?"

"We rode along the front edge of it until it caught us," Brianna said. "But by then we had cleared most of it to the north. The delay, it gave you and Dr. Harrison time to resolve the past? I was worried after you left Notlund that I had made a terrible mistake, telling you of him. That I should have devised another way out of the situation with Lord Newdale."

Lily stared at Garek's chest rising and falling in the dim light, debating about how much she could actually tell Brianna. "It was bad. Very bad in the beginning. But it also needed to happen as it did."

"And now?"

"As bad as it was, it is now a thousand times better. All that I had never dared to even hope for."

Brianna kissed the top of Lily's head. "I am glad for that. You truly do love him, Lils?"

Lily nodded. "I do."

"I am so sorry that I ever kept you two apart." Brianna's voice had softened to a delicate whisper. "I take all the blame for what happened a year and a half ago, and can only beg for your forgiveness, Lils. If I could go back to that time…"

"You would?"

"Yes. And change everything."

"As would I."

Brianna pointed to the bed. "Dr. Harrison—he was always a good, fine man. He saved me and I never gave him the proper credit for that. Never rightfully thanked him. Back then, after I awoke from the infection—I was not in my right mind. Not for a very long time."

Her head turning, Brianna rested her chin on top of Lily's head. "And you took care of everything during that time. Took care of me. I never did thank you for that either. Everything I have now—Sebastian included, is because of you, Lils. Thank you for that."

Lily craned her neck, looking up to find her sister's eyes. "You give me too much credit, but you are very welcome, Bree. I am happy you are happy. And I do forgive you."

Lily could feel the sigh of relief run through her sister's body. The edges of Brianna's mouth stretched backward in silent gratitude. "Now we just need to make sure you are happy, Lils."

Lily drew a deep breath, tucking her head onto Brianna's shoulder again. "You should go to bed, Bree, go to your husband."

"Nonsense." Brianna's hand came up, cupping Lily to the safe nook between her shoulder and neck. "I am absolutely right where I need to be at the moment."

Lily sighed.

Her sister knew. Still knew exactly how to hold her, ease the fears that consumed her. Lily closed her eyes, a tear sliding down her cheek.

"Thank you, Bree."

~ ~ ~

"How does it look?"

Lily's head popped up, knocking off the hand that had been curled around the back of her neck. There hadn't been enough room on the bed for her body, so she had dragged a chair next to the bed, settling herself with her head next to Garek's upper arm.

His hand that slipped from her neck landed on his chest, his eyes half-open, drowsy as he watched Lily right herself.

"How long have you been awake?" Lily's hands wrapped around his bare upper arm.

"Only a few minutes. I was not sure if you were truly sleeping or not."

Lily glanced at the one window in the room. Daylight shone through the thin curtains. "I checked it an hour past, maybe two. The blood stopped late last night, and now there is pus."

"Any color to it?"

"No. And no odor."

"Veins started?"

"No."

Garek nodded against the pillow. "Good."

His eyes started to slip, closing. Lily watched, waiting to see if he opened his eyes again. His head nudged into the pillow.

"Wait. Garek. Do not fall asleep on me."

His eyelids dragged open. "Anything you want, my love."

Lily found her feet and shifted to the bed, balancing her backside along the edge by his upper arm so she could lean over him. She set one hand just above the covers onto his skin, fingers curling along the middle indentation of his chest. "I only want one thing, Garek. But it is selfish."

He smiled. "I like that your list is so short, as I will not be moving well for a while. What is it?"

"To marry you. Now. The clergyman is downstairs, waiting."

"No."

Lily's head snapped back, stung. "What?"

He grabbed her forearm before she could move away. "No. Do not even let your mind skirt into darkness, Lily. It is a 'no' because I want to stand at our wedding, hold you. Not marry you as an invalid in a bed."

Lily groaned. "No. No pride, Garek. Do you want me as your wife?"

"Yes." His hand came up, fingers trailing along her face from her temple to her chin. "Since the night I met you, Lils. Since before I even knew you existed and fate lost me in those woods to find you."

She smiled, her palm capturing the back of his hand and clasping his hold to her cheek. "Then we are to marry now. I refuse to spend another minute without you as my husband. I understand these are short weddings, so you only need to stay awake and say 'I do.'"

Garek's eyes went upward, a beaten man. When they drifted back down to Lily, the green flecks within the hazel glowed, a small smile edging his mouth. "I may be proud, Lils, but I also would be crazy not to give you the world. And I am not a crazy man."

Her smile widened so far she could hardly speak. "I will go fetch the clergyman and Bree and Sebastian. They have been keeping him captive for us." She set his hand down onto his chest, getting up from the bed.

"Wait."

Already halfway to the door, Lily spun back to Garek.

"Send the earl in first—he can at least help me with the courtesy of a proper shirt."

Fifteen minutes later, Lily opened the door to the bedroom with Brianna and the clergyman trailing her.

Her slippered feet slowed to a stop.

Garek stood at the foot of the bed, proper trousers, crisp white linen shirt and a dark jacket draped over his shoulders.

Sebastian stood next to him, watching him carefully with his hands hovering at the ready to grab Garek should he start to fail.

"You should not be standing, Garek."

His left cheek rose in a smile. "And you will not be marrying me while I am bound to a bed. You said this was short?"

Lily scampered into the room, waving her hand over her shoulder to the clergyman and Brianna. "Let us hurry this then. I do not want my husband to over exert himself."

Lily sidled next to Garek's open side as his half smile broke wide at her words. He grabbed her hand as he leaned down, his mouth brushing her ear. "I like the ribbon in your hair, Lils."

Her eyes went up to him, smirking. "I went through your pockets."

"It is perfect, Lils."

His hand tightened around hers, solid, strong but gentle, just as he truly was. Had always been. A grip that promised he was never going to let her go.

She nodded as her smile softened, a complete sense of belonging, of raw happiness flooding her chest.

"As is this, my love."

{ EPILOGUE }

One hand on the linen wrap around his wrist, Lily looked up, wiping the last fat droplet of a tear from the cherub cheek. "Tell me you will take more care in the future, Robby. And on the horse, truly? Was that necessary?"

The little boy wiggled on the wooden chair, shrugging. "Sylvia said it would be a good idea. She said we could learn about fire. How high we had to drop the flame from for it to go out. The horse was the tallest thing near us."

Lily's head tilted, her blue eyes in full scold. Garek ducked his face, hiding a smile from her as he slid his surgical wallet into his black bag. Experiments.

"And does Sylvia usually have ideas that do not result in injury?" Lily asked.

The boy shook his head.

"So the next time Sylvia has a fine idea you would like to experiment with, you will wait to ask Lady Southfork? Or if you are afraid to ask an adult you can always ask Thomas." Lily tied off the linen and stood, rumpling the blond curls on his head. "Dr. Harrison and I will be gone from London for a month, and we will not be available to keep the lot of you mended and upright. So you will need to be extra careful. Promise me."

"Yes, m'lady."

"And you will keep Sylvia out of trouble?"

"I will try."

"Good. A hug?" The boy wrapped his arms around Lily's skirts and she squeezed his shoulders. "Off you go. We must be on our way."

"Thank you m'lord." The little boy threw the words to Garek as he scampered from the study in the Southfork's London orphanage.

Stepping behind his wife, Garek slid his hand along Lily's belly, his fingertips wide along the bump that had just started to harden within the last few days. "I expected him to ask you to sing to him again. I do believe that boy injures himself just so you will tend to him."

Lily chuckled. "Possibly so. That one is a scamp. At least your hospital is open now, so I can worry less about all of them while we are away." Her fingers tightened over his knuckles. "Did this delay us too long? I still need a few minutes to speak with Reanna as she had a letter for me to bring to Wynne."

"No. Even if we lose a few days in travel, we should still be to Notlund in plenty of time for the birth." Garek bent, setting his lips onto the irresistible spot on Lily's neck just below her earlobe. "I did not get a chance to tell you before we were requested here, that word came this morning from the duke. Wynne is still doing well, walking about, not bedridden yet from the weight of the babe on her belly. And Brianna and Luhaunt arrived at Notlund yesterday from the stud farm they were visiting on the continent."

Lily spun in his hold, wrapping her hands around his neck. "Good. I had hoped they would be back in time for the birth as well." Her blue eyes went serious. "You will miss the children while we are away?"

"Yes." Garek nodded. "This, working with the children, it is so different. Not to be surrounded by death constantly. I know Lord and Lady Southfork have said time and again how lucky they are to have us nearby for the children, but I am the lucky one."

Lily smiled up at him. "I think you are speaking of me, my husband."

"You are happy, my love?"

"Yes. Happy. At peace. With you. With our life." Her hand dropped between them, rubbing her belly as her voice cracked. "With this one. Happiness that hurts my heart it is so profound. And you?"

Garek smiled, his throat collapsing as his hands cupped his wife's face. He had no words that could cut through the pride, the joy that swelled his chest.

He nodded.

True since the moment he had met her, her happiness was his happiness.

And her voice still possessed the power. The power to take him to heaven and back.

~ About the Author ~

K.J. Jackson is the author of *The Hold Your Breath Series,*
The Lords of Fate Series, and *The Flame Moon Series.*

She specializes in historical and paranormal romance,
loves to travel (road trips are the best!), and is a sucker for a good
story in any genre. She lives in Minnesota with her husband,
two children, and a dog who has taken the sport of
bed-hogging to new heights.

Visit her at www.kjjackson.com

~ Author's Note ~

Thank you so much for taking a trip back in time with me.
Two special notes about the *Marquess of Fortune*. 1. If you haven't already
read Brianna's story, and want to know exactly how she travelled from bitter
patient screwing up her sister's life, to bettering herself and happily in love,
check out *Earl of Destiny*. 2. *The Last Rose of Summer* is the song Lily sang in
Chapter 6—an easy Google search will get you to its entirety.

My next historical will debut in late spring 2016.
If you missed the *Hold Your Breath* series or the first two
in the *Lords of Fate* series, be sure to check out these historical romances
(each is a stand-alone story): **Stone Devil Duke,
Unmasking the Marquess, My Captain, My Earl,
Worth of a Duke, and Earl of Destiny**.

Be sure to sign up for news of my next releases at
www.KJJackson.com (email addresses are precious, so out of respect,
you'll only hear from me when I actually have real news).

Interested in Paranormal Romance?
In the meantime, if you want to switch genres and check out my Flame
Moon paranormal romance series, **Flame Moon #1**, the first book in the
series, is currently free (ebook) at all stores. **Flame Moon** is a stand-alone
story, so no worries on getting sucked into a cliffhanger. But number two in
the series, **Triple Infinity**, ends with a fun cliff, so be forewarned. Number
three in the series, **Flux Flame**, ties up that portion of the series.

As always, I love to connect with my readers, you can reach me at:

www.KJJackson.com

https://www.facebook.com/kjjacksonauthor

Twitter: @K_J_Jackson

Thank you for allowing my stories into your life
and time—it is an honor!
~ K.J. Jackson